Copyright © 2022 Gill Merton

First published in March 2022.

All characters in this publication are fictitious and any resemblance to real persons, living or dead, is purely coincidental.

ISBN: 9798406909065

Entitled

by

Gill Merton

PROLOGUE

She is piling the usual Monday load of washing into the twin tub when a knock comes to the door. She sighs, knowing it will be Ewan McLeish popping in for a cuppa with her. She opens the door, the fixed smile reserved for the love-sick police sergeant set on her face. But it's not Ewan. Standing on the doorstep, hundreds of miles out of place in his expensive Savile Row suit, it's him...

PART ONE

UNIVERSITY (1958)

1

Unused to emotional farewells, Sally and her parents were uneasily awaiting the train that was going to take her away. Though that made it sound like a bad thing, she thought, as if she was going to the other side of the world for good, not to take up her hard-won university place – and medical school at that. Not many eighteen-year-old farm girls became doctors but that was Sally's plan. Her mum and dad were quietly so proud of her – surprised, too, she knew – and Sally had never seen either of them lost for words until they read her letter of acceptance. Even now, her mum was dabbing away tears with a clean white hanky and a shaky smile. As for her father, a real old soldier, who had seen and done things he never spoke about, even his eyes were suspiciously moist, his voice husky. The weight of being an only child, to an ageing couple who had once wanted a whole brood, hung heavily on Sally and now at the last – or first, really – minute, her eager expectation and excitement was giving way to fear and trepidation.

In a sudden flurry of whistles, chuntering and huffs, the train drew into the station, and in no time Sally and her luggage were on board. The platform now between them, Sally tugged down the window and leaned out, waving until the very last minute. As the train pulled away, she craned her neck to watch her parents cling to each other, smiles of encouragement fixed to their faces. Sally was not given to flights of imagination but she was sure that she caught a sniff of her father's tobacco and her mother's scent in the smoke that surrounded the carriage. It made her smile, gave her a boost, as she stowed her belongings and settled into her seat, and that frisson of excitement grew as the train's speed picked up.

From now on, Sally decided, she needed to grow up and take care of herself. She was an independent woman of the nineteen fifties, clever, pretty enough with the light behind her, and away to live a life she couldn't yet imagine. She wasn't going to be poor little Sally, the scholarship lass from the farm anymore, she could be whoever she wanted. It was a heady and scary thought. She would start with her name, she decided. She had been christened Sarah, and it was as Sarah, Sarah Jane Power – a much more serious, suitable name for a doctor – that she would start at the university.

So, over three exhausting hours later, when she was dragging her suitcase across the university quad towards the women's hostel, and a well-dressed stranger swooped in front of her and offered his help, Sally tried out her new name.

'Thank you. Thank you very much,' Sally stammered, suddenly conscious of her Northern vowels. 'I'm er, Sarah Power. I'm a first-year medical student.'

'Well, well. I'm very pleased to hear that, Sarah Power.' The young man smiled and made no secret of the fact he was running his eyes over her, head to toe. 'I'm Malcolm Harper-Smyth, final year medic, at your service. Is this all your luggage? Ah, well, what does a pretty girl need?'

He effortlessly picked up her case, leaving Sally blushing. There had seemed to be little point in buying a new suitcase when her father's battered brown leather one still served its purpose, but she couldn't help thinking it looked a little too shabby in the hands of the charming man with the double-barrelled name. Still, he had stopped to help, and he called her pretty … She hurried to keep up with him, running up the steps to the hostel to deposit the case with the porter, alongside the big and shiny trunks of the other girls.

'See you around, Dr Power.' Malcolm took her hand, squeezing it gently and brushing off Sally's over-effusive thanks. He winked at her. 'If you want to give me something in return, let me buy you a drink. Come, find me in the library,' he called over his shoulder. 'I'll be swotting there for Finals.'

Her heart thumping from the encounter, Sally found her room, and tried to settle herself by unpacking. She hung her few dresses and skirts into the single three-quarter wardrobe nearest her bed, folding her smalls into the top drawer and her blouses into the next. The open space below housed her spare pair of shoes and only pair of sandals; she'd heard the weather was warmer down south, and it was with glee she'd left her old gumboots behind. She carefully placed her travel clock, single family photograph and her dog-eared copy of Wuthering Heights on the bedside cabinet. The cupboard below would store her books and folders, when they were issued, and her mother had already collected some A4 notepads, files and a pencil case; she always said, the local WI was a goldmine.

Everything done in quick-smart time – Sally's (no, Sarah, remember, she told herself sternly) Sarah's Girl Guide training came to the fore – and now she was left unsure of what to do next. She would love a cup of tea, and maybe a slice of cake, but she wasn't sure what the cafeteria served this time of day, and she felt suddenly shy about exploring. Maybe she should change her clothes? She looked down, doubtfully; she was clean enough, and it's not like she had

7

anything different or fashionable. Instead, leaving the bedroom door open, she sat on her bed, resisting the temptation to bite at her nails, (something she'd never done, so why start now, she thought), staring at the other single bed and empty wardrobe. She wondered who she would be sharing this small room with. She couldn't decide if she was longing for the other girl to turn up or dreading it. It might be the chance to forge a bond with the sister she'd never had – or it could be a disaster. Sally didn't find it that easy to make friends, she had always been amongst the quiet, studious ones at school. Heavens, she'd never even been to the pictures or walked out with a boy, and she was very much afraid that the others in the hostel might find her a little bit old-fashioned.

As if she'd dreamed them up, she heard a door bang and the cadence of female voices in the corridor. They were singing snatches of something from the wireless, the Everly Brothers, she thought, growing louder with each step. Sally sat up straighter, gazing out anxiously as a group of three giggling students came into view. Immediately, she wished she'd got changed. Self-consciously, she smoothed down her neat blouse and blue pleated skirt, so different from the vibrant colours coming towards her. They looked like triplets; perfect hair in French twists and nice jewellery, wearing the modern shift dresses she'd seen only in fancy magazines. Even their stack-heeled shoes put Sally's sensible flats to shame.

And they stopped in their tracks when they saw Sally.

'Hello,' she managed. Her voice was barely above a whisper, croaky and she cleared her throat. 'Hello,' she said again. 'I'm Sal...Sarah. I'm new. Er, you can probably see that. Pleased to meet you.'

There was a second of silence as the trio looked at each other and back to Sally. Then, as if she'd passed some sort of invisible test – though how, she'd wonder later – the first girl smiled and marched into the room. She dumped her suitcase on the bed opposite Sally's, turned and said, 'Hi, Sal-Sarah. I'm Audrey – as in Hepburn. It seems we're sharing. This is Trixie and Cheryl hiding behind her.'

'Hello, nice to meet you all.' She gave them a little wave, knowing she was blushing and silently cursed her shyness. 'Are you all studying Medicine, as well?' she asked more boldly.

'Heavens, no. Are you?' When Sarah nodded, Audrey put her hands on her hips and looked at Sally with exaggerated curiosity. The other two giggled. 'Gosh. How thrilling. We three haven't enough brains between us, my dear. Cheryl and I are reading History, and Trixie, who's maman is from la gay Paree, is doing French.'

'Divine, Dr Sarah,' said the one called Cheryl. 'You'll be very useful if we get a pain in the night. You can tell us if it's our appendix or a simple bilious attack.'

Trixie nudged her and beamed at Sally. 'Forget that, darling. She can introduce us to all the handsome medical students. After all, why are we here, if not to meet our future husbands?'

'Don't mind them,' Audrey advised, her brow furrowing as Sally reddened. 'Some of us would like to get our degree first. Or at least at the same time. Though, methinks you, dear Sarah, might already have met an eligible one, hmm – say nothing, my dear!' She twinkled. Her gaze wandered around the room. 'Have you unpacked already?'

'Yes, I have. I can help you – all of you, if you like?'
Sally offered. 'I quite like tidying…' Why did she say that?
Oh, Sally, you utter idiot, she berated herself. Now she'd
forever be seen as the spinsterish dowdy one, who stayed in
darning her stocking while everyone else was going to
dances with the medical residents.

But Audrey appeared charmed. 'You do? What a treasure.
My mother says that I was at the back of the room when
neatness was handed out. If you help me, you can borrow
anything you want and I'll love you forever.' She looked
Sally up and down. 'And I'll share my very best skin care
advice with you. Yes?'

Her two friends laughed – and Sally joined in, relaxing for
the first time since she'd boarded the train in Ripon. 'Yes,
please,' she agreed.

That night, her first letter home – bubbling with
enthusiasm – written, Sally lay in her narrow bed, the thin
eiderdown pulled up to her chin, as she tried to accustom
herself to the strange noises of her new life. The bones of the
hostel building creaked, and the wind whistled intermittently
through the ill-fitting window-frame. The chintz curtains
were flimsy, but Audrey had begged that they left open the
ancient blackout blind, apparently a relic from the war,
because she was 'a frightful baby about the dark'. Sally
didn't mind, and she smiled to herself, as Audrey turned over
and snuffled like a baby in her sleep. She'd expected to feel
very awkward sharing a room, the whole problem of dressing
and undressing in company, but Audrey, fresh from the
confidence and routine of boarding school, acted without
thought and Sally simply copied her. It was as well, she
thought now, as the bed creaked underneath her, because

whoever heard of a doctor embarrassed about the human body.

Wide awake and very happy, Sally counted her blessings, and looked forward with a fierce longing for this new stage of her life to begin.

Amidst the flurry of the early weeks, every time Sally – would she ever get used to listening out for Sarah rather than Sally? She had to admit she would always be Sally to herself – entered the library, she sat down and found herself waiting/not-waiting for Malcolm Harper-Smyth to appear. She had seen him once or twice, either the life and soul of a group who was speedily ejected from the reading room or with his head deep in a textbook; he could have been asleep. She positioned herself where she could gaze at him without him knowing she was there and was delighted when he caught sight of her one day, and paused to pass the time of day. He didn't, however, suggest that drink.

Audrey, whom Sally had quickly taken into her confidence, thought she was ridiculous; she would square her shoulders and straighten her seams, and breathily offer him a cup of coffee at the Milk Bar in exchange for help with her books. 'But what if he says no?' Sally had objected, as the two of them, plus Trixie and Cheryl, had squashed on to Audrey's bed to paint each other's toe nails a dainty pearly pink. 'No?' Audrey had wrinkled her brow as if Sally were speaking a foreign language. 'No?' And Sally realised with a pang that neither Malcolm nor any of the other medical students – nor indeed any of the boys in the whole university – had ever said, would ever say no to Audrey.

It wasn't just that, Sally admitted to herself, as she opened her books and secretly watched Malcolm from behind her curtain of hair, there was an element of pride involved: Sally didn't need help with her studies, in fact it was true, even if she felt a little boastful to acknowledge, that she was consistently top of the class. It hadn't taken her a week to realise that to most of the professors – elderly, highly educated men – that the four women in the class weren't to be taken seriously. They were there to prove how modern and fair the university was, but they weren't considered genuine doctor material. It was quietly assumed that they would transfer to the nursing school when the going got tougher, or – as Trixie had said that first day – catch the eye of a young doctor and leave to get married. To the male students, they were a novelty, either awkwardly ignored or flirted with like dolly-birds. Sally kept her head down, worked quietly, and generally passed unnoticed. It suited her, even if Audrey was vociferous in telling her she was missing the whole point of university life.

Malcolm, though, was different. He was much older than Sally, perhaps even twenty-four, in his final year of studies, and already referred to as Dr Harper-Smyth. His tall, dark and handsomeness was almost too good to be true – brown wavy hair, sparkling blue eyes, with a fetching smile, and a muscular physique borne of rowing and rugby. He was charming, too, popular amongst the men, and always with a flock of girls surrounding him. Sally admired him from a distance, much as she did Cary Grant and Burt Lancaster in the films – until the day she tripped over and he rescued her. She'd been leaving an anatomy lecture, in a hurry and caught the hem of her skirt on a chair leg. She saved herself, but her books went flying and she was red-faced and mortified.

Those nearest to her sniggered or averted their gaze, but Malcolm caught her eye, gave her a sympathetic smile and bent down to pick up her papers. 'Happens to us all,' he said, as she stumbled through her thanks. 'I'm such a clumsy oaf, only last week I trapped my stethoscope in the sluice. Twice.'

It was nonsense, of course. He was too debonair, too sure of himself to have done anything of the sort, but that he'd made it up to comfort her was all the sweeter. 'Take care, my love,' he'd added. 'I haven't forgotten that drink.'

That encounter lasted seconds, before he went off taking the stairs two at a time, whistling tunelessly, but it was enough. Staid, sensible, Sally, swooned. She was in love. There was a word for it, Trixie told her, when she confessed to the girls later, wondering worriedly if it actually was possible to fall for someone instantaneously. In French it was a coup de foudre: love at first sight.

From that day on, Sally attached herself to the edge of his circle, feigned a sudden interest in rowing, and ensured that her turn to observe surgery at the teaching hospital was on a day when Malcolm was signed up as the assisting doctor. She didn't have a chance with him, of course, but she could dream, couldn't she? After all, he did remember her; he smiled when he saw her and once or twice even said, 'Hello, Sarah.' She hung on his every word. And slowly and steadily, with the persistence and hard work that had got her to medical school in the first place, and egged on by Audrey, Trixie and Cheryl, Sally became one of the flock. Within three months, she could genuinely say they were friends, and the day before she was booked on the train home for Christmas, he asked her to the Festive Ball.

'Why?' she'd asked in wonder, not convinced he wasn't

13

teasing her. 'Has your real date had to cancel?'

Malcolm had roared with laughter. 'That's why, my dear little Sarah. You just don't know how appealing you are, do you? Modesty and innocence are such a heady cocktail.'

The girls had squealed with delight, and they'd taken over. Sally had worn Cheryl's best frock, Audrey's fake pearls, and Trixie's French scent. She'd gone into the hotel ballroom on Malcolm's arm, like a princess, and if she'd noticed the raised eyebrows amongst some of Malcolm's friends and colleagues, she didn't care. Because everything else left her mind when he escorted her back to the hostel and, chivalrous, kissed her lightly in the shadow of the front entrance. Her first kiss. She was walking on air.

The mood lasted all the way home on the train. Sally had intended to study throughout the journey, but instead she stared out of the window and dreamed, occasionally doodling love hearts on her notepad. How would she manage three weeks without seeing him? How would she ever again focus on her studies? But thrown back into farm life, where the reality of university faded into baking and milking and feeding, she regained a semblance of self-control. Her parents had set time aside from her chores so that she could do her 'bookwork' and dutifully every afternoon, she sat at the desk in her bedroom and spread out her books. Spurred on by her parents' pride, and the photograph of Grandpa James on the wall in front of her, she tried hard to concentrate, to ignore the fizz of excitement deep in her tummy when she thought of Malcolm's lips on hers, and eventually found herself absorbed in her reading. Christmas itself was the cosy, familiar occasion it had always been, and when the holidays ended and Sally was back on the train, she felt both ready for her first exams – and for whatever other firsts Malcolm might ask of her. In fact, although she blushed at her unladylike thoughts, Sally couldn't wait.

2

'Being in love suits you,' Audrey said to her a few weeks into their new term. They had spent the evening applying Ponds Cold Cream to their faces, and circles of fresh cucumber to their eyes, as recommended by a beauty feature in McCall's magazine; Cheryl's cousin in America sent it to her every month and the girls agreed it was far more sophisticated than their mothers' copies of Women's Illustrated but not as unattainable as Vogue. 'Look at you, my dear Sarah, you're as radiant as a bride while I'm pale and wan.' Audrey wrinkled her nose at the reflection in her hand-held mirror, then looked up at Sally hopefully.

'You're beautiful,' she replied obediently, but honestly. 'You know you are. If I'm glowing, it's the result of hours out working in the bracing Yorkshire air.' But secretly, Sally was pleased. She thought Audrey was right; she looked better than she ever had and she'd flown through her exams and, as one of the professors grudgingly told her, 'Done rather well for any girl, not just a scholarship one.' She thought there was a compliment in there somewhere, and when she'd repeated the remark to Malcolm, joking about it, he'd said it was, 'High praise from old Barclay and well-deserved. Now come here and let me show you my appreciation,' and he'd taken her in his arms and kissed her thoroughly.

'Malcolm wants me to go to bed with him,' she blurted out suddenly to Audrey, causing her to drop the mirror she was holding on her toe.

Audrey yelped, 'Ouch,' quickly followed by a breathless, 'And? Oh, my gosh, Sarah, are you going to say yes? You are, aren't you? Oh, my gosh!' For all her veneer of sophistication, Audrey was as inexperienced as Sally. Her mouth was a round O and her eyes glittered.

Sally's face reddened. 'Do you know, I think I am,' she said slowly.

'Are you sure? Sarah?'

'I'm almost sure. I've thought about it a lot.'

'I mean, he hasn't asked you to marry him yet, though, has he? Wouldn't you at least want to be engaged?' Audrey sounded uncommonly serious.

'It's 1959. I'm almost nineteen. I'm going to be a doctor. And I love him,' Sally said. 'I've considered it all, and why not? I think it's the next logical step– What's so funny?'

Audrey's hand was at her mouth, stifling a laugh. 'I'm so sorry, darling,' she said, 'But only you could put the practical into romance. It must be the farmer's daughter in you.'

'I don't know about that,' Sally answered. 'But I do know what I'm doing.'

Did she, though, she asked herself, a fortnight later, as she rang the bell at Malcolm's private rooms. Tonight was the night, and there was no going back; her handbag contained a clean pair of white school-girl knickers, incongruously alongside a shockingly transparent and frilly nightie, that Audrey had said was called a baby-doll.

'I hope I don't get run over by a bus on the way,' she'd said as she folded them up, 'I'd be too embarrassed to explain that away.'

Audrey, clearly enthralled, envious and scandalised in equal measure, had pushed the St Christopher medal her older brother had given her before he joined the Navy in Sally's pocket. 'Go with my blessing, child,' she'd said.

It had seemed a game, back at their digs, a jolly jape, as Cheryl might have said, but it suddenly seemed something far more serious. This is the first truly grown-up thing I've done, Sally thought, as she waited for Malcolm to answer the door. Was she ready? It wasn't too late to change her mind…but actually it was. Malcolm hadn't said anything about them sleeping together, but it was clear that for him there was no decision to make, it was simply the next step in a healthy relationship. Sally knew, deep down, that if she said no, he'd be perfectly charming and understanding about it, and then move quietly on to the next girl who was more forthcoming. It was how men were. Even ones as special as Malcolm Harper-Smyth – especially one like him, if she were honest; men that were irresistible to women and so took their acquiescence for granted. Anyway, Sally gave herself a mental kick, she wasn't having second thoughts, this was her decision. She loved Malcolm and she was fairly sure he loved her. He hadn't mentioned a ring or marriage yet, but it was just a matter of time. Once his Finals were finished this summer, he'd be a qualified doctor, ambitious, and ready to start a career, and, she was certain, a family. By the time Malcolm came to the door, Sally was tingling with anticipation.

The wealth and opulence surrounding Malcolm, the extravagant furnishings and lush upholstery and the king-size bed were breath-taking. He wasn't ostentatious though, he simply acted as if it was the norm, and for him, she knew, it was.

He was very sweet and caring that night. He'd taken it for granted that she was a virgin, and she was thankful for that. When he asked her gently, if she was prepared, she swallowed and said that she was. She looked at him trustingly as he took her hand and told her not to be nervous, that he'd take care of her, of everything.

'We'll start with a glass of Champagne,' he said, clinking a slim, elegant glass against hers. 'Everything is enhanced with a glass of bubbly, is it not?'

She didn't tell him she wouldn't know – that for her, the Champagne was a first, too. Besides, she quickly saw the value of it. Slightly bitter to her tongue, she liked the way the bubbles bounced and made her a little giggly. When Malcolm gave her a second glass, a smaller one, and suggested he slip a little something into it to relax her, she thought she was probably relaxed enough, but she didn't argue. It was only a few milligrams of Phenobarbitone, and the first time was bound to hurt, she knew that. She didn't want to spoil it.

'That's my girl,' he said, taking her hand and leading her to the bedroom.

As he'd promised, Malcolm was in full control – like he always was and always would be, Sally thought. She liked that, she felt safe.

'You'll want to visit the bathroom,' he said, pointing to a door off the bedroom. An en suite; Sally was very impressed by that, she'd read of them but never known anyone who had one, and this was palatial. Fluffy towels and fancy soap adorned a very pale green basin and bath, and there was even a shower fitting above the bath, a frilly curtain tied up beside it. Sally had never had a shower in her life, just a weekly business-like bath. At home, their family bathroom was functional, white tiled and always chilly, and they still had an old barely-used privy outside. I must remember everything to tell Mum, Sally thought, then felt a pang. How could she tell her mother about this lovely bathroom, without explanation as to why she was here at all. Oh, well, there would be time enough when she and Malcolm were married; her mum and dad could see it for themselves.

Sally slowly undressed, folded her clothes into a pile, and put on the frilly nightie. She dithered over whether she should wear her knickers underneath, and in the end decided she should. Then she perched on the edge of the lavatory, the seat down, not sure what else she was meant to do. She titivated her hair and swirled some mouthwash around but hesitated to re-enter the bedroom. Was it time? Would Malcolm be in bed already or – she gulped – would he be naked, waiting for her? She paused so long, he tapped on the door.

'Sarah? The night will be gone if you hide in there much longer,' he called.

'Just coming,' she said.

In the bedroom, Malcolm had taken his tie off and unbuttoned the top two buttons of his shirt. Sally noticed his Rolex watch and cufflinks lay on the bedside table, the lights already dimmed. and the bed turned carefully down. She accepted another glass of Champagne and drank it in two gulps. She was both disappointed and relieved that he didn't comment on her skimpy outfit.

Instead, Malcolm said, 'Sarah, darling, I'll make this a most memorable experience for you, for us both.' He put his own glass down and took her in his arms. 'Relax,' he whispered, holding her tight. He kissed her, his tongue exploring her mouth murmuring to her to do the same. Tentatively, she did so, and gladly heard his, 'Hmm, you're a fast learner, I'll give you that.'

Malcolm's hands slid over her back, removing one thin strap, then the other, off Sally's white shoulders. He groaned, and swiftly, moved into her nape, kissing and drawing his wet tongue slowly along her curves and down towards her breast. She shivered, unresisting, and used her hands to stroke his muscular frame. He lifted his head and they kissed again, and again. Then in a swift, fluid movement, Malcolm picked Sally up and carried her to the bed, laying her down, before standing over her and undoing the buckle of his belt. She licked her lips, swollen with passion but dry from all the Champagne, and for some reason that made him laugh aloud. Then he lay beside Sally kissing her gently and undressing himself at the same time. She found herself getting impatient, and she squirmed with delight, eager now, to give herself to him.

'Well, well,' he said, as she attempted to unbutton his shirt but Malcolm moved again and sat himself astride her almost naked body. He pulled his shirt quickly over his head and reached down, tugging at her knickers, and twisting her nightie to one side with a suddenness that ripped the seam. 'I've waited a long time for this,' he breathed in her ear. 'For you.'

Sally shut her mind to how many girls, women, he had been with before. She wanted to feel special, and as he said her name, 'Sarah, oh, Sarah,' it was on the tip of her tongue to ask him to call her Sally… but the moment passed. She could feel him hard against her, a strange sensation, and she whimpered with fear and desire. Then she shut her eyes and let Malcolm take over.

It was the beginning of a glorious few weeks. Effortlessly,

Sally switched between dedicated medical student, the most promising female, the department of medicine had ever enrolled, to an eager and willing lover, the prize of becoming Mrs Malcolm Harper-Smyth dangling tantalisingly before her. It was as if she were split in two: of course, she wanted to get her medical degree, but increasingly, she wanted to be a wife and mother more. Why couldn't she have both, she argued with herself. Men had had careers and families forever, and times were changing fast, people were already looking to a new decade full of promise. Sally had heard it said that the 1960s were going to be the most exciting since the roaring twenties, and she wasn't going to be left behind.

Easter came and went. Sally was expected at home, and try as Malcolm might, he couldn't make her let her parents down. She was going, she laughed up at him, and he would have to manage without her.

'I'll find a way, I suppose,' he said, lightly enough, but it left a flicker of unease in Sally, sufficient for her to cut short the holiday, explaining – with a pang of guilt she pushed down – to her approving parents that there were extra lectures available for selected students. That was true in itself, and Sally was invited, but she had no intention of attending. She didn't need extra lessons to finish first in her class, but she did need to see Malcolm. And it seemed like he couldn't get enough of her.

'Smug,' Audrey teased her, more than once. 'I rather hate you sometimes, Sarah. You're so nice and so clever and you have a dreamy boyfriend. Do leave some crumbs for your pals.'

Had she been smug, Sally pondered as she sat in the university library, looking with unseeing eyes out at the cherry blossom dancing across the quad. She honestly didn't think so, or at least she hadn't meant to be. Open in front of her was her pocket diary, and she sighed as she fruitlessly flicked the pages over and counted the days, trying to make them add up to something different. Pride comes before a fall was something she'd had drummed into her since Sunday School. She'd let herself forget that and now she could be about to fall very far. It all depended now on whether Malcolm would be there to pick her up.

Sally slammed the diary shut, shoved it into her bag and stood up, all noisily enough to garner a sharp, 'Ssh,' from the duty librarian – who then looked surprised at who was the source of the disturbance. Sally mouthed a half-hearted 'sorry' at the woman as she left the safety of the book-lined cocoon and made her way purposefully to Malcolm's rooms.

Her nerve almost failed her as soon as she reached his front door, and when he grabbed her, pulled her inside and took her straight to bed, she didn't complain. If Malcolm noticed her heart wasn't in it, he didn't pause or comment. They were both dressed, and he was thinking aloud about an early supper somewhere or other, before she got another opportunity to speak.

'Malcolm?' Sally was quaking but she'd procrastinated for nineteen days already and could put it off no longer. She swallowed and dug her nails into clenched palms. She was interrupting him, which always annoyed him. 'I've something to tell you.'

'What is it?' He spoke sharply; he must have heard something in her tone.

'My period is late,' she said quietly. 'And I've been sick a few times. Malcolm I'm pregnant.' The last three words came out in a whisper. She took a deep breath and looked into his face, anxious as to how he'd react.

'Are you sure?' he asked, sharper still, his lips thinning the way they did when he was irritated. 'Sarah? Are you sure? Have you seen a doctor, had it confirmed?'

'No. Not yet. I–'

'Then common sense says you might not be. If you've not had it confirmed.'

Of all possible responses, she'd not imagined sarcasm. Strangely, it gave her strength. 'Malcolm, I know my body. I know I'm pregnant.'

'How long?'

'About seven weeks. Perhaps a little more.'

'Oh Christ, Sarah. Christ. Let's think.' He turned away from her. 'Bloody hell. We need to stay calm, think this thing through.'

'This thing,' Sally repeated. 'Malcolm we're talking about a baby.'

'I know that.' Malcolm was pacing from window to fireplace and back, his hand held to his forehead. 'Although medically speaking, that is negligible. It's a cluster of cells.'

The sobs that unexpectedly racked her body stopped his pacing and he turned to her and sighed. 'Come here,' he said, his arms held out.

Sally laid her head gratefully on his shoulder and let her tears fall.

'Don't worry.' Malcolm handed Sally his handkerchief. 'It's regrettable but I'll sort it out.'

'Sort it out?'

'I'll take care of things.'

'Of me?' Sally felt a twinge of hope.

'Sit down.' Malcolm guided Sally to the brown leather Chesterfield. 'This isn't what you want, is it, Sarah?' he asked.

Sally looked at him, confused. 'It's certainly not what I planned, but it's happened.'

'What will your parents say?'

Sally's tears welled up again at the mention of her mum and dad. 'Oh, Malcolm, I can't bear to think about that.' If there was a promise of marriage... she wanted to add, but Malcolm was pacing now, and she didn't dare.

'Ssh. Don't cry. For Christ's sake, don't bloody cry, I'll sort it, you'll see. You'll make a great doctor, you know.' She could see he was forcing his smile. 'Doctor Sarah Power, sounds good, doesn't it?'

'That probably won't be possible now.' Sally was struggling to speak. 'Time off. A baby–'

'Sarah, you know very well that if you have a child, you will be asked to leave the university and it will be in disgrace. Medicine is no place for a mother and especially for... well, it would be churlish to spell it out.'

His 'an unmarried mother' went without saying and Sally's last vestiges of hope, that Malcolm would do the right thing by her, began to trickle away.

'It could still happen,' he said taking Sally's hand in his.

'You mean–' Optimism flared.

'We've got a lot to offer, you and I,' he said earnestly. 'We've each got a great future ahead of us. This pregnancy has happened a bit too soon for us, that's all.' Malcolm leaned towards Sally and ran his finger down her cheeks, wiping the tears away. He sat down again and took her in his arms, placing his lips to hers. 'In five years, it will be something to celebrate. But now? No, Sarah. I cannot be a father now.'

'And me?' she whispered. Optimism died.

'And you can't be a mother,' he added hurriedly. 'You'll be a wonderful mother to my children, Sarah. No one better. But when we can do it properly. No hole in the corner nuptials for the Dr… Doctors Harper-Smyth clan, hey? Come on, give me a smile. It's not so bad,' he added, as if to himself. 'Now that the first shock is over, it's not so bad.'

After a pause, Sally spoke mechanically. 'You said you can sort it out.'

'That's my girl!' She knew she'd said the right thing. 'I promise I'll take care of it. Of you.' Malcolm pulled back and looked at her. 'Your parents never need find out about this, you know. No-one need ever find out about this. We can go on as we were before. Sarah, I can make this all better.'

'It's going to be alright,' Sally repeated to herself, over and over, all the way back to the women's hostel. 'Malcolm's going to take care of me.' But she thought it dully, apprehension already gnawing away at her. How could she have been so stupid?

3

She had expected a private clinic, and a doctor, one Malcolm knew personally, one who would keep the secret – the awful secret – a sort of filial Hippocratic Oath. The clinic was unnecessary, apparently, and the man he had in mind was a doctor, Malcolm assured her, in all but the ink on his qualification drying. He knew the procedure and, after all, he was top of the class and best student of the year, every year. He had researched carefully…

It was only at that point that Sally realised, with disbelief, that Malcolm wasn't talking about a colleague of his from the hospital. No, he was talking about himself. He intended to operate on her himself.

He, personally, intended to abort their child.

'No, no, no, lovely, Sarah, don't say that.' He'd held her to him when she'd asked him outright. 'Don't think of it as a child. It's a scraping of cells. It's called a D&C, you know that. Minor surgery. I've watched several women cured of their menstruation issues this way.'

'Watched? Not done it?' she whispered.

'Darling Sarah, the difference is negligible.' With distaste she thought he looked almost enthusiastic; proud to show off his ability, at any rate. He was getting impatient with her, too, she could sense his frustration barely masked by the kind words and carefully curated bedside manner. She was losing him, Sally knew it. Not only was she losing their unborn child, she was losing the man she loved.

'Alright,' she agreed. 'Alright, Malcolm. Do what you think is best.' She was too tired, and felt too sick, to argue any more.

Firstly, he administered a sedative, following that, a painkiller. She soon felt numb, in body now, as well as mind, and then drowsy as the anaesthetic worked. Sally watched as Malcolm stripped his bed and spread out a huge plastic sheet out over it, and then she let him take her by the hand and lay her down on top of it, her head propped up with two pillows. The vision of Malcolm, donning surgical greens and gloves, before he pulled a mask over his mouth, was the last thing she remembered.

Sally woke sometime in the afternoon, alone and frightened. She wasn't prepared for all the blood. Malcolm must have cleaned up, but this was fresh blood, oozing out of her and she had a pain deep in her belly. She attempted to stand up, but dizzy and nauseous, she couldn't make it even to the bathroom, and she collapsed back onto the bloody bed, wet and sticky, and wept heaving sobs before falling back into a troubled sleep. She dreamed that Malcolm was operating on her with a long, iron knitting needle with a skein of coarse thread; when she tried to break the nightmare to tell him she was awake, he pulled his mask over his eyes and turned away.

Malcolm woke her hours later; it was dark again. He said, 'You needed stitching, so I gave you more pethidine, before carrying it out earlier on. You were quite restless. The bleeding has stopped and the stitches will hold if you stay lying down and rest, give your body time to recover.'

'Did you do it?' she croaked, her mouth dry. 'Is it gone?'

He nodded briefly, before turning away, to fill her a glass of water. Sally noticed his hands were shaking as he helped her sip it, and he looked strained. She felt a pang of – what?

Sympathy? Empathy? Followed by one that bordered on satisfaction; he was suffering, too. As he should. It was something, for good or bad, that they would share forever.

'I'll be back later, and maybe you will want to eat something.' He said it in the dispassionate tones of a doctor, distant, authoritative. She couldn't bring herself to ask him where he was going, please not to leave her.

He did come back, but Sally couldn't eat, she was in too much pain. She wanted to ask Malcolm questions but she felt too tired and then he left again. He didn't sleep in his rooms that night, or the two following, simply visiting her morning and evening for the next three days, bringing tinned soup and bottles of milk. When she was conscious, Sally grew resentful at his actions – nothing but a dutiful doctor doing his rounds – but she got steadily weaker and still was spotting fresh blood.

'Might I have an infection?' she asked Malcolm. 'That would explain the aches and fever…' She stopped when she saw her attempt at self-diagnosis was irritating him – everyone knew doctors made terrible patients – and didn't comment when, on his next visit, he started her on a course of antibiotics. They helped, but not much.

Eventually, Malcolm said, 'This is not working, Sarah. I can't give you the care you need. Your friends are asking for you. I told the bossy one you have influenza and are in isolation here whilst I lodge at the hospital – that much is true – but we need to avoid any hint of rumour.' He cleared his throat. 'Speaking as a doctor, I think it best if you go home to recuperate.'

'Home?' Sally was confused. 'Back to the women's hostel? The superintendent won't take a… a sick student back, surely. Not even to the infirmary, if Audrey tells her I'm infectious.'

'I mean, your proper home, Sarah. Home to your parents in Yorkshire.'

'But what about you?' She meant, 'What about us?' but was afraid to say it.

'I'll be fine,' he said shortly, and if she wasn't sure whether he was being deliberately obtuse, his next words confirmed it. 'Quite frankly, my dear, I haven't time to look after you, and my real patients, and concentrate on my Finals. There's no reason why all this, your operation, hasn't gone exactly to plan. You should be fine by now.'

'You're saying it's my fault I'm not better?'

'I'm saying I think there are emotional and psychological elements to your recovery, and that you're not doing yourself any good, wallowing here.'

'Wallowing in my own mess,' she said flatly.

'Stop it, Sarah. That's not what I meant, but your attitude is. Look,' he relented, 'I expect you are also anaemic. Better to go back to the country, hmm? Fresh air on the farm, where your mother can look after you. You can say that you contracted scarlet fever. I'll write you a medical certificate, shall I? That way you avoid any unsavoury questions. In a couple of months, you'll be right as rain, and you'll forget any of this unpleasantness ever happened. Sarah?'

When she didn't reply, didn't meet his eyes, he cupped her chin with his palm and, gently enough, forced her head upwards. He smiled at her. 'It's for the best, Sarah, you know that. We can't go on like this.'

Sally nodded, too weak, too lost, to argue. Malcolm told her he had already arranged for Audrey to pack her belongings and send them on, and had asked her to tell the Lady Superintendent at the hostel. He couldn't do any more, he said, she would need to give notice of medical leave of absence to the university.

'But I have got you this,' he said. 'To make things just a little easier on you.'

She took the envelope and opened it. Inside was twenty pounds and a first-class train ticket for the next day.

That was the last time Sally expected to see Malcolm Harper-Smyth.

Sally knew that the effort of getting to the train would be too much for her, so she'd made her way slowly to the telephone box on the corner of Malcolm's street and booked a taxi.

With tuppence to spare she wondered whether to phone the farm and tell them to expect her, or Audrey to say goodbye. In the end, she did neither, afraid that her mother or her friend would hear something in her voice and she would shock them, blurting out horrors she could never recall. Instead, she took paper and stamps from Malcolm's desk, and wrote to them, Cheryl and Trixie, too, saying how much she would miss them, three girls who had, against all the odds, become such good friends to her. Then, on the final sheet, she slowly drafted a letter to the Heads of the Medical School. There was no question of a leave of absence, Sally had known that the moment Malcolm unveiled his plans to send her home. Instead, she carefully and with finality, withdrew from her studies and relinquished her scholarship. Her heart would be breaking if it wasn't already in tatters. Sally would never be a doctor now.

The next morning, she was grateful to the friendly taxi

driver, for carrying her case, small as it was, to the platform. There, the porter took charge of it, and her, and found her a seat in a quiet corner. Sally wasn't sure if that was because she looked so thin and ill or whether first class passengers were always treated that way. On board the train, the carriage felt cold, and she tightened her jacket around her slight frame. She then pulled her luncheon box from her bag and stared at it sitting on her lap. Her inclination for food had left her since that day. 'You have to eat,' she said aloud; she didn't want to terrify her parents. Sally nibbled at the cheese sandwich, in the hope that she would feel better. 'Feel better? Will I ever feel better again?' she said bitterly, wondering whether talking to herself was the first sign of madness.

Her thoughts travelled to home, and her mother. Her lovely mum. The mum who made her the pink princess dress for her ninth birthday party. The mum who served up her favourite pudding, apple crumble and custard, when Jason Bishop tripped her up on the way home from school. How she wanted to be that child once more. But what if her mother figured out what had happened to her? They seemed to have a sixth sense for things like that... not that she would know that now. Sally tried to distract herself from her racing thoughts by looking out of the window. The train was still alongside the platform; fearful of being late she had been half an hour early. She watched the blonde woman hug the dark-haired gentleman. She noticed the young woman, with the red-cheeked baby sitting upright in the Silver Cross pram. Probably teething, Sally thought bleakly. It was then that her heart began to race, panic surged through her. She started trembling; she wanted to get off the train, she had to get off the train, right now. She needed to feel safe. She needed to turn the clock back. Turn it back… Sally's mind went blank. To when though: before the abortion or before him?

'Is anyone sitting there?'

Sally jumped as the grey-haired woman in the gaberdine coat addressed her. She didn't answer. She couldn't.

'Are you alright love?' The woman's face creased into a concerned frown. 'You're looking very peaky.'

Sally managed a small nod and sank back in her seat.

'That's right, love, you relax. You look like you're glad of a seat. My legs are killing me, too. I can hardly wait to take the weight off them,' she said, plonking her ample body clumsily next to Sally. 'Is it me, or is this carriage a bit parky?'

Sally gave her a weak but genuine smile and felt her heart rate slowing slightly.

Ordinary everyday conversation, that's what she needed. She was grateful to her fellow passenger who was still chattering on.

'Maybe I shouldn't have put my winter's coat away just yet.' She glanced down at Sally's lap. 'Oh, you've started your lunch early, I see.'

'Yes, I felt a bit peckish.' A lie. They tripped of her tongue these days, Sally thought.

'I'm going to my sister, Mabel's, for lunch. What that woman can't do with potted meat, isn't worth knowing.'

Sally felt a giggle rise within her but stopped its escape.

'Tuesday's her day off. She's a cleaner at the Southern General, you know. Her house is like a new pin. Wish mine was.' She laughed heartily at that. 'Where are you off to, then, love?' she asked. 'Oh, pardon me, my manners. I'm Mildred.'

'Sally.' The firm, working woman's hand was solid, reminded Sally of her mum again – but this time it was comforting. 'I'm going home,' she said. 'I've not been well. I don't think the city agrees with me.' She closed the lid on her sandwich box and put it back in her bag. Resting her head against the back of the seat, she listened to Mildred chatter on. Her stories were as jumbled as Sally's thoughts: Frank, the hapless husband. And Gerard. Sally still hadn't figured out who Gerard was when she was asked her opinion on his pigeons. She realised she'd dozed off. Fortunately, like most of Mildred's questions, it was rhetorical, and her struggle to give an opinion pleased the older lady.

'Exactly.' She beamed. 'I was lost for words too.'

Sally couldn't imagine that. She drifted off again.

'Well, this is me,' Mildred announced, sometime later, startling Sally from her sleep. 'Seems a shame to wake you, but I didn't want to leave without saying ta ra. You look after yourself now, do you hear?'

'Nice to meet you,' Sally replied. 'Enjoy your lunch.'

'Oh, I will, haven't had a lunch yet, I ain't enjoyed.' Mildred rubbed her generous middle.

Sally watched as she made her way down the train. She was pleased when they caught each other's eye and Mildred waved to her from the platform. Maybe, Sally thought, she wasn't all spoiled; Mildred had seemed to think she was still a normal girl with a normal life.

The train crept on and thoughts of the farm crept back into Sally's mind. They would have got the letter first post, along with the early milk, to say she was on her way back. Time enough to get to the station to meet her, but not too much left over for them to worry. She hadn't written she was giving up the course permanently. That was still to come. Scarlet fever, she reminded herself. She'd caught scarlet fever and it had taken her badly.

Sure enough when the train eventually trundled in to Ripon Station, her parents were there already, as Sally knew they would be. She had made her way out of the first-class compartment, and climbed down from the ordinary end, not wanting to invite questions. Her stomach lurched at the sight of her mother in her best hat and her father in his only suit, looking as awkward as he had at Christmas and at Easter. He always did when he was away from the farm. And there was Auntie Vi; Sally hadn't expected Auntie Vi. She was to be greeted by a welcoming committee. It was all she needed.

Sally took a deep breath and stepped from the train.

Her mum, holding her hat in place, ran to meet her. She stopped before Sally and her eyes teared up. 'Oh, love, my poor love. You have been in the wars. What has happened to you?'

4

As such, Sarah's life was woefully short-lived. After the abortion, she went home, back to being Sally. Or what was left of the old Sally. Her mother fussed over her like the proverbial hen, worried by her weak and wan daughter. Gradually, fed by fresh farm produce, Sally's physical health did improve, and she strived to put the whole unhappy university period behind her. When she'd built her strength back up, she took on more and more of the farming duties; caring for the animals was a substitute, albeit a poor one, for caring for patients in the medical career she'd lost.

Offley Farm had been in the Power family for generations. It was medium-sized, on the edge of the Dales: a small herd of cattle, a handful of pigs, saddlebacks, hens and their two dogs, both Patterdales. Sally's parents were God-fearing Christians, kindly folk, whose Bible was read religiously every evening after supper. Churchgoing was taken for granted and Sally fell back into adorning her Sunday best and sitting silently in the congregation, watching her father playing the organ, and politely refusing to help out with Sunday School until she was 'fighting fit again'. She had no qualms about sitting in God's house, after what she'd been through, what she'd done. She had never been a committed believer but if she was certain of anything, it was that her abortion was driven by man not God.

After her recuperation – physically that is, she had a long way to go emotionally – Sally broke it gently to her parents that she had decided to stay on at the farm and give up any notion of becoming a doctor. City life, academic life, wasn't for her, she told them, meaning it. She was sorry more than she could say if they were disappointed in her but at least she'd tried it out and she knew now what her life would – should – be. Mr and Mrs Power accepted her decision equably; they just wanted their only girl to be happy, and if her mother guessed there might be a boy – man – involved, she soon stopped fishing. Sally mentioned Audrey occasionally, and Trixie and Cheryl, and her mum urged her to have them visit. When it never happened, and no post came, she stopped asking about that too. Sally knew her mum probably thought she was ashamed of her humble beginnings, but it wasn't that. She simply hadn't left her address with them, sure that a clean break was the only way.

The one person who could have found her, never did. Since the day Malcolm handed her the envelope with the four £5 notes and her train ticket, Sally knew their relationship was over. He had sorted her out, looked after her; saved himself and his reputation at the same time. She'd shoved the money under her mattress on her first night back at home. She didn't want it, it made her feel dirty, but it would be a bigger sin to burn it. Sally wrote to him, once, twice, going into Ripon to stamp the letters, so that the gimlet-eyed postmistress, her mum's bosom-friend Sally called Auntie Vi, couldn't comment. There was never a reply, no apologetic contact, no remorseful visit. Eventually Sally gave up hoping for them and reluctantly realised that the suave and entitled Malcolm Harper-Smyth had lived up to his reputation, after all. Disappointed and sad, she accepted her destiny as a simple life on a farm.

As the months drew on, her mother urged Sally to go out more: the weekly social in the local dance hall; the pictures in Ripon. Walking the hills with only the dogs for company was no outing for a lovely young lady, Auntie Vi agreed. After all, she'd added coyly, it wasn't as if Sally needed to be alone, did she? Sally pretended to misunderstand, until the well-meaning pair came right out and said it.

'Sally, love, of course you remember Robert. Robert Brown,' Auntie Vi reminded her.

'He was always sweet on you, even at school,' her mum added.

Of course, she knew who they meant. A local farmer's son, he'd been in the year above her. A tall, gangly lad with reddish hair and shy. Shyer than she'd been, even. Sally suspected his being sweet on her was poetic licence, and she sighed inwardly, knowing the matchmaking was inevitable. If Sally were to live on the farm long-term, she needed to be a farmer's wife – she would inherit Offley but she couldn't run it alone – and Robert was conveniently in the wings. He and his brothers now took care of their own family homestead, a dairy farm with over 100 Friesians and a milk bottling plant on site. Robert was the youngest of the four and as such, unlike Sally, he would never inherit the farm solely. It was the original match made in heaven.

Sally decided she could do worse. Marrying Robert would keep everyone happy, and her happy enough, she supposed, and that was as much as she'd ever hope for now. Her mother, always with a soft spot for their neighbour's mild-mannered boy, set up a plan of campaign: cake after church for the two of them, then dinner on the farm, then blatantly encouraging Robert, to ask Sally to the WI tea dance, to the Parish picnic, to the pictures.

Whatever he offered, Sally accepted without demur, and soon it was taken for granted they were courting. Robert was nice. He was safe, and that's what Sally wanted. Slowly, their friendship blossomed to a gentle romance. Robert remained the perfect gentleman, bringing her bunches of flowers, a box of chocolates, and a certain contentment she'd never thought she'd find.

On one sunny afternoon at a picnic two and a half years later, Robert knelt down and proposed marriage.

'I love you, Sally,' he said. 'I always have. You know that.'

'I love you, too. Yes, I'll marry you.' Sally agreed without hesitation. It wasn't a lie; she'd said nothing about being in love. She'd never again wanted that.

They announced their engagement, set a date for early the following year, and the whole village clapped and cheered them through their simple wedding day. When the kegs of cider were empty, heralding the end of the wedding breakfast, Sally threw her bouquet, and with it, she hoped and prayed, all the shadows that had been Malcolm and Sarah.

Gill Merton

PART TWO

MARRIAGE (1963-1968)

5
MALCOLM

Dr Malcolm Harper-Smyth. M.D. F.R.C.S.

Admiring his personal letterhead, the man himself signed his name with a flourish and sat back with a sigh of satisfaction. Those qualifications and the nameplate on his office door were evidence of his success: like grandfather, like father, like son. Malcolm was entitled to use 'Mr' rather than 'Dr' these days, but it was his personal choice not to; he liked being a doctor and liked that calling himself such made him stand out amongst his colleagues. The Harper-Smyths had always been medical men, and Malcolm had known from prep school days what was expected of him. And here he was, a private cardiothoracic surgeon – heart specialist, to the hoi polloi – at thirty-three. He'd drink to that, and in fact, he often did: work hard, play hard – another motto of the Harper-Smyth medical men.

Speaking of which – Malcolm glanced at his Omega watch – he was meeting his father at the Club for lunch, and the old man couldn't abide tardiness. There was no value in pleading emergency because in Dr Harper-Smyth Senior's world of General Practice, patients toed the line and suffered their weak chests and nerves and bilious attacks during prescribed surgery hours.

Malcolm pressed his state-of-the-art intercom button and listened for the tinny voice of his secretary. 'Any messages, Susan?'

'Nothing that can't wait until after your luncheon appointment, Dr Harper-Smyth,' came the efficient reply. There was a slight pause, followed by a silkier, 'Is there anything else I can do for you, Doctor?'

Oh, she was no kitten. Classy chassis, too, under the respectable twinset. Malcolm enjoyed a self-satisfied smirk. Susan was the subject of much ribald speculation amongst the younger doctors at the Club, but Malcolm kept the upper-hand. She was Cheltenham Ladies College, through and through, and her ma had been his ma's bridesmaid or some such nonsense; there had been many women, many, but one didn't sully one's own patch. Regretfully, Malcolm had slipped up once or twice with youthful indiscretions (come on, it was a rite of passage!) but none had ended well. As for that regretful time back in his university days. Silly, silly girl – even now he gave a sigh. Sandra, or Sarah, wasn't it? Something that like. He'd done her a favour really, he'd reasoned, after the event; she'd never have made a doctor, given she'd failed even to take care of herself.

Malcolm realised Susan was still waiting patiently for his answer. 'No, thank you,' he said, pulling himself together and regretting the discreet pout of disappointment he imagined on her rosebud lips. Oh well, it wasn't as if an eminent physician was lacking in opportunities and, Malcolm straightened his tie, some might say he was entitled to them.

By four o'clock he was ready to call it a day. The food at his pa's club invariably disagreed with him, and today's mulligatawny soup and then steak and kidney were dancing an unholy tango somewhere south-east of his gall bladder. Thank Christ the place laid on a decent wine list and soothing waitresses, well-stacked and comely.

The old man had been on top form, Malcolm thought. A bit high-coloured – though woe betide mentioning BP to his father, 'Young upstart,' he'd grunt – but firm of foot and handshake. He had an agenda, too, and wasn't afraid to broadcast it.

'Time you made your way down the aisle, my boy,' he'd boomed. 'Anything suitable on the horizon, huh?'

'Haven't been looking for a wife, pa.' Malcolm ploughed his way through the spotted dick and custard. 'Too busy.'

'Hmm.' The old man had lowered his voice at that. 'Too busy chasing bits of skirt who're no better than they ought to be. Or so I hear.' The raised eyebrows were ominous.

Malcolm hadn't expected that; he was always discreet. 'Pa–'

'Pa, nothing. Doctors talk, Malcolm. Medical school is all very well for high spirits and a spot of wild oats sowing, but when a man is in his thirties he's expected to settle down.' He'd tossed back his brandy and landed the glass on the tablecloth just a little too hard. 'See to it,' he'd barked.

The point was made and Malcolm had taken it: what was sauce for the medical student was poison for the new consultant; thank Christ, the old man had given him the nod. Patients liked their doctors to be married men, he mused, family men. Two children, he thought, to start. Maybe four if his wife didn't manage boys first time round…Wife. Yes, indeed, time to choose the future Mrs Malcolm Harper-Smyth, and he knew exactly where to start looking.

6

Sally's honeymoon, delayed 'til after lambing season, was the first real test in her marriage to Robert. Her dad had driven them to the station, an occasion that warranted his best suit again, looking a little frayed now, and with an overlooked gravy stain on his tie – Sally's mother, beside him in her wedding hat and gloves, was mortified. The newlyweds were catching the London train, and the older woman was concerned whether the old Thermos would keep their tea hot as far as Peterborough, when they could chance the British Rail buffet.

London had been Robert's idea; a surprise that had made her gasp but not with the joy her fond husband and parents had imagined. How could she face London again, after what had happened at the university? She'd have to, she'd thought bleakly, Robert had never been to the capital before and was beaming with pleasure.

'You can show me the sights,' he said, squeezing her arm. 'The Crown Jewels and Tower Bridge…'

What did he think she'd done during her two and a half terms at medical school, she thought irritably? She'd been there to study, not to gallivant all over the city. But she discarded the thought as quickly as it came; she hadn't studied, had she? The only sights she'd been interested in were those inhabited by Malcolm Harper-Smyth. Even now, she felt a jolt of nausea at his name, and she hoped to God, he was miles away being a highfalutin doctor like he'd promised. With effort she tuned back in to Robert, just in time to hear him say,

'We could go and look at your old college, Sally, love–'

'No!' She hadn't meant to sound so sharp; Robert looked at her strangely, almost as if she'd struck him. 'I mean, no, let's not.' She took his hand. 'Let's look to the future. concentrate on us. That life wasn't for me, Robert. This one is.' She could have cried, the look of love he gave her, and the more he chattered happily on, the more she could feel the horror of those awful days, almost five years ago now, nibbling at her edges as if it were yesterday.

Sally composed herself as they grouped on the platform, Robert checking his top pocket for the tickets and her dad looking anxiously for the minute old Fred Postlethwaite, the station master, would wave his flag. If she looked strained, rather than the radiant bride they were all expecting, she would put it down to worrying about her mum, who was dabbing her eyes with her hanky and calling Sally 'my little love'. It was like leaving for medical school all over again, she thought, and was glad when the train puffed into the station and they had to board. They left in a flurry of waves and last-minute warnings to be careful 'down there', then Sally settled thankfully into a corner seat, and let Robert solicitously wrap a blanket around her knees. He was such a kind man, Robert, her Robert, he always had been; she needed to shape up, Sally told herself sternly.

She had grown up in the last five years, matured in a way the naïve girl of her university days had never dreamed of; the glamorous Audrey, Trixie and Cheryl wouldn't recognise her in a line-up. This Sally would let nobody, certainly not Malcolm, spoil her life. It had taken every last day of their engagement for Sally to teach herself that she was entitled to be happy, and if she was, then Robert certainly was, too.

'Thank you, Mr Brown.' Sally smiled, watching Robert

fold his overcoat carefully and lay it beside them. 'It's always a bit draughty on these trains. Is it too greedy to start on the egg sandwiches, do you think?'

'Whatever you say, Mrs Brown.' Robert got up again and reached for the wicker basket. 'Your wish is my command.'

'Now, you're to have a good rest, while we're away,' he went on, as they munched the soft bread. 'You work too hard, Sally, what with the farm and your folks and the WI and all your good deeds running you ragged!'

'You work just as hard,' she protested. 'And I love what I do, even if it is hard work at times. We'll both have a good rest,' she compromised.

'That we will. We best make the most of it – you never know,' Robert flushed faintly, 'on the way back we might have an er… little one cooking. Wouldn't that be a turn up?'

Sally nodded, the sandwich suddenly dry in her throat. Please let it happen, she prayed to a God she still didn't believe in. It had happened once and been taken from her. For both of their sakes, please let it happen again. Properly, this time.

7
MALCOLM

Despite his confident plotting and planning, Malcolm had no idea it was Martha Beaumont he was searching for, until he saw her, ice-cool and perfectly turned out, taking her place behind the much-coveted podium.

The speaker couldn't have failed to notice the ripple through the ranks – the overwhelmingly male ranks – as she smoothed her long, tapered fingers over her skirt and lent towards the microphone. More than one of the assembled medics, Malcolm included, scrambled to consult their programmes, confirming that this was, indeed, Dr M Beaumont – Martha Beaumont, as she introduced herself, not Michael or Matthew or Mark. Even more surprising to the audience, there was neither challenge nor apology in her introduction, she clearly had eyes for nothing but the speech in front of her.

Malcolm didn't hear a word of it. His image of the docile, motherly, house-proud wife, ignorantly supportive of his career, was busy taking a 360-degree turn. In front of him was a woman who could take him places. Fine-looking, if not beautiful; a slim and healthy body, ideal for child-bearing; a faint American accent that was bound to open doors; and as an MD working as a genetic research scientist, she would be esteemed but no professional threat to him. Oh, she'd be a challenge, but that was all the better. He almost groaned aloud, frantically wondering how best to inveigle a speedy introduction.

Malcolm was smitten.

'Dr Beaumont?' At the end of the lecture, Malcolm was

one of the first out into the foyer. Ahead of him, Martha, alone, was moving swiftly towards the lifts. Just the ticket, he thought, increasing his own stride. 'Dr Beaumont,' he called again. Christ, was the woman hard of hearing or being fabulously difficult?

Only when she'd reached the nearest lift and pressed the Call button, did the figure turn to look at him. 'Can I help you?' she asked crisply.

Definitely American, he decided, but of the right sort: Boston, perhaps – Harvard-educated, with any damn luck. Malcolm summoned his most charming, boyish smile, the one that never failed with ladies of any age or standing. 'I do hope you can,' he said earnestly. 'You see, I'm a great admirer of your work. I'm a cardiologist, myself, so don't profess to have your level of knowledge but I am interested in er… the relationship between genetics and er…the outcomes of cardiac surgery in er… geriatric female patients.' He was improvising wildly in the face of her impervious stare; he'd never given any remote thought to genetics in his work, and he prayed she'd put his hesitation down to being overawed. Who could resist a spot of hero worship?

Apparently, Martha Beaumont could. 'Really?' She didn't even sound interested.

Desperate measures. Thinking rapidly, Malcolm changed tack. 'Yes, really, Doctor. And, well, there's something else.' He hung his head momentarily, then looked back at her, locking his gaze on hers, his tone hardening slightly. 'I don't know anyone else here. I don't want to know anyone here. And to that end, I'd rather like it if you'd do me the honour of sitting beside me at dinner.' Confident, he waited for her to crack, but his smile was forced by the time she finally spoke.

'I'm afraid not,' she said. 'I have a prior invitation with the Dean of Studies, Dr–' She flicked her eyes towards his name-badge, 'Dr Harper-Smyth. Good afternoon.' She gave him a brief nod, stepping into the lift, the doors closing behind her before Malcolm could sufficiently collect his wits.

Far from being rebuffed, though, he was suffused with anticipation, excitement, even. If there was a problem with having one's choice of girls at beck and call, it meant that the majority were dolly-birds; easy come, easy go, or those breathless little nurses who would happily get themselves into trouble for the prize of a well-heeled doctor husband. The chase was lukewarm at best, a trap at worst.

He'd give Dr Martha Beaumont a run for her money alright, he decided, retracing his steps to swing through the fire door and down the stairs to Reception. There, he busied himself smoking two cigarettes, lighting the second from the remains of the first, whilst he watched the lie of the land and eventually came up with an infallible plan to meddle with the seating plan for the evening's formal dinner.

8

'We've tried everything, Sally, love. Your mum, well, she thinks it's time we went to the doctor. Robert looked uncomfortable, either at admitting to his private conversations with her mother, or at the embarrassment of seeing old Dr Harris together.

She had known this was coming. Everyone, it seemed, had crossed their fingers for a honeymoon baby, and the veiled comments came thick and fast when a year went by and there was no rounding of Sally's tummy coyly hidden under a Peter Pan-collared maternity smock. Slowly, the little niggle of fear inside her began to uncoil and Sally faced the fact that maybe her insides weren't working the way they should. Maybe it was the… the procedure – she no longer gave the other word the time of day – or the subsequent infection. She never had gone to a proper doctor. Maybe it was a punishment, divine retribution.

'You know I really want a baby, too,' she told Robert, and she did, she really did. It wasn't just to right a wrong, there was a deepening streak of maternal instinct inside her, but she was scared to let it fly free. He cuddled her into him, their eyes jointly tearful, before he bent his head and kissed her.

In the doctor's surgery a week later, their doctor listened to Sally's halting story – Robert was silent and red-faced – harrumphed and told them to let nature take its course. 'Mr and Mrs Brown, these things take time,' he said, not unkindly. 'And the more you worry, the less things work.'

'It's been more than a year, Doctor,' Sally said quietly. 'We thought, perhaps, there are tests we could have. To reassure us.'

'Young lady, the National Health Service is about
treatment, not reassurance.' Dr Harris looked at her over his
half-moon glasses. 'If we went about reassuring everyone it
would be bankrupt in a decade. However,' he leaned back
and seemed to soften in the face of her downcast gaze, 'in
your case, there might be something I can do.'

He paused and Sally's heart quickened. In her case. What
did he know? Sally was so busy seeing her carefully-
constructed life crashing around her, she didn't catch what
the doctor was saying. She blinked and saw both of them
looking at her oddly. This was the end, she knew it.

Robert touched her hand gently and said, 'That's great,
isn't it, love?' He was smiling at her encouragingly, and Dr
Harris was nodding along.

'Sorry,' she said weakly. 'Can you just say that again?'

'You're the young Power girl, as was, aren't you?' The
doctor said patiently. 'I know you did a while at medical
school. I'm sorry you couldn't continue – we need more lady
doctors. Bad bout of scarlet fever, wasn't it? Anaemia, too, I
heard. I hope those London doctors treated you well.' He
fixed her in his glare again. 'You should have come to see
me when you got home. That aside, I was saying, I think all
those are sufficient grounds to refer you to a specialist. Not
that I think anything is wrong other than impatience! And,'
he twinkled at Sally, and looked twenty years younger. 'Your
grandpa was a great friend of mine at school; Jimmy Power
did a lot for me. Least I can do is help out his worrying
granddaughter.'

'Thank you,' whispered Sally.

'I can send you to London –'

'No! I mean,' Sally attempted a laugh. 'Is there anywhere nearer? The farm and everything…' The medical world was a small one, even her limited experience told her that, and nothing could be permitted to get back to Malcolm.

'Very well. There's a good man in Leeds.' Dr Harris was writing as he spoke. 'Name of O'Rourke. We trained together,' (See? Sally thought, everyone knows everyone) 'And he'll do me a favour. You'll have your ovaries and uterus checked, Mrs Brown. Some blood tests, too.'

Robert coughed. 'And, er, Doctor, what about me? Will I have, that is, do I need to be tested? Somehow?' He looked mortified.

'A sample of your sperm may be required, Mr Brown. But all in due course. Let's start with your wife.' As he ushered them to the door, he added, 'You'll receive a letter with an appointment. Until then, go home, carry on as normal, and don't worry.'

But Sally was worried. How could she have fallen pregnant so easily when she was eighteen, and now, married and desperate for children, was struggling? She had to face it that he had likely damaged her insides. Scar tissue, or a malformation… And if so, that would be visible – but would the cause of it be clear? She was fuzzy on reproductive details, it hadn't come up during her brief studies, and there was no way of checking now. The local library's resource stopped with a set of the Encyclopaedia Britannica, and she was too self-conscious to go into a bookshop. She could do nothing but wait and see.

It transpired that Dr O'Rourke saw patients at Leeds Royal Infirmary, and where Sally and Robert travelled to a few weeks later. They'd taken the day off from the farm, letting it be known that they fancied a day out in the city. Sally ignored her mother's knowing look and her father's offer to drive them. They took the bus.

In the waiting room, they both fidgeted until Robert ducked out for a cigarette, a habit Sally hated. She sat alone, trying not to bite her nails but couldn't sit still. She shifted her hands, her position, and began to perspire. Beads of sweat erupted on her forehead as she felt her face reddening.

Robert, temporarily calmed by his smoke, took this to be nerves and attempted to comfort her, 'It will be alright, Sal, love. Bound to be. The tests won't hurt and we'll have the answers soon enough.'

How would you know? She wanted to scream, but none of this was Robert's fault. Instead, she stammered out, 'What if...?'

'No, Sal. No what ifs. I know, let's concentrate on baby names. You can choose a girl's name and I'll choose a boy's one. How about that?'

When the nurse called her name, Sally stood nervously. Robert, half rising, was unceremoniously told to remain where he was while Sally was examined. 'Your wife does not need an audience,' the nurse said tartly. 'Hurry, now, Mrs Brown, if you please. We don't want to keep Doctor waiting.'

The doctor, portly and bearded, was waiting for her. 'You're Harris's patient.' He held up a letter. 'Good man, Harris. Real tinker in med school, but that was a long time ago, of course. Right. Well, let's see what we're dealing with. Nurse, prepare my patient, please.'

'Of course, Dr O'Rourke.' The nurse was cooing now, all sweetness and light, and despite herself Sally wanted to laugh. Would people have been so silly over Dr Sarah Power, or was it a preserve of male doctors? 'Come along, Mrs Brown, and undress behind the curtain. Nothing to worry about, Dr O'Rourke is a marvel. And we have one of the newest ultrasound scanning machines in the country. Only Glasgow's Yorkhill has had one longer. You are a very lucky lady to have been referred to Dr O'Rourke.'

Sally murmured something non-committal, earning herself a wounded glance from the nurse, unable to explain why a brand-new radiography machine was both good news and bad. Under the nurse's watchful eye, she removed her clothes and donned a gown that opened at the mid-section. She settled herself on a narrow couch and the nurse placed a folded towel over her lower abdomen. Thoughts of Malcolm came rushing back before she could block them: him laying a plastic sheet over his bed, leading her to it, cutting her child away…

'No need to worry, Mrs Brown, you're in safe hands here.' The nurse must have seen, and misinterpreted, Sally's shiver. 'Ready for you, Doctor,' she trilled.

'Relax, Mrs Brown,' was all he said, as he positioned a light over her body, and twisted and turned different knobs on the gently humming machine.

Sally tried not to wince as his cold hands poked and palpated her abdomen, his eyes fixed on the screen of the scanning machine. Sally looked at it too, but she could see only something that looked like a snowstorm on a grey day, the sort of fuzzy interference she'd seen on televisions. Dr O'Rourke seemed pleased though, humming to himself, and when Sally stole a glance at the nurse, she was positively transfixed.

'You may help my patient dress now, nurse,' the doctor said after several moments of silence. 'Leave the equipment. I've asked Wilkins to drop in and take a look.' To Sally he said, 'That's all, Mrs Brown. I'll see you and your husband in room 3. Nurse will accompany you there.'

'May I see you alone? Without my husband?' Sally said quickly. She ignored the four immediately raised eyebrows and persevered. 'Robert, he, well, he's a little embarrassed, squeamish. He won't want to hear details of, er, well, women's bodies...' Forgive me, Robert, she added to herself. It worked.

'Very well.' Dr O'Rourke said. 'Nurse, please.'

Five minutes later, he was firing yes and no questions at her: 'Did you have polio as a child? TB? Are you on regular medication? Have you had surgery? Any irregularities in your monthly cycle? Do you have pain on sexual intercourse?'

Sally uttered an honest, 'No' so many times that when it came to the more difficult questions, the ones she was preparing to lie about, it was easier than she thought.

'Have you been pregnant before? Have you miscarried?' he asked.

'I'm... I'm not sure,' Sally said slowly, wondering if he could see or hear her heart thumping. 'There was a time, early on, when I thought, perhaps...I was late, just a few days, and then when it came the bleeding and cramps were worse than I'd usually expect. I never told my husband,' she added hurriedly. She held her breath; it wasn't really a lie at all and it might be enough to cover her, if there was anything that needed to be covered.

'I see.' The doctor didn't seem perturbed by her reply, and

Sally let out her breath slowly. 'Well, we have no way of knowing. Nature has a way of weeding out the bad eggs, as it were, Mrs Brown, but as it happens, I don't think it has any bearing on your case.'

'Does that mean you've found something?' Her heart pounded again.

'I believe I've found the problem, yes. I would like my colleague, Dr Wilkins, to confirm it. Nurse?'

She scuttled off, leaving Sally and the doctor in a not unfriendly silence, returning a few minutes later with a young doctor wearing a laboratory coat, a stethoscope hung loosely around his thick neck. He smiled almost apologetically at Sally and her heart sank. She watched him and Dr O'Rourke, as they conversed in an undertone, pointing and nodding at several papers on a clipboard. Dr Wilkins then signed something on the clipboard, smiled again at Sally and left the room.

'Mrs Brown.' He sighed. 'It appears that you have damage to your cervix and left Fallopian tube. You understand those terms, I think? Dr Harris said you had had a modicum of medical training. Good. Well, this would create fertility problems, I'm afraid.'

'Is… Can you fix it?' Sally asked.

'I regret to say I don't think so. There is evidence of trauma to the uterine wall. It may be congenital. You may have had an undiagnosed infection. Perhaps your original miscarriage – if that's what it was – left scar tissue. I honestly can't say.' Dr O'Rourke stroked his beard and looked at her sympathetically. 'I really am very sorry, Mrs Brown.'

Sally stared at him, numbly trying to take it in. 'It

shouldn't have happened like this,' she whispered, the words out before she could stop them.

The doctor shook his head. 'No, it shouldn't. You're a young healthy woman, you and your husband should be entitled to as many babies as you can bring up. But these things happen. There's often no explanation and it's not your fault. You must not blame yourself and neither must your husband blame you.'

Hearing the kindness with which he said that, Sally's tears fell. How wrong he was. The nurse clucked and handed her a square of white linen to wipe her nose.

'Would you like me to explain, in simple terms, to your husband, Mrs Brown? It might be easier for you?'

Sally nodded. Even amidst her anguish there was a little flicker of relief that nobody, especially Robert and their families, would ever hear about what she... what Malcolm, had done. She sat there, wooden, and watched Robert grow ashen-faced as the doctor explained their hopes of ever having a child were futile. That it was one of those unfortunate things and for them, adoption was the sole solution to their dreams of a family.

9
MALCOLM

Safe behind his wedding band, and in the confines of their sumptuous home, Malcolm was happy to bow to Martha in the majority of decisions. In public, he frequently joked about the way his wife had led him a merry dance before he'd won her over and got down on one knee, and Martha never contradicted him, even though it was clear to anyone who knew them both, that she had only been 'won' because she wanted to be. Malcolm knew it too, but he didn't care; even the old man had been impressed. 'Brains and breeding,' he'd approved, although Malcolm had heard on the Club grapevine – and ignored – that being translated as a cold fish. 'Handsome woman, too, if you like them buttoned-up, and a man in your position doesn't want beautiful anyway – too much bloody trouble, m'boy.'

'We're happy, Pa,' Malcolm had said, meaning it. Well, he was happy with the way things had turned out: their lifestyle, professional reputations and social standing were excellent alone, put together made them impeccable – enviable, he hoped. It seemed to work for Martha too; she wasn't really a happy or sad person, indifferent to most things outside her research but ruthless in her pursuit of progress. And if she was a bit of a cold fish, that came with the territory of being orphaned young, educated via a trust fund at boarding school, and working between laboratories in England and America. Malcolm could live with that. After all, if he found himself in need of the occasional extra-marital womanly comforts – comforts performed dutifully rather than passionately by his wife – he had a very discreet little black book, and a tacit belief that Martha chose not to notice or care as long as her career wasn't compromised. It was even possible, Malcolm thought, that he was more worried about maintaining their respectability than she was. She hadn't turned a hair when whispers of a mutual acquaintance's dalliance had led to a rather salacious divorce, whereas the fallout from the Profumo scandal – for Christ's sake, they had dined with John, and with Stephen Ward – and his old man's beady eye, kept Malcolm from veering too far off the romantic straight and narrow.

Theirs wasn't a business arrangement as such, nothing so crude, but it was a version of an arranged marriage. Martha was wedded to her work, she'd made that abundantly clear in the wake of Malcolm's all-out wooing at that first conference. 'I like you, Malcolm,' she'd said, 'but I'm not looking for a soulmate, my work fulfils that role entirely. But it's not the swinging sixties in this medical world of ours, and a single woman at the top of her field is still a single woman. What I need is a partner, one who will open doors for me.'

And that's what Malcolm agreed to, literally and figuratively, the payback being Martha treated him as an equal in career-stakes; his practice thrived.

The one sore spot was the children Malcolm was entitled to. He'd agreed to put the idea of a family on hold for a couple of years, while they built mutually beneficial, lavish and wide-ranging social and professional networks, but when that landmark passed and Martha still seemed to dally, Malcolm's father noticed and told him to put his foot down. Malcolm knew the old man was right. It was no matter that Martha didn't have a maternal bone in her body; that's what maternity nurses, night nurses and nannies were for. All she had to do was grow the baby like one of her precious lab specimens, but it had to be soon; his wife wasn't getting any younger and he didn't want problems from her end – he knew he was fine, of course, that was the one good thing that had emerged from that unfortunate little episode with whatever the girl had been called.

10

The night after seeing Dr O'Rourke and being given their devastating news was the first time Robert got drunk. While Sally nursed a small medicinal brandy, he poured himself a large drink, then another and another, eventually slipping into a maudlin, paralytic stupor. It was Sally who hauled him to his feet and slung his arm around her shoulders, trying to wake him enough to walk him to their bed. Dead-weight, he flopped onto the mattress where Sally removed his shoes and socks, loosened his trousers and shirt, and threw the blankets over him. Fully-dressed, she lay beside him and listened to his heavy breathing. That was the first time, too, she had put him to bed.

And what started out as a one-off drinking binge to drown his sorrows, slowly turned the teetotal Robert into a hard-drinking man. First it was one or two beers in the evening, and a round at the village pub at the weekends. Robert's brothers had often enjoyed a tipple and with their encouragement, rarely a day went by without something to 'celebrate'. The alcohol made Robert taciturn and weepy in turn, and as the months went on, the farm suffered, and their marriage even more so.

There was no question of adoption, Robert had made that clear: if they couldn't have children of their own, they weren't going to bring up other people's rejects. Sally was shocked by that, unaware Robert had such a bitter streak, and unsure whether he'd always harboured that opinion, or if it was the drink talking. Even if he never said, she was sure he resented her. She couldn't blame him.

They struggled on, neither of them happy but not knowing

what to do about it. Sally, desperate for an outlet from the farm, and the heavy atmosphere between them, spoke to Robert about taking on a little job in the village. The postmistress's cousin, Mrs Giles, a widow, was in a bind. She had the opportunity of full-time employment as manageress in the department store in Ripon but needed someone to care for her children for an hour after school. It was less a job and more about being a good neighbour, Sally told him; Robert, sober or drunk, still took his role as bread-winner very seriously, but, she explained, Mrs Giles had her pride and insisted on a small payment for Sally's trouble.

'What do you think?' she asked Robert as she served their midday shepherd's pie. 'It wouldn't interfere with my chores here, and I'd like to feel helpful.'

Robert – his hand shaking, she noticed – helped himself to a liberal serving of cabbage and turnip before he replied. He thought she didn't know he'd recently taken to hiding a bottle of whisky in the rafters of the farthest barn. 'Are you sure it won't upset you?' She knew what he was going to say. 'You know, looking after someone else's littl'un.'

'I think it will help,' she said. 'I like to be around children, and I am used to it – have you forgotten how often Auntie Sally minds your brothers' broods?' It was meant as a light-hearted remark but she bit her lip as a mutinous look crossed his face; Robert didn't want to be reminded how easily and regularly his sisters-in-law carried on the family name. 'The money will come in handy over the leaner months, too,' she continued, adding insult to injury. She didn't care; she was trying to make the best of things, why couldn't he?

'We don't need the money, Sally. Do it if you want to, but not for the money.' He clattered his knife and fork down and scraped his chair back. Sally winced. 'I need to get back to work. Thanks for dinner but I'm not hungry. You can heat it up later. I'll be late.'

She watched him stride over towards the barn and sighed. Everyone had always called Robert, the sensitive, profound one of the Brown brothers, Sally included. It was only now, when times were tough, she saw not a caring and easy-going man, but a weak one. Sally was not weak. She had been, once, but no longer. Never again would she suffer for a man, or a woman for that matter. Sally took off her apron, deep in thought. It would be a delight to care for the three Giles children a few hours a week, and she would walk into the village and give the good news to the postmistress to pass on to Mrs Giles. Halfway down the lane, Sally was already engrossed in plans for the fun they would have.

Sally soon realised that her love for caring, particularly of children, outweighed any residual duty she felt to working on the farm. She did it for her parents, but once they – first her father, and eighteen months later, her mother – died, she gave up all pretence of interest. Robert remained nominally in charge but agreed that they should take on a 'manager' for the day to day running of the business. In fact, they employed a local lad, Tom, a farmhand with them since he was fifteen. He and his new wife, Louise had a baby on the way and were thrilled with this stroke of good fortune; they were loyal too. There would be no gossip about the 'strange' life led at Offley Farm when Tom and Louise Parks were within hearing.

While Robert was drinking at home, or lurching around the fields with one of the dogs, Sally's reputation as a childminder – or nanny, in fancier streets – was second to none and she was in high demand. By the time Robert's drinking was at its peak, she was working nigh on full-time, and revelling in it. She had never got the chance to see if she'd make a good doctor but finally it didn't matter, she was, for the first time, since she was nineteen, contented. If married life wasn't ideal, Sally and Robert had come to a truce: Robert pretended he didn't drink and Sally pretended she believed him. Their quiet times together, though few and far between, given Sally's work, weren't unpleasant, and in their way, they loved each other – even if that did make them, at barely thirty, sound like a couple in their twilight years.

Afterwards, Sally tried to piece together what had happened the day of the accident. It appeared that Robert had finished his last bottle of whisky and then taken it into his head to go out and get another from the local grocer. It was only a few miles along the back lanes, and Robert had thought nothing of getting into his old Austin A30 starting it up, and driving drunk.

At the inquest, the police statement reported that a tractor pulling a trailer load of hay bales was already on the same single-track road when Robert came around the bend. The tractor driver realised that the oncoming driver, later formally identified as Robert, was distracted – tuning the radio, they guessed – and subsequently swerved, then performed an emergency stop far too late. The tractor struggled to stop, too, the weight of the trailer load and the forward momentum on a downward hill, too much. The resultant collision was head on. The tractor driver managed to break free and get help, but by the time the ambulance arrived, Robert was dead at the scene.

The police sent the local bobby, PC Dawkins, to knock on the door of the small farm, but there was nobody about. Dawkins returned to the station and made a few phone calls, soon finding out that Sally was at the vicarage, where she looked after the vicar's twins. At this time of the evening, she would be cooking them supper, bathing them and putting them to bed. She cleaned and tidied the house while waiting for the Reverend Spence and his wife to return; Sally would be back at Offley Farm around nine o'clock that night.

Dawkins called into the church and had a quiet word with the Reverend, and Mrs Spence went home alone to relieve Sally. And so, it was the vicar and the policeman gravely waiting at the farm when Sally arrived home. Her automatic greeting faded on her lips.

Dawkins spoke first. 'Mrs Brown... Sally. May we take you inside, please?'

Sally licked her suddenly dry lips and nodded briefly. She felt strangely calm, as if she'd been expecting this visit. 'It's Robert, isn't it?' she asked.

'If we could just go inside first, Sally,' the PC insisted gently.

In the kitchen, the breakfast dishes still draining beside the sink – as if it was any other day, Sally was to marvel later – he broke the news. 'Sally, I regret to have to inform you that earlier today, your husband was involved in a serious car accident. He died instantly. I'm so sorry.'

'Would you allow me to make us all a cup of tea?' Reverend Spence asked in his quiet voice. 'And is there anyone I can fetch to come and sit with you, Sally?'

'Yes, please.' Then, 'No, no there isn't,' Sally said. 'There's milk in the larder, and some biscuits – I'll get them, shall I? Oh, and I need to tell Tom and Louise. Someone will have to see to the locking up–' She made as if to leave the kitchen, but the vicar put a gentle hand on her shoulder.

'Please sit down, Sally,' he said, 'You've had a huge shock. We'll take care of everything. PC Dawkins will see to the farm, and you will come back to the vicarage with me for the night. Penelope would insist, and the children will be a great comfort to you.'

Sally sank down onto the nearest chair, the words turning around in her head, confused, why hadn't Robert waited for her to come home? Where was he going? 'Had he been drinking?' she asked abruptly and saw Dawkins and the reverend swap an uneasy glance. She raised her voice. 'Was Robert drunk, Constable?'

'We think so,' he said.

'But it was…' Sally hesitated. 'It was an accident? He didn't plan…' She couldn't go on, but Dawkins was quick to reassure her. 'We're satisfied it was an accident, Sally.'

'Was anyone else involved? I mean, did he hurt anyone else?'

'No,' the PC reassured her. 'Bill Mullins was in the tractor he hit. He got an awful fright and a bit of bruising but he's fine.'

'Good. That's good,' Sally said absently. Then she looked up at both men watching her. 'Poor Robert,' she said. 'Poor, poor Robert.' Then she burst into noisy sobs.

11
MALCOLM

Martha did not suit pregnancy. A woman who was never sick, never suffered from nerves or fainting or weakness, like most of the female patients Malcolm met, she had become pregnant on cue and they had both expected her to sail blooming through three trimesters. She didn't: hyperemesis, varicose veins, anaemia, they all assailed her without remission. Hanging on grimly, she underwent a long, painful labour, and never again, she told Malcolm, who had the rare insight to concentrate on the washed and dressed baby in the nursery crib, rather than point out she was reneging on their two children deal. It was, at least, the required boy: Jeremy William, after her father and his.

Martha – Malcolm had no say in the appointment – employed a maternity nurse from day one; in fact the thickset dragon, as Malcolm thought of her, had barely unpacked her Gladstone bag before his wife was established back in her laboratory. And in no time The Dragon was replaced by an earnest and very plain – maybe Martha wasn't as oblivious as he'd believed – Norland Nanny. She didn't work out at all. The girl seemed to expect a level of parental involvement that was alien to Martha and impossible to fit into Malcolm's schedule. He loved his son, no question, but surely he couldn't be expected to see him for more than an hour, clean and tidy, before supper time? Martha agreed – she visited the child in his nursery, after breakfast – and they interviewed a second applicant, and a third... The fourth girl ('Norland will be running out of dull, plain girls, with lank hair, at this rate,' Malcolm muttered to his father and was rewarded with a rare burst of laughter and a clap on the back), was a little older. She proved neat and tidy in her dull brown uniform, adept at manoeuvring the monstrous Silver Cross pram that Malcolm had proudly ordered – all the infant's equipment was from Harrods; appearances mattered – and, to Malcolm's secret delight, had been in service with minor royalty. Best of all, possibly primed by the principal of the college, she understood that little Jeremy's mother and father were just that, they did not expect to care for the child as well.

As such, the little boy's first few months jogged along quite happily, Malcolm took pride in referring to 'my son and heir', in conversation with wealthy and gushing patients, and Martha was relieved that half of her bargain was over. The sticky issue of child number two was, however, in both of their minds. Malcolm, keen as he was to crack on and sire the daughter that would make them a proper family, calculated that Martha would need several years, probably 'til Jeremy was five, he thought, but before the boy was sent off to board at prep school when he was seven, to forget the indignities of her first go around. It irked him, but as his old man said, 'Even the best of us must face adversity sometimes, m'boy. Best keep that wife of yours on side. I wouldn't put it past her to close for business altogether if you're too heavy-handed at this stage.'

Malcolm curbed his angst by combining a coveted speaking engagement in Paris with the ministrations of the wife of a French colleague – no strings; the husband was rich, old and a closet homosexual; the wife was bored and willing, with her eye on being a society widow. It was all above board in a very French way that Malcolm found both scandalous and splendid. So when he arrived home, with

Chanel parcels for Martha and a Cartier christening set for Jeremy, he was astonished at his greeting.

'I'm well aware of our agreement to have two children,' Martha began. She was sitting at the dressing table, brushing her hair for one hundred strokes before plaiting it for the night, and she watched Malcolm through the mirror.

Malcolm, in a state of post-Paris bonhomie, appetite sated for all things, shook his head, intent on being magnanimous. 'Darling, I know pregnancy was a trial for you, and I wouldn't dream of inconveniencing you until Jeremy is, say, five years–'

Martha raised her hand, effectively silencing him. 'Thank you. I appreciate your sentiment but I am an honourable woman and I want to get this over with.' She closed her eyes and gave a faint shudder. 'The sooner I have the second child, the sooner we can get on with the next phase of our lives. By my reckoning, she should be born when Jeremy is thirteen months old, and looking ahead, it's only seven more years when both will be off to boarding school. As you know, my lab is looking at research studies and grants on a five-year plan, so it works for me.' She swung around and faced Malcolm, who was still catching up with such organisation. 'Does it work for you?'

'Well... yes. Of course.' Malcolm couldn't believe his luck.

'Good. There is one stipulation.'

'Yes, darling?'

'Immediately I deliver the second child I am booked for a sterilisation operation. I will not have further children, Malcolm.'

There was no argument from him; once his family was

complete let her do with her body as she wished – she would anyway. 'Naturally,' he said, adding cautiously – and knowing the answer – 'You are sure you don't want to wait?'

'Quite sure. My biological clock is against me. And,' she went on, looking, what for Martha, passed as vulnerable, 'I don't like to fail, Malcolm. I won't fail. A second pregnancy will be a challenge to myself to do it better.'

Cold fish, his old pa's voice came to mind again, but he just nodded.

Martha rose and went towards the bathroom. 'Saturday night,' she said. 'My cycle should be at its most amenable then. Perhaps Sunday, too, to be sure.'

Thank Christ, thought Malcolm. The French colleague's wife was quite a woman; he didn't think he'd be up to performing before then.

Nine months from Saturday, when Jeremy was just shy of thirteen months old, Martha and Malcolm looked down on their daughter, Rosemary Ann, and shared a rare smile. Their family was complete.

12

After the funeral, Sally wiped her tears away, and with Penelope Spence and a lot of determination began to gather up the remnants of Robert's life. The Salvation Army would make good use of his clothes, shoes and coats, and Sally folded them neatly into bags and heaved the bags to the front door. As she turned, Sally noticed his cap on the coat rack, she brought it down, clenched in her hands before bagging it too.

The next few weeks were spent sorting out paperwork, and finalising plans for the future of the farm. Sally had decided almost immediately to sell Offley Farm. It was run-down, none of the Brown family wanted to take it on, but the land was valuable and there was no shortage of businessmen willing to take a chance on it. Tom and Louise Parks were taken care of, and found a new position with Robert's oldest brother over in the next Dale, and Sally was lucky to make a profit – a good profit. Invested carefully, that and Robert's Life Assurance policy would keep her very nicely–

'Until you remarry, and, indeed, beyond,' the solicitor had observed smoothly. 'You are now a very comfortably off, young woman.'

Sally said nothing. Money really didn't interest her, although it was nice not to have to worry and she was pleased that plenty remained of her parents' legacy; they would have liked that. She wouldn't want to think Robert had drunk away generations of Powers' hard work. As for remarrying? That was something she had no intention of ever doing.

Sally was going to look for permanent work as a live-in nanny: caring for children, that was her calling. She could have none of her own, an aching bitterness she would never, ever get over, but to compensate she would devote herself to other people's children. And it was true compensation, a way to find the surrogate family she knew she was entitled to.

With her years of experience, her glowing references, her independent financial means, and that first year of medical school behind her, Sally had her pick of jobs. She would start nearby, she thought, look in the Ripon Advertiser, take something local while she found her feet, then she'd branch out; The Lady always had interesting opportunities. As it happened, the Reverend Spence asked if he could recommend her to an acquaintance of his, a wealthy banker in town. Sally was gratified, and two weeks later had her first position as a live-in nanny.

Sally enjoyed life in Ripon, working for a Bank Director, Mr Wallace, and his three school-age children. His wife, always delicate, had died suddenly of pneumonia the year before and a cousin had stepped in, but she was needed by her own ailing parents. Aged thirteen, eleven and nine, the three girls required overseeing rather than babysitting. Money was no problem and Sally took them shopping every Saturday, followed it with lunch and an afternoon at the pictures. It wasn't all smooth sailing, as Lucy, the eldest, attempted to assert herself, and the youngest, Eleanor, desperately missed her mother. In the middle, Philippa was full of life and couldn't learn enough, continually asking questions. Sally never tired of answering to the best of her knowledge, or showing her how to find the answers in the library. Sunday was Sally's day off and she generally treated herself to a bus trip, or a lovely walk along by the river with a picnic.

By her first anniversary with them, Sally realised two things: firstly, much as she had grown to love the Wallace girls, she yearned to cradle a baby or two, to hear the gurgling sounds and to watch a toddler taking their first steps. And secondly, Mr Wallace was ready to remarry. Once Sally had kindly and honestly put a stop to his tentative overtures towards her, he had found a lovely middle-aged woman, a bank customer of his, who was happy to take on his daughters as her own. Sally said goodbye the week after the new Mr and Mrs Wallace returned from their honeymoon.

As she'd promised herself, she read through the adverts in The Lady and quickly found Professor and Mrs Anderson, and their little daughter, Gwen, a toddler. A Yorkshire family, they were moving to Bath, they told her, where the Professor would take the Chair of Chemistry at the University. Would leaving her roots be a problem? No, Sally decided, it wouldn't: it was the 1960s, society was changing, travel was not so difficult, hemlines were rising and Sally felt it time for another change.

Gwen was a delightful child, bright and happy. She was extraordinarily gifted for her two and a half years and attended a special playgroup three times a week, so she would learn ahead of school; the Andersons were academically gifted themselves and wanted their darling daughter to shine. Sally sat in on music appreciation sessions, dance classes, and with 'Mam'selle' for French. On fine days, Sally and Gwen helped Mrs Anderson in the garden, weeding, deadheading flowers, and arranging the summer blooms in the beautiful modern house. Gwen had a tiny easel, too, and all three of them set up on the terrace, painting the beautiful views. Sally was no artist, but she loved the peace. She was the happiest she'd ever been, playing the doting nanny, and she blossomed in the care of kindly Evelyn Anderson's household.

Moving south brought up none of the trauma Sally had experienced when Robert had announced London for their honeymoon. Time heals, she thought – although it hadn't really, had it, not in any physical sense. It never would. Emotionally, well, she simply refused to think about Malcolm and about what might have been. If truth be told she had no feelings for him any more beyond distaste. She'd been brought up to forgive, and if she couldn't exactly do that, she didn't hate him anymore either. Nor did she miss him, he hadn't been the love of her life that silly little Sarah had thought he was, but she did miss the children she wouldn't have because of him. And so, she lavished all her spare love on the adorable little Gwen.

Ironically, it was little Gwen who indirectly brought Malcolm back into Sally's life, or to the periphery of it, anyway. The little girl was hale and hearty, ate well, slept well, and rarely lost her sunny personality, but she was prone to a touch of eczema behind her elbows and knees. Professor Anderson had a good friend, a dermatologist, who kept an eye on Gwen, making her laugh, magicking pennies from behind her ears, and the visits to his surgery always coincided with teatime. Sally whiled away the time reading the magazines in the waiting room, an eclectic mix of The People's Friend, The Lady, and back copies of The Lancet. It was there, she first came across Malcolm's name, author of a scholarly article about advances in the treatment of thrombosis. Sally didn't let it bother her then, or the next couple of times she saw the name. He lived in Cambridge now, she learned, a cardiac specialist, his wife was an equally eminent scientist. They travelled regularly to the United States of America and holidayed in Europe. Fine, Sally, thought, it was exactly as she'd expected.

What she wasn't expecting was to get to the end of a story she was skimming about a charity ball for Dr Barnardo's – to see a photograph of Dr Malcolm Harper-Smyth, accompanied by his American wife, Dr Martha Beaumont, receiving an award for their joint patronage. He was jowly, the rowers' physique missing; she looked clever, serious. In retrospect, Sally was pleased she'd stumbled across it and read the piece before she realised there was a photograph below. If she'd had warning, she would have agonised over whether to look at it. As it was, she felt… she wasn't sure what she felt. Empty. A little regretful, even a little nostalgic for what might have been, but mostly empty. She wasn't sure what made her carefully tear the picture from the journal, but she did, and she folded it neatly into her bag. Then, when she and Gwen left, she stopped at the nearest waste bin and threw it away.

Something had started in Sally though, with that discovery. She took to scanning medical journals, browsing society pages of the newspaper press, even looking at the Anderson's television if there was a high-profile event. It was a compulsion she hated, and somehow couldn't deny but it was curiously emotionless. She saw Malcolm and Martha once or twice, checked her feelings and was reassured to find nothing untoward. And then, a few months later, something happened to change that.

It was a Tuesday, French day for Gwen, when Sally saw a

feature in The Lady. It waxed even more lyrical than usual about the 'charmed and charming Harper-Smyth family: inspiring doctors and charity patrons' – so far, so good, Sally smiled to herself, but the smile drained from her face as she read on. The words danced in front of her eyes, and for a second she really thought she might faint. 'Blessed with adorable toddlers, Jeremy and Rosemary, the Harper-Smyth's are the perfect family", she read. It wasn't a good picture of the children, but it didn't matter. Sally read the words and felt as if her womb had been ripped all over again. Not only her womb, but her heart, as well. It was as if the clock had been turned back to her eighteenth year.

Sally did the only thing she could. She turned to little Gwen and the Andersons for solace. It was, then, hard to know who was more distraught, the Andersons en masse or Sally, when the Professor's work took him to Hong Kong. It was perfect for the family really, an excellent position, and Evelyn's sister and mother were there – she had spent the first fifteen years of her life in Hong Kong. But going 'home' to an established family, with plenty of cousins for Gwen and help for Evelyn, meant that nobody, least of all herself, could justify Sally accompanying them. Instead, Professor and Mrs Anderson promised to spend the next four months doing all they could to find Sally the perfect nanny position.

The advert which caught Sally's eye was one of several possibilities, and it had been specifically highlighted by Evelyn Anderson: Required immediately: full-time live-in nanny for two children aged 18 months and 2 ½ years. Sole care.

Even as Sally paused to make a note beside it, she wondered – again – at those words, sole care – what kind of mother was happy to hand over her babies completely to a stranger? Maybe there was no mother, of course, she shouldn't judge, she told herself, and wasn't this a family that the lovely Mrs Anderson said she knew of personally? One of the select positions for which she'd recommend Sally unreservedly, and ensure the Professor wrote a glowing reference. Sally carried on studying the advert and as she did so, her heart gave a jolt. Busy professional medical couple, she read, Cambridge. Apply Box 502.

It was nothing out of the ordinary, but at the same time it was too much of a coincidence. Intuition or fate, Sally just knew it was him. Him and his high-flying wife.

'Malcolm,' Sally breathed. A name she had followed but not uttered aloud for ten years – more than ten.

Her first thought was, definitely not. There was absolutely no way she would – or could – face Malcolm, let alone put herself forward as nanny to his children. Not that he would allow her to do so, once he realised who she was – how could he ever face Sally? And then face his wife? As for his children… Sally felt a sharp knife twist in her stomach, and her heart plummeted. His children. His. Not hers. Never hers.

She couldn't sleep that night. She sat up, needlessly watching over a slumbering, snuffling Gwen, resisting the urge to pick her up and hold her tight. In waves, Sally's feelings sliced through grief, anger, disappointment, guilt and everything in between. And somewhere in that clash of emotions, she acknowledged openly the part of herself that she had shut off. Sally wanted children. She wanted children above all else, her own children, born of her own flesh and blood, suckled at her breast. That was what she wanted.

And she could not have them.

Sally grieved anew for the baby, her baby, who had been torn from her by the man who said he loved her. Not only that but who was supposed to care for her, for their baby, and for all people, under his doctor's oath. By morning, Sally's mind was so jumbled, only one clear thought emerged through her sleep deprivation. She hated Malcolm Harper-Smyth. Hated him. And she wanted him to suffer as she had – was still – suffering.

She carried out her duties in such a lacklustre way that day, poor Mrs Anderson was concerned. Sally – truthfully – pleaded a bad headache and Mrs Anderson ordered her to lie down, virtually marching her to the pretty bedroom, giving her tea, and switching on the radio for Women's Hour.

'Relax, dear Sally,' she said. 'I'll take Gwen to music and cook her supper, and some for you too. Coddled eggs, perhaps?'

When the house was empty, Sally cried at the woman's kindness. Then, exhausted, she did sleep. She woke to eat her eggs, clear-headed and calmer. An idea had come to her, one she could barely countenance… It didn't go away; it grew and developed, ebbing and flowing, leaving her frightened and elated in turn. It consumed her and she desperately needed counsel, but there was nobody she could turn to.

'Sally?' Mrs Anderson asked a couple of days later, over their breakfast kippers. 'Have you given any thought to those nanny positions I showed you? I don't want to rush you, dear, but time is marching on and I can't bear to leave for Hong Kong without you settled.'

'I've given it a lot of thought,' Sally replied, honestly. 'There are two I think would suit perfectly–' She got up slowly and fetched the magazine from Evelyn's writing desk.

Opening it at the advertisements section, her heart thumping – was she really, really going to do this? – she pointed with a shaking finger.

Evelyn put on her reading glasses and peered down. 'I see. Excellent. I think both are ideal positions, and both would be very lucky to have you.' She smiled up at Sally. 'I would like to make the first approach for you, my dear. I feel responsible, and it's much easier not to have to put oneself forward to a stranger. I can telephone to both and give you a glowing reference in advance.'

Sally nodded, swallowing. 'Thank you.' Her voice croaked, and she cleared her throat. 'Thank you,' she said more steadily.

Evelyn nodded, too. 'Right we are, then. I'll contact Reverend Templeton in Bromley, and Dr Beaumont in Cambridge immediately.'

Sally was on the train hurtling towards Cambridge when, out of the blue, she remembered one of her beloved grandpa's favourite phrases. 'Grow steel in your backbone, child,' he'd say to her. 'You can do anything, hear me?'

I don't know if I can do this, grandpa, she thought as the train rushed through the countryside, but I do know I certainly shouldn't. She would get off at the next stop, she vowed, take the position in Bromley with the buoyant Reverend Templeton, his sweet invalid wife and their brood of jolly daughters. But the next station came and went and Sally sat on, playing one scenario after another in her head.

She had no intention of becoming the Harper-Smyth's nanny, of course. Since that day, she'd always thought she never wanted to see Malcolm again, but something had changed when she found out he had children. Now she wanted to look him in the face and see – what? Guilt? Regret? Apology? Or indifference; that would be hard to bear. She wondered if he would even recognise her. It was more than a decade since they had parted, and the brief blooming of the star-struck student, Sarah Power he knew, had long withered and died. A competent nanny, a Sally Brown he had never known.

Sally looked down at her neat dress and sensible shoes, and patted her long hair, curled into its equally neat French plait. She was a far cry from the bobbed, fashionably-dressed – courtesy of Audrey – young student that even Sally herself barely remembered. She'd pulled out all the stops for Malcolm, make-up and that beautiful pale-silk baby-doll slip, a girl full of promise. Now she was a dried-up matron, leaning to plump. A tear slipped from Sally's eye, which she brushed away hastily, and told herself fiercely to behave.

As the train pulled into Cambridge, Sally still hadn't decided, which would be worse: whether Malcolm did recognise her or whether he didn't.

He didn't.

Martha, poker-faced and efficient, but clearly impatient to be elsewhere, carried out Sally's interview. She referred to the Andersons' glowing endorsement, and read a previous reference from Mr Wallace, nodding impatiently. She then asked a few peremptory questions about routines and basic childcare that Sally, even sick to the stomach with nerves and expectation, could answer easily. Their meeting had started at noon, and as the study clock chimed the quarter hour, Martha had finished.

'Do you have any questions, Mrs Brown?' She looked at

her watch, then the door, as she spoke.

Just one: how can any woman be so disinterested in the care and welfare of her own children? That's what Sally wanted to say, but of course, she didn't. She forced herself to ask about the two children she would never see, let alone look after – there was no offer to meet them, Sally noticed – replaying their names. Jeremy and Rosemary. Rosemary and Jeremy. Pleasant names, not Sally's choice though…

The door opened brusquely, and Sally stumbled to her feet.

'Ah, Malcolm. We're actually finished, I think,' Martha said pointedly. She gave a flick of her hand. 'Sally Brown, my husband, Dr Harper-Smyth.'

Neither of the doctors appeared to notice that Sally had been struck dumb, waiting for the axe to fall. But Malcolm simply looked her up and down once before smiling benignly and saying. 'Good afternoon, Mrs Brown.' It could have been greeting or dismissal, his eye had already moved to Martha. 'We need to leave now, if we're to make the train.'

'I will write to you in due course,' Martha said to Sally. 'Thank you for your time. Can you find your own way out?'

'Yes. Thank you. Goodbye.' Sally fiddled with her gloves as Malcolm held the door open for her, avoiding the possibility of catching his eye. Any thoughts of confronting him were long gone. She hurried to the front door, fumbling with the catch in her eagerness to leave, and barely took a breath until she was down the path, along the road and had turned the corner. What had she been thinking of? She must have lost the run of herself altogether. She'd got away with it, at least. Though she had no idea what, if anything, she'd achieved.

Slowing her step, Sally made her way back to the station; she had no inclination to wander Cambridge, beautiful as it was reputed to be. There had been no hint of recognition in his eyes. If she'd said anything both doctors would have thought her quite mad. She wouldn't have recognised him, she thought, if she hadn't been primed by her little compilation of newspaper cuttings. He was still good-looking, but bearded now, and slightly more overweight than his photographs displayed. Bespectacled, but no doubt vain about it in public. But his roving eyes hadn't altered, nor his arrogant way of standing – that was the man who had coldly aborted their child then cast Sally away with twenty pounds and a train ticket without a second thought.

'Bastard,' Sally said under her breath. 'Bastard.' It was an alien word to her, one she never used, but it was the only word for him, and saying it made her feel better.

13

Thoughts of Malcolm, the very image of a respectable doctor, and of the interview plagued her as she went about her daily duties. Gwen was a distraction and the comfort to Sally that she always was, but soon she'd be gone. What would she do without her, Sally wondered. Was hers to be a life of transience; a life of joyous little charges who came and went? Dear Gwen. Would the emptiness of the little girl's departure finally consume her? 'You're made of sterner stuff, lass,' her grandpa's words came to her again.

What should she do? She wouldn't get that job. They'd want a Norland nanny; Martha had interviewed her only out of deference to Professor Anderson's standing. Sally shivered. She should never have gone there anyway. After working so hard, over so many years, to move on, she was resentful of the space Malcolm was back occupying in her mind.

On Thursday the 12th, Evelyn Anderson handed her a letter, the quality of the paper identifying the sender. The playroom fire danced behind the guard and Sally felt tempted to place the envelope in the flames and watch as it disappeared into ash. Her hands fumbled to release the contents: I am pleased to offer you the position... The words jumped out at her. Her hand groped for the seat by the window and Sally eased herself into it. The letter rested on her lap and her thoughts were overwhelmed with him.

'Nanny, Nanny,' Gwen's call startled her. Sally forced the letter clumsily back into the envelope, and then into her pocket; Gwen needed her.

As she and the little girl walked to the park later on, Sally was still distracted by thoughts of the letter. Imagine working for Martha, the Ice Queen, in their perfect home, looking after their perfect children. And watching Malcolm play the perfect husband. She couldn't take the job; she wouldn't take the job.

Gwen tugged at her sleeve. 'Hurry, Nanny. Feed the ducks.'

'Yes, let's,' Sally replied. As she released the bread, one slice at a time, from her bag, she laughed at Gwen's anticipation.

'Another, please, Nanny. They are hungry ducks.'

'Oh, my darling, the ducks will always appear hungry, when there's bread on offer.'

'Really, they are.' The little girl's earnest face looked up at Sally. What would she become without Gwen?

That evening, with all the storytelling and talk of ducks over, Gwen lay sleeping. Sally crept from the child's room to her own, where she took the letter from the envelope and re-read it. What should she do? In spite of herself, Sally relished the frisson of power that was hers. She knew who they were; she knew his secrets. They had no idea who she was. But that was how it had to stay. There was no other way. That night Sally followed the hours on the clock until somewhere before 4am. She woke again, just after six, feeling out of sorts.

She and Gwen sang as they walked by the river. As she looked down at the little girl skipping along the path, hand-in-hand with her, Sally's heart felt bruised at the thought of losing her too.

That evening, defiant, she wrote to accept the position of nanny to the doctors' children.

PART THREE

THE NANNY (1969-1971)

14

Departure day dawned early and restlessly. Sally had been swimming a perilous sea to save Gwen, she'd reached for her little, outstretched hand time and again to be thwarted by the swelling tide that took the little girl just out of her reach. There had been other dreams too, darker ones she couldn't recall, and Sally knew that was for the best. She turned in bed to face her brown case, its neatly packed contents waiting to be compressed and contained. She rolled back to her waking position and wept into the pillow.

'You must take tomorrow morning to prepare yourself,' Mrs Anderson had instructed her. 'I will see to Gwen, then we'll have breakfast together.' Her chin had wobbled. 'Oh, my dear, how shall we bear it?'

The house echoed as Sally made her way to the dining room; so many of the familiar ornaments and much of the furniture were already in transit to Hong Kong. Mrs Anderson's smile was strained. Little Gwen sat opposite chewing at her marmalade toast. She greeted Sally with a generous smile and a wave. The professor, one eye on The Times, was rushing through his cooked breakfast, until finished.

'Excuse me, everyone, for I have much to do.' He paused at the door. 'I won't see you again before you go, Mrs Brown, so I'd like to thank you for your loyal service to my family. You will be missed, my dear.' And with that he was gone.

'It's so much simpler for men, don't you think?' Evelyn Anderson said quietly, leaning towards Sally. 'I will miss you greatly, Sally, I want you to know that. As much as Gwen will, perhaps more. The truth be told, I wanted to ask you to come with us, but Professor Anderson is such a prudent man and couldn't agree. He's right of course, my family will want to be involved with Gwen and we can employ someone over there if needs be, but it won't be the same.'

The breakfast rolled around in Sally's mouth. Was it too late to beg, she wondered, half seriously. Or, she had money, she could follow the Andersons, make a home in Hong Kong. It was a ridiculous idea, of course – but why, a little voice in her head said. After all, it was an idea far less ridiculous than what she was planning.

'We can feed the ducks today,' Gwen interrupted Sally's random plans.

'Oh, darling, not today. I'm leaving after breakfast, remember? We talked about you going to Hong Kong and me going to meet a new family.'

'But I don't want you to go, Nanny.'

'You have such an adventure ahead of you, Gwennie, much, much better than feeding the ducks.'

'Don't want a'venture. I want to feed the ducks. With you.' Her bottom lip protruded and tears sprang from her baby blue eyes. She turned and hid her face in her mother's skirt.

'Will you excuse me, Mrs Anderson?' Sally rose from the table and ran up the two flights of stairs to her room. She closed the oak door behind her, and leaning against it, she sank to the floor and cried.

The storm over, her goodbyes were controlled. Gwen held onto her hand and then to her coat. 'No, no. I don't want you to go, Nanny. Why do you have to go?'

The child was bewildered, never had she been so out of

sorts and Sally was grateful when Mrs Anderson took charge, lifting Gwen, cuddling her and wiping the tears from her face. Relieved to be in the taxi and sheltered, at last, from Gwen's distress, she waved until she could see them no more. Sally wondered how long it would be until the little girl forgot about her? She could never forget Gwen.

Sally had taken no notice of her surroundings on the day of her interview, but now she remembered how she had holidayed in Cambridge with her mum and Auntie Vi when she was about ten. It was the furthest they'd ever travelled together and Sally thought it was abroad, it was so far and so hot. She remembered walking to Grantchester to have tea in the Orchard, where poets had gathered so many years before. Auntie Vi made up poems that day; 'I'm inspired,' she'd informed them. She'd been quite put out when Sally's mum laughed and Sally, encouraged by her mum's reaction, had joined in. She also remembered punting on the River Cam Auntie Vi got so sunburned that she peeled for weeks after they got home.

But that was then and this was now. What were you thinking? What are you thinking? Sally chided herself, as she had done so many times since she had made her decision. She left the station, clumsily lugging her heavy case, to wait. Someone called Patrick, the housekeeper's husband, had been instructed to pick Sally up in Martha's car but Sally, afraid of being late, had taken an earlier train, so she settled on a bench outside the station, waiting for the red and white Vauxhall Cresta PA to arrive – Martha had been quite detailed in her description of the car, though not of Patrick. When the flashy vehicle arrived Sally was struck by what an ordinary-looking man he was; never had Sally seen a driver so unsuited to a vehicle.

Her suitcase was soon edged into the boot and Sally took her place beside him. He was a man of few words and she a woman of many worries so the conversation was stilted at best. Sally didn't mind how long this went on; part of her hoped they might never arrive.

'We're here,' Patrick announced, all too soon, turning into the gravel driveway she remembered from her interview.

Oh, my lord, we're here. What have I done?

Patrick eased the case from the car. 'What have you got in here?' he grunted.

'Not all that much really,' she replied, whilst thinking, I'm sure he doesn't dare speak to Martha like that.

With ill grace he carried her case to the door and rang the bell, summoning his wife. Mrs Somerville's face was set equally at sour. There would be no allies in them, Sally thought, glumly. 'Mrs Brown. You're expected,' she said, a tight smile settling, clearly out of place, on her lips.

Sally was ushered along the generous, parqueted hall and up the green-carpeted stairs. Her room was in the attic, and a breathless Patrick plonked the case outside her door, pointedly no further. Duty done, he slipped away without a goodbye.

Mrs Somerville didn't delay either. After a terse, 'I'll leave you to settle in,' she followed her husband. Sally could hear the murmur of voices as they made their way downstairs.

Hers was a generous room, with ample head height despite the coombed ceiling and the view extended from two dormers, over the rooftops to a church beyond. Along the hall, between two further attic rooms, Sally found the bathroom. As she unpacked, she hoped she didn't share this floor with the Somervilles, and she was also surprised at how far away from the children she appeared to be. Unsure what to do next, she waited uneasily until summoned by Mrs Somerville.

'Mrs Brown, Dr Beaumont is ready to meet with you now,' she called from the foot of the attic steps.

'Are the children with her?' Sally asked, heart pounding.

'I believe so.'

Sally followed the housekeeper to the drawing room, where Martha sat, two small children, perfectly turned-out and demure, by her side. The little girl was no more than a baby, but Martha wasn't holding her, she was propped up on a cushion between her mother and – Sally just held in a gasp – a slightly older boy who looked so like his father, it hurt her.

Martha wasted no time on greetings. She nodded stiffly and beckoned Sally further into the room.

'Children,' she said, 'this is Nanny Brown. She's come to look after you. Do you understand?'

The boy looked uncertainly between his mother and Sally, then nodded.

Martha turned to Sally. 'This is Jeremy, Mrs Brown, and the girl here is Rosemary. Say hello, children,' she added.

'Hello,' Jeremy said obediently.

'Hello, Jeremy,' Sally said, with a warm smile. 'My, aren't you a big boy. I can see you will be a great help to me.' She turned her gaze on Rosemary, placidly playing with her fluffy knitted booties. 'And Rosemary…' Sally instinctively went to pick her up, saying a belated, 'May I?' to Martha.

'By all means,' was the clipped reply.

Sally stepped forward and scooped up the unprotesting Rosemary. The little girl gripped on to her like a baby monkey, seemingly content with this stranger, as Sally breathed in her innocent baby smell. She held out her free hand towards Jeremy, who edged off the sofa and took it gingerly.

Martha watched them for a moment – as if she were observing us in a laboratory, Sally was to think later – and then indicated a document placed in the centre of the mahogany coffee table. 'I've had my secretary type this up for you,' she said. Sally assumed it was a contract of employment that Martha required her to sign but the doctor went on, 'It's information you may need about the children: their routine, the household rules, their likes and dislikes, that sort of thing. It also contains contact details for myself and Dr Harper-Smyth, though I stress these are for emergencies only. As discussed, you have sole care of the children and we expect that to be upheld.'

'Certainly,' Sally murmured, when she saw some sort of response was required.

Martha went on, 'On page two you will see that when at home, my husband likes to have the children presented to him in the drawing room at 5.45pm. They should be bathed and in their night clothes. I am more spontaneous than my husband,' she gave a brittle laugh, 'and will pop in to see them in the nursery when I can.' Martha's check that you are doing everything by the book,' was unspoken but Sally heard it and couldn't resist saying coolly, 'I will appreciate that as much as the children. You'll want to be satisfied I'm carrying out your wishes.'

Martha's eyebrows went up slightly and Sally was sure she saw a flash of respect in them. 'Then we shall get on very well,' was all she said. 'Now, unless you have any questions, that will be all.' Without waiting for Sally to speak, she added, 'Off you go now with Nanny, children. I have work to do.'

Never had Sally been so relieved to close a door behind her. The smell of Martha's perfume lingered around her as she carried little Rosemary up the stairs. Jeremy toddled ahead.

'Can you show me where the nursery is?' Sally asked him, realising too late that no-one else had. But Jeremy, who Sally thought, might prove to be more precocious even than Gwen, led her gravely through the house – Sally trying to get her bearings in the sprawling Queen Anne building – and reached a door on the floor below Sally's attic room. On tiptoes, Jeremy reached up and twisted the door knob, frowning with the effort, and then stepped back for Sally and Rosemary to enter the room first. He put out an arm, as if showing them in.

'You do have wonderful manners,' Sally said to him, wondering if the doctors had insisted on this very adult action or if Jeremy was copying his father. 'How old are you, Jeremy?'

'Two and a half, Nanny.' He held up two fingers on one hand and one on the other, and spoke very distinctly. 'Rosemary is one and a half. She's a baby.'

The nursery was subtle, splashes of childhood colours only in the pictures and toys. The work of a designer's hand, Sally thought – closely guided by Martha's, no doubt. Everything a nanny and her charges could possibly need was provided, but there was nothing ostentatious; these were not spoiled or cosseted children. If anything, the beautiful room was like the rest of the house, impeccable in taste but strangely sterile. There was no personal imprint anywhere that Sally could see. It was a far cry from Malcolm's rooms whilst at University, she thought, with a flashback to his luxury furnishings. Martha clearly had the upper-hand in all matters domestic. Cocooned in the nursery, time passed comfortably, much to Sally's surprise. Jeremy chattered away as he showed Sally his favourite toys: small cars and a cumbersome, old-fashioned rocking horse – Neddy – that took pride of place in an alcove beside the fireplace.

'He was my daddy's horsey,' Jeremy told her proudly as she helped him climb on. Rosemary, in the centre of the rug with her alphabet building blocks, clapped two together with excitement as Jeremy rocked back and forth, and soon all three were laughing happily. It came as a surprise when the starched Mrs Somerville came to let her know that nursery supper was waiting for them in the morning room.

'Should I eat now, with the children?' Sally asked the housekeeper, as she pulled out a chair for Jeremy, and settled Rosemary in her high-chair. She had been too nervous to eat earlier in the day, and now her stomach rumbled as she surveyed the table: bread and butter, tiny round scones, salmon sandwiches, and tinned peaches with evaporated milk. There was a pot of tea under a cosy and a jug of milk.

'That's for you to decide, Mrs Brown,' Mrs Somerville told her. 'Cook will leave you a hot meal in the kitchen if you prefer to eat after the little ones are asleep. I took the liberty of providing the sandwiches for you today. I expected you would be tired after your travels.'

'How kind of you, thank you,' Sally said. 'I'm very grateful for the tea and sandwiches.'

Mrs Somerville inclined her head slightly. 'If there's nothing else, Mrs Brown, I'll return to my work. There's no need to clear. Patrick will see to that later.'

She was making her way out of the room, when Sally screwed up her courage to ask, 'Do you know…that is, is Dr Harper-Smyth at home? Dr Beaumont said he liked to see the children in the evenings when he's at home.'

'The doctor is currently away until Thursday,' was the reply, and hearing it, Sally let out a long breath. A reprieve. Once Jeremy and Rosemary had been helped to eat, Sally tucked in, too.

Jeremy chattered away as he followed Sally around 'helping' her. He liked to run, he said, and showed her how. He liked to kick a ball – would Nanny kick it back? She would, and he was beside himself with excitement. At the park, he liked the swings, and Sally pushed him as he frowned in concentration and pumped his little legs as hard as he could to go higher and higher. All the while, placid little Rosemary, who could totter around quite happily, clinging onto Sally's skirt, burbled away in her own language.

In looks, neither child favoured Martha, but Jeremy's mannerisms were Malcolm's: already, the toddler had the exaggerated upward curl of his lip on the left side and the way he ran his fingers through his hair. There was no doubt in Sally's mind that he was inherently his father's son, it wasn't something learned; within two days, she realised that their parents were relative strangers to Jeremy and Rosemary. They met strictly by appointment; Martha's idea of 'popping

in' to the nursery was as tightly scheduled as Malcolm's
sessions were reputed to be. Sally read the document Martha
had given her with incredulity. There was no affection or
humour or allowance for the tinies being tiny, they were
treated as mini-adults – or, Sally thought suddenly, little
wooden soldiers whose intermittent displays were pleasing to
watch from afar. Why on earth had the doctors ever had the
children in the first place, Sally wondered. Suitable heirs to
carry on the Harper-Smyth line, she supposed. The poor little
souls were starved of proper love, the way they'd
immediately taken to Sally confirmed that. With a pang, she
reached out and affectionately settled Jeremy's ruffled hair
and stroked Rosemary's plump pink cheek. What was she
doing, Sally thought again. Living in someone's house was
very different to a three-minute encounter at the end of an
interview. Because he hadn't recognised her then, was no
guarantee it wouldn't come to him now or in the future. She
hadn't seriously considered how Malcolm would react if he
recognised her, other than that she would be dismissed
forthwith. That would be… well, she had no real idea what it
would be to Malcolm, but to Martha it would simply be an
inconvenience, and Sally herself would survive – she had
come through worse. But what would it mean to the
children? She was uncomfortably aware that her madcap
scheme hadn't taken their innocent needs into account; she
hadn't thought any of it through at all.

They were uncommonly good children, and Sally was left – as
Martha had outlined – very much to her own devices, in fact all
three of them saw the doctor only once, and then fleetingly, in
the three days following Sally's arrival. With the Somervilles

and Cook taking care of all the household duties, Sally had ample free time for thinking, and she did have a plan, of sorts. If – when? – Malcolm recognised her, she would neither explain nor apologise; she'd heard someone, somewhere proffer that advice and decided it would work in her favour. She would simply affect embarrassed innocence: her dealings had been via Mrs Anderson and with a Dr Beaumont; nervous, she had not caught his name on their brief introduction; she had not recognised him as he hadn't, then, recognised her; of course their position was untenable – what would Dr Beaumont think if she knew of their former... friendship (Sally was banking on the likelihood that Malcolm hadn't shared the sordid details of what he would probably call his 'youthful indiscretions' with his wife); Sally would leave immediately if Dr Harper-Smyth wished, or as soon as they could find a replacement nanny. She ran through it over and over in her head: clean, unemotional and inarguable. Not watertight, but the best she had.

On Thursday evening, as she bathed the children and prepared them for bed, a knot settled in Sally's stomach. She had heard the car arrive, then the front door open and close, a half hour or so ago, followed by voices from the drawing room. Malcolm was home. Sally hadn't dared move to where she could glance down the staircase to the vestibule, and the children showed no interest in the possibility of their father coming home. But then, she thought, it wasn't 5.45pm, they weren't expecting to see him.

As the audience with him drew close, Sally felt a headache pound at her temples. Would they be summoned or were they to make their own way there? Perhaps a little bell would be rung, or Mrs Somerville might come for them? Maybe he wouldn't request his children's presence at all.

'Dr Harper-Smyth is expecting you promptly.' It was Patrick who brought the news as he arrived to clear their tea things. 'You know where the drawing room is?' He nodded at Jeremy. 'The boy can find his way there.'

'We knock and my daddy says 'Enter',' Jeremy piped up. He made a knocking motion on the tablecloth and growled the Enter in imitation.

'Then we must be ready on time.' Sally got up stiffly. 'Come, children.'

They left the nursery with precisely two minutes to spare, and stood before the closed mahogany door on time. Sally raised her hand to knock, aware of her body trembling. She took a deep breath and steeled herself. She would not let her nerves show, nor would she allow herself to feel second-rate. A phrase she'd learned long ago at school came to her: knowledge is power. Sally rapped smartly on the drawing room door.

'Enter,' a voice instructed.

Sally opened the door, ushered Jeremy ahead of her and held Rosemary's hand as she toddled in. Sally waited for the children to run to Malcolm, for him to hold out his arms in welcome. Instead, all three huddled dutifully inside the door.

'Ah, Nanny…er, yes.'

He clearly had no recollection of her name, Sally understood. Why would he? She was staff, not a patient or colleague.

'Sally Brown, sir,' she said quietly.

'Of course, of course. My wife keeps me informed, but I'm not always listening.' He gave a roguish smile, leaving Sally thinking a braver man than he would ignore Martha. 'I hope you're settling in, Nanny Brown. Is she, children?' he boomed at them. He rose from his chair and beckoned them over. Sally gave both a little push, and Jeremy took Rosemary's hand and led her across the room. Sally stayed by the door and fiddled with a long thread sticking from the button on her cuff. Malcolm took Rosemary on his knee, and asked Jeremy, 'Have you had a good day?'

'Yes, Daddy,' the little boy replied.

'Good.' There was a pause. 'Have you…er, let's see…have you been at the park?'

'Yes, Daddy,' Jeremy repeated. 'On the swings.'

'Excellent. And you little lady, cat got your tongue?' Malcolm turned to Rosemary, whose fat little finger was tracing the Paisley pattern on her father's tie.

It was painful to watch. So, Sally thought, the man who could use his charm to win over the weak and the willing was struggling with each word he directed at his children. Uneasily, Sally played with the thread again, stopping only as the button fell from her blouse to the floor. From across the room, three pairs of eyes followed its progress.

'I'm sorry,' Sally murmured, stooping to retrieve it.

'Well, I'd better let you go and sew that back on, Nanny,' Malcolm said heartily. 'Behave yourselves, children.' With that he placed Rosemary on the floor and patted Jeremy on the head. They made their way back to Sally, who grasped their hands tightly. 'Say goodnight to Daddy, children,' she encouraged them, leaning down.

'Goodnight, Daddy,' Jeremy parroted obediently, and Rosemary opened and closed her hand in a little wave.

The other side of the door, Sally leant against the wall for a second and closed her eyes. The first hurdle was over.

15

Two months passed into three, into six. As Sally grew to love the children in her charge, she also learned to relax and let her guard down just a little. It was clear, in her limited interactions with Malcolm, that nothing in the competent and deferential Nanny Brown reminded him of the trusting young medical student, Sarah Power. She was simply the homely figure that presented his children to him, and removed them ten minutes later, his fatherly duty done.

Sally didn't see much of Martha either. That also suited her just fine, although she never stopped finding it hard to believe that a mother – and a father, for that matter, although there was some affection in Malcolm's eye when he gazed on Jeremy and Rosemary; Martha was nothing except cool and dispassionate as if they, Sally too, were specimens in her laboratory – could have such little interest in her own children. If they were mine … Sally often found herself thinking, but she always stopped the thought right there, because they weren't hers. Even though they should have been.

'They should have been yours.'

The voice came from nowhere as Sally was folding towels and placing them in the nursery airing cupboard. She jumped, and for a wild second wondered if her nerves were playing tricks on her again. She knew her cheeks were staining red with embarrassment – and guilt; Martha might as well have read her mind. How long had she been standing there, silently watching?

Just because Sally didn't see much of her, it didn't mean that Martha didn't watch them. She did. Those cool,

appraising eyes followed Sally; the professional smile hid a
multitude; the carefully held body suggested polite distaste.
To Sally, it was clear why Martha had gone into medical
research – she didn't like people, and that included the little
ones. Martha didn't hold them with affection but as a doctor
would, efficiently checking for a fever or a sore tummy.

'They should have been yours,' Martha repeated. It was
the most conversational she'd ever been.

'I beg your pardon, Dr Beaumont?' Sally stammered. 'The
towels –'

'You're smarter than that, Mrs Brown.' The woman leant
against the door frame, her beige cashmere twinset as neat at
7pm as it had been at breakfast.

'I don't–'

'The children.' Martha shrugged gracefully. 'It's nothing
to be embarrassed about, my dear. Some of us are born to be
mothers, others of us are not. I made an error of judgement
and I should have known better.' She stared at Sally for a
long minute. 'So did you, I think.'

What was she insinuating? 'My husband died.' Sally's
tone was flat, trying to mask her racing heart. 'I know how
lucky I am to care for your children.' The emphasis rang out
stronger than she'd meant it.

'I don't want your gratitude, Mrs Brown. Although,'
Martha brushed away a non-existent hair from her sleeve.
'Although, I believe you deserve mine.' She paused again,
and Sally couldn't move. She felt caught in a strange trap, as
if it were one of her own making. 'I just wonder,' Martha
went on, 'whether you are really cut out to be a nanny.'

Sally's head swam. She grasped the nearest shelf for
support. 'Are you giving me notice?' she managed to ask.

What would she do without Rosemary and Jeremy? Losing their father had damaged her in so many ways; losing the children would kill her. What had she done?

'Heavens, Mrs Brown. Firing you? Of course not.' Sally closed her eyes in sheer relief, registering the genuine surprise underneath Martha's humourless laugh. 'We couldn't possibly manage without you. Dr Harper-Smyth speaks very highly of you.' Does he know? Sally thought. 'Why, you're the stay-at-home wife he should always have had.'

Twist the knife, why don't you, Sally's heart said, whilst her practical nanny's voice found its way through. 'Dr Harper-Smyth is very generous to me – and the children. As are you, Dr Beaumont.' She wasn't lying; money was no object. Time and love? Well, that was a different matter.

Sally wished the woman would just go; Martha was making her uncomfortable. She wasn't the type to gossip over a cuppa, even within her own circle, and she usually called a spade a shovel in clear diagnostic terms, but tonight Sally was confused. 'If you don't mind,' she began, but was saved by a cry from the neighbouring bedroom.

'Nan, nan,' Rosemary's little voice quavered. 'Nan.'

The two women looked at one another. Sally wasn't sure of the protocol. 'Would you like to go to her?' she offered. 'I think it's a tooth. You might be able to help her more than I can.'

'Nan. Nan?' The plaintive little cry came again.

Martha raised her eyebrows. 'Dear Mrs Brown, I think Rosemary has made it very clear who it is she wants,' she said. 'Off you go.'

Dismissed, it was all Sally could do not to run. As it was,

Martha called her back.

'Mrs Brown?'

'Yes, Dr Beaumont?' She turned and looked back.

'We have stood on ceremony long enough. Sally – may I call you Sally?'

'Why, yes. Yes, of course.' Sally was more flummoxed than she'd been since she arrived.

'Or is that a diminutive? Are you a Sarah, perhaps?'

'What? Oh, excuse me. No, no. I'm simply Sally Brown, Dr Beaumont.'

'Good. Well then, Sally, we need to talk again. It's … illuminating.' Martha nodded, more to herself than Sally, it seemed. 'Yes. We'll talk again soon.'

Entering the night nursery, Sally had already switched automatically to 'Nan' – all little Rosemary could manage of nanny – but the undercurrent of discomfort didn't leave her. It was as if Martha had been testing her somehow –

Oh. She stiffened, even as she brushed Rosemary's curls away from her red-spotted cheeks, murmuring, 'Hush, darling, hush. Nan's here now.' Martha couldn't know, could she? About the past. Sally shook her head and lifted Rosemary out of the cot. No. The woman was a cold fish and she didn't suffer fools, but her principles were tight. If Dr Beaumont had discovered Malcolm's actions and Sally's part in them, both would be packing their bags before the General Medical Council had heard even a whisper.

'Isn't that right, Rosie-Posie?' Sally murmured soothing nonsense to the little girl, letting Rosemary's soft breathing soothe her as they rocked together in the low nursing chair beside the fireplace. She pulled the candlewick bedspread over them both, settling in for as long as Rosemary needed her. It was as well, Sally thought with a glint of humour, that Martha locked herself in a laboratory; if she'd just come up to the nursery as a dutiful employer, imagine her breaking bad news to a patient. With that, she hugged Martha's daughter, her beautiful and oblivious daughter, all the more tightly.

Rosemary, once she slept, did so deeply, and Sally eventually eased them both up and settled the child into her cot. Rubbing her stiff neck, Sally watched her for a few moments and then moved across to check on Jeremy, whose eiderdown slithered towards the floor at least once each night. Sally's heart-strings tugged: such privileged children, missing out on so much love from their unaware parents – though was Martha actually unaware? Sally thought not. Wideawake now, Sally padded to the kitchen and made herself a cup of hot milk. She picked up Mrs Somerville's Women's Own, and the house copy of The Lady and took everything back to her own room, where she undressed and climbed into bed. Out of habit Sally skimmed the Situations Vacant columns, her eyes lingering not on the jobs but on the beautiful locations: a Girl Friday wanted on the Isles of Scilly off Cornwall; a tutor in the Isle of Man; a companion on a Hebridean island…They sounded lovely. Each one a wonderful hideaway for a family, Sally thought, as her eyelids finally started to droop. She fell into a deep dream: travelling hopefully, stepping off a boat – and feeling as if she were coming home.

16
MISS MAUD CAMPBELL

'You can't just up and leave,' said Miss Maud Campbell indignantly.

'I'm not just leavin'. I'm givin' you five weeks' notice.' Margaret, Maud's housekeeper for many a long year, stood her ground. She wasn't intimidated by the old lady.

'What good is that to me?' Maud glared at her. 'I need you here.'

'I'm gettin' too auld to look after a house this size, you know I am. You need somebody younger. I'll mention in the village store that I'm leavin', see if they know anybody who might want the job.'

'You most certainly will not mention it in the village store. I don't want them knowing my business.'

Margaret – Maggie to everyone but her employer – sighed. 'But you need help, you know you do.'

'Clearly that is now my problem not yours and I'll thank you to leave me to solve it. Good day to you, Margaret.'

The conversation with Margaret, her housekeeper of nigh on twenty years, upset Maud more than she would ever let on. Margaret did far more than clean and cook for her, she was one of the few links Maud had with the village. Margaret knew everyone and everything, and much as Maud professed to abhor the petty gossip inherent in a small community, one of her first thoughts was who would keep her up-to-date with all the news? Annoying she might often find it, but miss it she would. 'Wanting to spend more time with her grandchildren', indeed. Maud snorted; more likely that daughter-in-law of Margaret's wanted free childminding while she was off gallivanting on the mainland. What was next? Maud thought indignantly: Sandy Mac, sixty if he was a day, finding himself a lady-friend and taking up growing azaleas and turnips in his own garden instead of hers? Sandy, ostensibly Maud's part-time gardener and handyman at the Big House, but in actuality her general factotum, was Maud's lifeline as much as Margaret.

Margaret and her notions. She just needed to ride it out, Maud told herself. If she didn't do anything about finding a replacement, Margaret would never leave her in the lurch.

Despite herself, though, Maud was uneasy, and sleep was difficult that night. She had to face the fact that even if Margaret stayed this time, neither of them was getting any younger, and island life was relentless on the fit and healthy, so what would happen when one of them succumbed to the vagaries of old age? By first light, as she rose to tend to the fire, Maud acknowledged that maybe this was a blessing in disguise. She wouldn't let Margaret have the satisfaction of the upper-hand, but she would give some thought to the future. Maybe find a younger woman, someone who could live in.

'Have you done anythin' about findin' my replacement?' Maggie asked the following Friday.

'Not yet, I've been far too busy,' Maud lied. She could hear Margaret's unspoken, Doing what?

'Well, I'm leavin' on the 14th. I'm spendin' a few weeks with Gillian, John, and the children over at Nairn,' Maggie said. 'I'll leave you set up as best I can.'

So, she was serious. Maud was mildly surprised but pleased that she was no longer so put out. She'd had an idea, and she thought it was a splendid one. Maud had no family, something she'd not ever regretted, but the Big House was increasingly lonely at times. It was getting old with her, she thought, and it needed new life. She, Miss Maud Campbell, spinster of the parish, was going to place an advertisement in the newspaper and find herself a family. A 'distant great-niece' would be most suitable. She spent several days doing her research. She'd thought to use The Telegraph, but it seemed from a leader she'd read, that a paper called The Lady was far more suitable. Maud wrote off for a copy, and whilst waiting for its arrival on the mail boat, passed the time composing a 'Companion Wanted' notice. Finally, happy with her efforts, Maud asked Sandy Mac to post her letter.

'Writing to The Lady, I see,' Sandy commented. 'Knitting patterns and suchlike, Miss Campbell?' He knew Maud had never knitted a day in her life, and he knew Maud knew he knew – but they understood one another.

'Just post it, Sandy. Or I'll be buying seed catalogues and sowing them myself next.'

'Yes ma'am.' He clicked his heels and gave her a mock salute.

'And Sandy? There's a letter for Mr Conti, as well, if you wouldn't mind dropping it into his office?' Maud had written to Alisdair Conti, the local solicitor, first thing, to let him know that replies to an advertisement she had placed would be addressed to him and FAO MC. It was about all he was fit for, in Maud's opinion: post boy; he hadn't the brains to question her. 'Don't open them,' her letter instructed the hapless Alisdair. 'Just give them to Sandy Mac in a plain, brown envelope. He'll bring them to me.'

Maud took her morning coffee that day with the satisfied air of a job well done. Maggie could remain in the dark.

Alisdair Conti's lack of interest in the law made for a poor solicitor but meant – unique on the island – he was the soul of discretion, and Sandy Mac was her ally. All she had to do was sit back and wait to welcome her long-lost family member home to the remote isle of Inniscuillin.

Two weeks later the large, brown envelope arrived. A lady less genteel than Maud might have snatched it out of Sandy Mac's hand; she was not known for her patience. In the privacy of her sitting-room, jotter and letter-opener to hand, she sat down to read and re-read the replies. There were six envelopes in a variety of hands, all postmarked a different location. Maud said a silent prayer - she might not believe but it could do no harm - that one of these young women would be what she was looking for.

It didn't start out promisingly. Ada Mackie at fifteen was a child; Diane Chambers at seventeen, was still too young, and more worryingly, was seeking 'travel and adventure'. Maud cast those letters aside. Daisy Donaldson, also seventeen, was pregnant, and needed to leave home quickly. Her writing was assured, her tone educated. She would, she said, do anything in exchange for a safe place for her and her baby. 'Oh dear, the poor girl,' Maud muttered to herself and kept that letter separately; Inniscuillin was no place for such a young – and unwed – mother. Had the young woman been ten years older... Maud shook her head. No, it wouldn't do, but maybe there was something she could think of to help Miss Donaldson; a sum of money perhaps sent to the almoner in her local parish. Maud made a note to herself.

Three down, three left. Maud repeated her prayer and attacked the final letters with renewed purpose: Molly

Nugent, at sixty-four, was only a year younger than
Margaret, and sounded as if she might be looking for a cosy
retirement home. Nan Douglas, aged thirty-one a widow with
two children…Maud paused there. She'd been thinking a
niece, but wee ones might work. Or she might be setting
herself up for a tremendous fall. Oh dear, this was a
minefield. Maud sighed and turned to her final option:
Jessica Montgomery aged forty-two, with fifteen years'
experience as a housekeeper in a very minor stately home.
'Unmarried and unencumbered,' Maud commented to
herself. 'Miss Montgomery sounds ideal. Though the Big
House on Inniscuillin might be too much of a come-down, of
course.'

Her father's advice to sleep on a decision had always
stood Maud in good stead, and she retired early, letting the
letters and the circumstances of the applicants play on her
mind. By morning she woke early, refreshed and very clear
about what she had to do. For years she had listened to
Margaret boasting about her Gillian and her Peter, and then
the grandchildren when they came along: Amy, Katie, and
little what-was-his-name? Now Maud would create not just a
niece but her own ready-made family.

For the position of Companion, Maud Campbell was going to
interview Miss Daisy Donaldson and Mrs Nan Douglas.

17

Had Sally been planning it from the moment she realised who had placed the advertisement that Mrs Anderson circled? No. No, she hadn't. That had never been her intention – Sally was certainly clear about that. For better, for worse, back then she had just wanted to see him – Malcolm. Why? That she certainly wasn't clear about. It kept her awake at nights; it kept her on the hop as she carried out the more mundane chores of her nannying life. Of course, there had been the element of curiosity in her decision to attend the interview, and maybe even a hint of defiance – something she wished the long-gone Sarah had harnessed back then – and surely that could be forgiven. But to have gone as far as actually taking the job? Slowly Sally admitted to herself how much more it was.

She'd wanted revenge, that was it. She wanted to get back at him for what he had done to her, the empty life he had inflicted not only upon her, but on the innocent Robert, and on her parents, who would have doted on grandchildren. The vindictive streak she hadn't realised ran through her – and now a little scared of – had led her to do the unthinkable. It brought her into the Harper-Smyth home where she could affect Malcolm's life as he had affected hers, but Sally would be subtle.

She would get to know his children, get them to like her – to love her – and then she would turn them against him, their own father. He wouldn't even know she was doing it. If she'd had a plan, that was it. She'd imagined the boy precocious, a charming and entitled brat, just like his father, and the baby girl? Well, she was likely a cosseted princess learning from her brother. Sally would pretend to like them, to be impressed by them, and in doing so would gain their trust and make them love her more than they loved their superior parents. Sally's ultimate influence would manipulate them to feel for their father what she felt for him: utter contempt.

If she hadn't known all of that at the time, she had worked it out in the months she had lived with the family. She was shocked at herself, a little ashamed – not at her desire for revenge, who wouldn't feel that? but that she would use the children as chess pieces to such an end – but she wasn't going to deny it. Not now. The problem was, Sally understood, as she pushed Jeremy on the swings, brushed Rosemary's hair, read to them, dressed them and sang to them, she hadn't expected to genuinely allow them into her heart, to hold them so dear. She'd expected her love for them to be forced; she'd expected to feel affectionate at best towards his children. She hadn't expected to fall in love with them. Sally wanted the world for Jeremy and Rosemary. Like a true parent she wanted all that was good for them. And, she was increasingly aware, she – she, Sally Brown neé Power, nanny – she was good for them. She was their world, and they were hers.

Sally could pinpoint exactly when her big – breath-taking – idea had come to her. It started as a fleeting thought, preposterous and immediately swatted away, with a bittersweet if only. That was the evening she'd been so unsettled by Martha's ambush – that's how it had felt – in the nursery, when they had been interrupted by Rosemary's teething cries. Martha's low-voiced, 'They should be yours,' echoed in Sally's mind. From the mouth of anyone else, it would have been an off the cuff remark, but Martha was never flippant. She gave the impression of never uttering a word before silently double-checking it, and Sally was certain she meant it – theoretically, of course. It had never been repeated; Martha had initiated three or four equally brief encounters since that night and Sally always felt tested or challenged in some obscure way – as if she were the focus of a social experiment, she thought – but Martha didn't refer directly to the children's parentage again.

It was, then, the alignment of Martha's interaction and Sally's casual reading of the Situations Vacant column of The Lady, which led to Sally's fantasy. The more she dismissed it, the more it grew. It kept her awake, driving her half-mad in the middle of the night, and putting her off her food. It started to consume her.

Those dear, dear children should be hers. Hadn't their own mother said so? Hadn't their own father (if inadvertently) behaved as such. Sally had already, subconsciously, started to create an alternative world in which it happened: a car crash, something quick and painless, leaving her the obvious person to adopt the orphaned Harper-Smyth children. But life had taught her that waiting for things to happen didn't work. She had to be proactive to get things done; look at Martha Beaumont: a woman who knew exactly what she wanted and would do anything, make any sacrifice to get it. Not that Sally would dream of harming the doctors, of course, that wasn't what she wanted. What she wanted was her and the children cocooned on a desert island, their own happy family trio.

That wasn't going to happen, but it was that Positions Vacant column in The Lady which put islands into Sally's mind. The magazine page was creased and stained, so frequently did Sally pour over it. She could picture the shape of a small and remote Scottish island home to an elderly woman who was seeking a companion. The image became as clear as day: apple-cheeked and sweet-natured, with a gentle Scots brogue. She lived in a stone cottage, surrounded by an expanse of sea Sally recognised only from the radio Shipping Forecast. Maisie? Margaret? Morag? – fetched eggs from her hens and tended her cottage garden with green fingers but an increasingly painful hip and an inclination to forgetful had resulted in her carefully writing to The Lady... So real were these images that sometimes Sally had to stop what she was doing with the active half of her brain and remind herself that this woman and that island idyll were no more than a figment of her imagination.

With a rashness similar to that which had brought her to interview with the doctors, Sally eventually decided there was only one way to chase the dream away. She would apply for the job. She was well-qualified and, after all, she had a precedent... Of course, this time she wouldn't take the position, even if offered – one mad act driven by passion was forgivable, a second, done in cold blood was not. Anyway, once she had been in contact with the real islander – likely crabby and querulous on a bleak hunk of rock in the midst of a cruel sea – Sally was sure the fascination would vanish in a puff of tempestuous Scottish winds.

Calling herself Nan Douglas – Nan because that had been adopted by both children, less of a mouthful than Malcolm and Martha's invariable Nanny Brown – and Douglas because...well, because it had vaguely Scottish overtones and wasn't at all memorable, Sally applied for the position.

Nan was a widow with two young children, interested in a new start, and replies should be directed to her via a newly-opened Post Office Box in an area of Cambridge Sally Brown never had reason to frequent. A fortnight later, it was there that Sally found a slim white envelope, addressed in neat cursive, awaiting a Nan Douglas.

'If Mrs Somerville is in agreement, then I can find no objection.' Martha looked up at Sally with what could only be described as surprise, when Sally politely asked if she might take an afternoon off. 'I will leave it with you to make the arrangements.'

With a quiet, 'Thank you, Dr Beaumont,' Sally closed the study door behind her, amused rather than offended that her request for an afternoon off appeared tiresomely beneath the good doctor. Had it not occurred to her – to either of them – that Sally had neither asked for, nor been offered, a day off since she had become nanny to the Harper-Smyth children? Sole care really meant sole care, in their eyes. The Somervilles were in a similar position, Sally knew, and to be fair, Martha herself worked endlessly. Malcolm, well, he was always busy, frequently away, and often on the fringes of the public eye; the generous-minded could suppose it was all duty and no play.

Mrs Somerville raised no objection to babysitting for an afternoon. If, for once, it meant Rosemary spending the time peering through the bars of her playpen and Jeremy climbing in and out of it to collect the toy animals she had recently taken to 'making fly', Sally decided it couldn't be helped.

The fictitious wedding Sally was attending, that of her second cousin, Elsie, was taking place the following Saturday at noon. It coincided perfectly with the invitation she had received to telephone Miss M Campbell in relation to the position of companion which Nan Douglas had applied for. It was something of a charade, Sally acknowledged, as she dressed in a pretty frock, let down her hair and put on some lipstick, but it felt strangely less dishonest than popping down to the local phone box with Jeremy and Rosemary in tow. That, should she be seen, was not easy to explain away – there was a perfectly good telephone at the Harper-Smyth's that she could have asked to use – whereas blending in, briefly, with the attendees of a wedding or a tea dance at one of the bigger hotels, would not be noted. Still, as she hurried her way into the safety of one of the public booths in the foyer of the Regency Hotel, Sally half-expected to feel the tap of a police constable, calling her out for impersonation.

Ever since she had received the brusque instructions to contact Miss Campbell – two lines and a telephone number – Sally had been practising what she would say. She'd rehearsed it so often, she felt it had left grooves in her mind: Nan Douglas; widowed with two children – twins was a nice touch – looking for a fresh start somewhere quiet; in need of simple accommodation. She was still running it through her head now, heart thumping, whilst she waited for the operator to connect her to the long-distance number. There was a delay on the line, and Sally imagined her Miss Campbell, stumbling in from the garden, humming a little tune – a hymn, perhaps, and wondering why the telephone was ringing...

'Hello? Hello? Is that Mrs Douglas? Speak up, if you're there,' was enough to jolt Sally from her reverie. It was not the start she imagined, nor was the rest of the conversation. Miss Campbell was forthright rather than forgetful, smart rather than sweet, and it sounded as if she, as much as Sally, were reading from a well-rehearsed script.

'I haven't done this before, Mrs Douglas,' the Scottish voice said bluntly. 'I need to be assured of discretion. I don't like idle gossip – the island is full of it – and I won't be pitied. In fact, the woman gave a little cough, 'I have no family of my own. Therefore, I was hoping I might introduce my new companion as a distant niece…'

It was the first sign of hesitation and Sally spoke instinctively, as herself rather than Nan Douglas. 'I think that's a very good idea. As you know, Miss Campbell, I'm a widow. I'm also, originally from a small village in the north of England, and I know all about gossip and pity. I don't have family either – oh, except for the children,' she added hurriedly.

'We need new life about the place,' Miss Campbell replied abruptly. 'What are your wee ones called?'

'They…' Sally thought quickly. She couldn't have her madcap behaviour identifiable. 'Jay. And Mary. They're twins, a boy and girl of two-and-a-half.'

'Would they take to a great-aunt, do you think?'

'I… yes. They're good children, mostly.' What am I getting myself into, Sally thought. Stop it, now. She didn't, though.

'Och. All children need a bit of spirit. Well, Mrs Douglas, can you cook and eat a lamb you last saw gambolling in the field? Can you put up with dreich weather, draughts, and old crotchety ladies?'

Sally laughed. She liked the sound of Miss Campbell, there was humour in her tone, and in different circumstances, the promise of comradeship – Sally realised with a sudden pang she'd never feel that way with the doctors. 'I'm not sure what 'dreek' means,' she said, 'but I'm a farm girl at heart, nature doesn't frighten me –'

The pips went at that point. 'Would you like another two minutes, caller?' interrupted the bored operator, and the last thing Sally heard was a definite, 'No. I'll write to you, Mrs Douglas,' as the call ended.

Sally hung up, and slowly made her way back to the bus stop. She'd been going to treat herself to a cup of tea in the hotel lounge, but she had too big a lump lodged in her throat. There was no question that she'd chased away a ghost, but she'd replaced her with a no-nonsense, warm and real person. An image of her Grandpa James swam into her mind, he would have got on famously with Miss Campbell, Sally was sure. Sally herself would have got on famously with Miss Campbell… but instead, she'd misled her. Sally might argue that the doctors deserved being fooled, but this lady didn't. If only…

As the bus hove into view, Sally hauled herself towards the stop, wishing with all her being she'd never set off down this ridiculous path. When Miss Campbell wrote to offer her an interview – and Sally was certain she would – she would decline with genuine thanks and regret.

In actual fact, when Sally collected Nan Douglas's letter four days later, Miss Campbell didn't offer her an interview. When she explained precisely why that was, Sally's world was turned upside down.

Although… that was really only the second half of the story, Sally was to think later on. Of all people, it was Martha who was to send Sally off in a direction she'd not believed possible. And while none of them expected it, that too was coming to pass the very afternoon Sally didn't go to a wedding.

18
MARTHA

A transatlantic telephone call was virtually unheard of, even amongst the hallowed confines of their Cambridge set. Martha tapped her fingers on the desk in front of her, trepidation vying with impatience; if only her colleagues could see the implacable Dr Beaumont now, she thought wryly. Come on, come on. She glanced, again, at the wall clock; surely in this day and age, one could depend on the international operator.

When the call came through, Martha refrained from snatching up the receiver, she even took a second to appreciate the soft burr of their newly installed trimline telephone – so much more refined than the old rotary instrument. After a spot of interference and what Mrs Somerville would, no doubt, call faffing, an American accent echoed across five thousand miles.

'Dr Beaumont, Ma'am? Howdy. Professor Royston Mills III here. Call me Royston. How are y'all this fine day?'

'Good afternoon… Royston.' Martha frowned, reminding herself of something Malcolm had said; what was vulgar to an Englishman was friendliness to an American. She made an attempt to soften her clipped tones. 'This is Martha Beaumont.'

'Well, hey, Martha – I might call you, Martha, yes? We don't stand on ceremony here.'

She winced at the full-bodied guffaw that boomed down the line and swallowed. Royston Mills was clever, rich, a new breed of scientist, he didn't need to be a gentleman, too. 'Of course,' she managed.

'Good. Good. Y'see, Martha, we in the Cardinal Institute, wouldn't want to offend your British sensibilities when you come to join us.' The man paused; he knew what he was offering and he knew she knew. 'And you will come and join us, won't you, Martha?'

Very slowly, Martha let out a long breath; a lesser woman might have let out a squeal or punch the air with a heartfelt yes! Nobody, nobody – not even Malcolm – knew how much she wanted this, how long she'd canvassed for it, the extent of her plans and her sacrifices. She pulled herself together. She didn't point out she was, by birth, as American as Royston III because by inclination she was British and it suited her, she'd worked harder than anyone on her accent. 'I would, indeed, be very interested,' she said, curling the phone lead around her fingers, and banking on her reputation, 'If the offer is beneficial. To me.'

There was a faint whistle. 'My people said you were no fool, and they were right.'

The man sounded impressed – and so he should, she thought. He might own the best research institute in the world, but she, Martha Beaumont, was the best of the best. And she badly needed him, and his people, to know that.

'Sure, it's beneficial,' Royston went on smoothly. 'You have, Martha, been what we Yanks call head-hunted. Let me be blunt: we want you, Martha. Your terms, give or take. You come. Bring that husband of yours – cardiologist, right? I can find a real sweet deal for him. And your kids. America's a great place for kids. We'll love 'em. So, what d'you say, Martha? A new start in the Land of the Free appeal to you?'

'Yes, Royston,' Martha said, allowing herself a rare smile.

'It does.'

'Swell! Welcome on board–'

The line crackled, bringing her to earth; she was keen to seal the deal, as Royston would put it any second now. Martha reached across her desk and pulled a piece of paper towards her. 'Thank you,' she said briskly. 'Here, then, are my conditions.' Again, she held her breath.

'Bring 'em on, Dr Martha Beaumont,' was the cheerful response. 'Bring. Them. On.'

Martha began to speak.

19
MISS MAUD CAMPBELL

Maud had never been a ditherer; when something was right, it was right. Saturday lunch cleared, she summoned Sandy Mac to drive her down the hill, where she made herself at home in Alisdair Conti's empty office, taking advantage of his desk and direct telephone line. The island's solicitor was rarely at work between noon on Friday and elevenses on a Monday, leaving his long-suffering secretary to close up for an altogether more traditional weekend break. On a Saturday afternoon, it was an open secret that Alisdair and the resident police Sergeant, Ewan McLeish, had a long-standing engagement, putting the world to rights over a wee coffee that led naturally into a not-so-wee dram. Maud, aware that weekends on the mainland tended to report higher levels of crime, had once asked both men what they did if there was a police – or, indeed, a legal – emergency. She was assured by the precise bobby that this had occurred only once in the last decade, on 30th July 1966, when the young Stewart boy had taken exception to England winning the World Cup. Inebriated, he had 'borrowed' Nurse MacIntyre's bicycle, where his grandfather had later found it abandoned with a flat tyre, young Stewart sleeping peacefully in one of the rowing boats tied up on the harbour end of the beach. Old Stewart had dragged his grandson to the police house, apologised for interrupting the McLeish-Conti summit and insisted the boy spend the night in the island's holding cell (a barred room off Ewan's scullery). By this time in the story, Maud very much regretted her tongue-in-cheek remark, and had never again willingly engaged the sergeant in idle chatter.

On this afternoon, she knocked on the office door for form's sake, because there was no sign of Alisdair and the keys were swinging merrily in the lock. She entered the silent outer area where Miss Brady sat – on the days she wasn't teaching - and discovered this, and Alisdair's inner office, were remarkably tidy. A less observant woman than Maud would have assumed that was down to Helen Brady's filing skills, but Maud was fairly sure that if she opened a drawer in the metal filing cabinet it would be virtually empty. Save the odd last will and testament, or a simple conveyancing task, legal work was minimal on the island and if anyone did have a problem they would – cheerfully encouraged by Alisdair – approach a branch of Conti solicitors on the mainland. Maud knew of old that as the last of the Conti clan, nobody had expected much of the young Alisdair. His older brothers had taken over the family firm, his sister carefully married off to a potential rival, and Alisdair had been somewhat lost in the mix. 'A strange one,' people had said about him, although Maud thought that just meant he was disinterested in the law and so easily distracted; he wasn't brainless, that was for sure. He could, if he wanted, run rings around the solid Sergeant McLeish.

There was a rumour – more than a rumour – that money and land had changed hands to ensure Alisdair got his legal qualifications. Certainly, Conti family money had provided the ideal set-up for the youngest son on Inniscuillin; the postmistress could tell you that a private income supplemented his meagre earnings and paid Miss Brady.

Maud stopped her musings, resisted the urge to pull open a file cabinet and see if she was right, and mentally wished Alisdair and Sergeant McLeish a good afternoon. She set herself to a productive hour's work, determined that by the time Sandy Mac came back to collect her, she would have received two long distance phone calls, written three letters, and counted out money for use of the office facilities and the purchase of stamps and a postal order – Maud was punctilious about settling her debts – with a note asking Alisdair's secretary to oblige her.

Her telephone conversations came first. These completed, Maud took great care over her letter-writing. The first letter required the utmost tact, the second calling upon an old Glasgow friend, an almoner, for a favour regarding an expectant unwed mother. It had been immediately clear to Maud, and, indeed, to the girl herself, that Miss Donaldson would not do at all as a companion; Daisy was not ready for island life, and Maud guessed that the island was not ready for her. Maud, too, decided she would benefit from a young woman who had embraced the 1970s with a little less vigour.

If she had wanted any further proof of that, it came within a few minutes of speaking with Nan Douglas. Maud, known for her common sense, was also shrewd enough to set some store by intuition and even – on occasion – to take a calculated risk. She thought deeply for a few minutes before pulling Alisdair's jotter towards her, sliding a new piece of carbon paper into place, and composing her third letter. This one, clever as it had to be, was equally written from the heart:

My Dear Nan,
I am writing to invite you, and your dear twins, Jay and Mary, to come and make your home with me here on Inniscuillin. As you are aware, I live alone, and the Big House has, as you might infer, sufficient room for you to

have your own quarters. I would be grateful for some light housework in lieu of rent, and more so, will welcome the companionship of my widowed niece, and the grand niece and nephew I am yet to meet.

I see no reason as to why this arrangement won't be of mutual benefit and indefinite. However, mindful of the change this will be for both of us, I propose that you come north for a short holiday, say three weeks, and in the event we do not take to one another, we can part company with mutual well wishes.

Directions to Inniscuillin are enclosed. You will require some time to close up your residence in London, so might I expect you on this day four weeks? Please confirm by return, and I will arrange for you to be met at the ferry. You can send your belongings ahead, care of Inniscuillin Post Office.

I further enclose a postal order to the value of ten pounds only. This will cover your expenses. In the event that you decide not to accept my invitation, I leave it to you to put it aside to do as you wish for the children.

With fond regards from,

Your (Great) Aunt Maud Campbell

Maud read through the letter one more time, then sat back in satisfaction. If, as she had long suspected, the postmistress enhanced her quiet life by steaming open private letters (and sitting at the switchboard listening in to telephone calls via the island exchange – one more good reason, Maud thought, for not installing a party line at the Big House) she would find nothing untoward in this affectionate missive to an impoverished relative. It did, of course, require a certain level of understanding on Nan Douglas's part, but if Nan was the young woman Maud thought she was, this would not be a problem. All Maud could do now, was wait and see.

'Ye're looking mighty pleased wi yersel', Miss C,' Sandy Mac commented, as he opened the car door for her a while later. 'A guid time, weel spent?'

'I think so, Sandy.' There was no time like the present to try out the idea, Maud thought, and on a friendly audience. 'I'm hoping a great-niece of mine might like to come and stay at the Big House with me, now that Margaret is retiring.'

'A great-niece, you say?' Sandy's bright eyes sought out hers, as he put the car in gear.

'Yes, indeed. That's the simplified relationship of course…' Maud waited.

Sandy pulled out onto the island's one main road before speaking. 'Weel, now, isn't that grand,' he said finally. 'An' here was me thinkin' ye were in Mr Conti's office turning ower the Big House tae the kirk.' His eyes twinkled as Maud gave a loud snort.

'Over my dead body,' she said.

20
MARTHA AND MALCOLM

When Martha put the phone receiver down on Professor Mills – Royston – her list of requirements was, without exception, ticked off, and they had the makings of a draft contract scribbled down – in her own, indecipherable to anyone else, form of shorthand – and the leisurely promise that, 'We'll finalise it when you're out here, Martha, no sweat.' Martha, giddy equally with success and the unheard-of gamble of agreeing to something without having dotted all the 'i's and crossed all the 't's, gave herself a moment to gloat. Then she took a fresh sheet of paper and picked up her pen once more.

It took her another hour to prepare the version she would show to Malcolm. She didn't think he'd have any objections, but she was taking no chances. Nothing and nobody, including her family, were going to stand in Martha's way.

Precisely at six o'clock, Malcolm knocked on the study door. She capped her fountain pen carefully and slid her private notes into her desk drawer and turned the key, slipping that into her pocket. 'Come in, Malcolm,' she said, as he opened the door. 'I have news for us. Excellent news.' Martha couldn't help the small smile that crept across her lips.

'Tell me all.'

'Darling,' she said. 'We are going to America.'

'Yes!' Malcolm had no compunction about sharing his feelings. He strode across the room towards his wife, sure that, for once, she'd welcome an unsolicited embrace. 'Congratulations, Dr Beaumont. Exactly as you deserve.'

Malcolm was desperate to see America, and if it took Martha's coat-tails to get him there, what was the harm? He'd soon make his own mark – the first, his ego swelled – of his colleagues to do so outside Europe. The old man mightn't hold much truck with the Yanks, but even he had to admit that was where progress was being made these days. Money, too, of course, but one didn't talk about the vulgarities.

Martha accepted his hug, and even reciprocated with a kiss on his cheek – that was how excited she was. 'Well done, old girl.' He laid it on thick. 'When do we leave?'

'Ah,' Martha said, stepping to one side. 'There are one or two conditions insisted upon by Professor Royston Mills III,' she lied. 'If you're agreeable.'

Malcolm gave a bark of laughter. 'Hmm? Nothing Malcolm Harper-Smyth the First can't accommodate, I'm sure.'

She turned towards her desk, and picked up her sheet of paper, holding it out to him. Malcolm ran his eyes down the half a dozen points as Martha spoke.

'As you can see, they'd like us to go out for an initial six-week period,' she said. 'They will arrange for us to fly BOAC to Los Angeles and will put us up in a respectable hotel. If we're happy after that, we will return indefinitely.'

'Nothing to rail against there, is there?' Malcolm nodded. 'The children?'

'We can't take the children,' Martha said. 'The travel and accommodation wouldn't be suitable, and neither would we have the time or inclination for them. Sally Brown is a capable enough nanny and the children like her, and she them.' Martha paused as if that was an interesting thought.

129

'She has the Somervilles, here, and she can take the children to the sea for a week's holiday.'

Malcolm nodded again. 'Absolutely. First class thinking. Maybe Nanny Brown will come with us when we go permanently, she's not a bad sort, is she? Mousy, but willing.'

'Let's not get ahead of ourselves just now, Malcolm.' Martha took her notes back and glanced at her watch. 'I'll have a word with Sally in the morning.'

'Good idea. You do that,' Malcolm decided there was no better time to push his luck. He reached out and, with great daring, squeezed Martha's waist. 'In the meantime, what say we celebrate with a glass of something extravagant and an early night?'

There was a pause, then, 'I think that could be arranged,' she said.

21

Sally was nervous; she hadn't been summoned to see Malcolm and Martha together since she had first become Nanny Brown. She might have fallen in love with the children but she certainly wasn't comfortable around their parents – Malcolm for obvious reasons, and Martha, well, Martha reminded Sally of drawings of Queen Elizabeth I; autocratic and distant, someone you could admire from afar but never warm to.

She hesitated before knocking on Martha's study door, smoothing her hands over the plain grey dress that Martha liked her to wear. She remained sure that Malcolm hadn't come close to recognising her, and she couldn't think of anything she had done that would cause the doctors to give her notice, but she knew she could never, never become complacent.

'Come in,' was the crisp response to her tap on the door. 'Ah, Sally.' Martha looked up from a neat sheaf of papers on her desk, but Malcolm, lounging on the Eames chair by the fireplace, didn't stir from behind his Times.

'Good Morning, Dr Harper-Smyth,' Sally murmured; her eyes flitted between the two, the greeting encompassing them both.

'We're going away,' Martha announced without preamble. 'I've been invited to participate in an extended research programme in America.'

'Away?' Sally repeated faintly. 'America?'

'Yes.'

She understood from the pause that she was expected to comment, but how? Her mind was immediately reeling. What did Martha mean? Am I going to lose the children, Sally thought, pushing down a twist of panic, or do they expect me to go with them, and if they do, I'll have to get a passport in my full name and he'll know…

'Sally?'

'It's quite an honour for my wife,' Malcolm put in.

They were both looking at her oddly by now and Sally pulled herself together quickly. 'Yes. Yes, of course. Congratulations,' she said as warmly as she could muster. 'They will be very lucky to have you.'

'Yes, Well.' Martha looked mollified. 'We won't be leaving until next month,' she went on. 'We'll leave it to you to take the children for a holiday of their own. We thought a week at the coast – Eastbourne, perhaps.' She frowned suddenly. 'What is it?'

'I'll be staying here? With Jeremy and Rosemary?' Sally was holding her breath.

'Well, of course. You weren't expecting to come with us?' Malcolm gave a snort of laughter.

'The nanny position did stipulate sole care,' Martha added.

For all her anxiety, Sally didn't miss the faint looks of horror on her employers' faces, at the thought of their children – with or without a nanny – accompanying them halfway across the world.

'I understand,' she said quickly. 'I'm very happy to care for the children alone here. I was just concerned that you might miss them too much.'

'It's only for six weeks – perhaps a little more to incorporate travel. Certainly not more than three months. We'll be very busy.'

Six weeks. Six blissful long weeks. Maybe, even more. That was all Sally could think about when she was dismissed a couple of minutes later. She closed the study door gently behind her and ran lightly along the hall and up towards the nursery. Six weeks. The things they could do; the places they could go. She imagined a week – could she even push it to two – beside the sea; sandcastles and paddling with little Rosemary, Punch and Judy and donkey rides for Jeremy. No doctors. No Somervilles. Just Sally and the children. It would be almost as if…

No. Sally stopped suddenly. She couldn't let her thoughts go there. She mustn't. Yes, she could, a little voice in her head said. Why not? It was a game, what harm could it do? To dream. To pretend. To be a real mother, just for a little while. *They should have been yours… they should have been yours…*

When, the following morning, she collected Miss Campbell's letter from the PO Box, and read what the old lady had to say, Sally's starry daydreams took on long, strong legs – to the point where there was no going back: Nan Douglas was a real mother, devoted to twins, Jay and Mary; Nan Douglas was a real niece, solicitous of her elderly aunt, her only other relative in the world. And if Nan Douglas had six weeks to spare, she wouldn't hesitate to travel north, to a remote Scottish island, to introduce her children, Jay and Mary, to their Great-Aunt, Maud Campbell. So why should Nanny Brown be limited to a week in Eastbourne? They'd be there and back well within a month, Sally told herself. With any luck, they would have a lovely, memorable holiday, she'd find empathy in Miss Campbell when – the only part of the plan that made Sally hesitate – she refused the housekeeper's position, and best of all, Sally's own restlessness and yearning for real-life motherhood would be assuaged.

22
MARTHA

Martha planned her forthcoming trip to America with the same level of meticulous care lavished on the longitudinal experiments she oversaw in her prized laboratory. In fact, that was where most of her efforts were placed. The house would be fine with the Somervilles in charge; their life would be easy, so much so... Martha didn't believe in idle hands, so she decided the couple would take a holiday for two weeks – no, she calculated the time she and Malcolm would be gone – four weeks. No doubt they had a relative or friend somewhere to stay with. Obviously Cook would go on furlough; the woman cycled in from one of the villages each day and Martha rather thought she had an invalid husband or sister or suchlike, so would appreciate the break. Malcolm would grumble but she'd arrange a small stipend to ensure loyalty; he'd grown up in the days when servants were tied to grand families, but Martha knew how lucky they were to have staff these days. The doctors deserved them, of course, they needed them, and Martha had no doubt that the Harper-Smyth household was a coveted place to work.

Martha made a note to speak to the Somervilles and Cook, and then started on a list of things she needed to take with her (she paused to make another note to remind Malcolm that he had to do likewise). Mrs Somerville would be in charge of the packing, and Patrick could run extraneous errands. Royston had the paperwork in progress, and there would be visas and documentation to collect from the American Embassy in London. Malcolm would have to wire money over, which meant a bank account... Martha frowned. The level of administration was tedious in the extreme. Even so, she reminded herself, it was worth it. This trip was going to highlight Martha as one of the leading scientists of her generation, and with the right connections she was stepping ever closer to establishing a lab in California. Martha gave herself to a rare moment of daydreaming, before returning to her list and writing rapidly. When she sat back, twenty minutes later, and cast an eye over it, she was pleased at its comprehensive nature. Something niggled though – what had she forgotten? It would come to her, the important things always did. In the meantime, she rang for Mrs Somerville.

The housekeeper took the news with equanimity. They had no relatives, she told Martha, but she and Patrick had a small pot of savings and would enjoy the luxury of a small guesthouse by the sea–

'Yes. It sounds delightful,' Martha interrupted. 'You may use the telephone to make your arrangements, if you wish.' She handed over one of her lists. 'You can start packing. We leave in three weeks and I'd appreciate the items on the left being shipped in advance. They'll need to go imminently, preferably by one of the American flag companies – get Patrick to check that out.'

'Certainly, Dr Beaumont. I'll start immediately. May I ask about the remainder of the household? Cook–'

'Ah, yes.' Martha nodded. 'You might tell her she's to be given leave for the duration? I'll arrange to speak to her myself before we go. Thank you, Mrs Somerville.' It was a dismissal, but Martha was irritated to note that the housekeeper still stood there. 'Is there something else before you get on?' she asked.

Mrs Somerville looked at her somewhat strangely, Martha

thought, though it was hard to tell – she'd always had a slight strabismus of the left eye that should have been checked in childhood. That was something she must ensure never happens should either child develop a weakness– Oh. That was it. Martha remembered what it was missing from her provision at exactly the same time as Mrs Somerville said quietly:

'Mrs Brown and the children, madam. What is to happen to them whilst you're gone?'

'Mrs Brown will be taking the children on holiday for a week or two. Eastbourne has been mentioned, but I am leaving all the arrangements in her capable hands. In this case, I am happy to say that Nanny knows best.' Martha gave a tight-lipped smile. 'Don't you agree?'

'Oh, yes, Dr Beaumont. And when the holiday is over?'

'Nanny will look after the children here. She will add laundry and light household chores to her duties during that time. Your leave is unaffected. Now I must get on. Thank you, Mrs Somerville.'

'Yes, madam.' Mrs Somerville inclined her head and backed out of the room but Martha barely noticed her. She was thinking about the big house, that it was tiresome they couldn't close it up for the duration; Nanny and the children would do perfectly well in a small flat somewhere, in fact, Sally Brown would probably prefer it. Maybe if she spoke to Malcolm… But no, regretfully, Martha accepted it was too near their precious departure time to think of the upheaval of shutting up the house or renting it out. It was certainly a thought for the future though; Martha made a note in her desk diary. If – no, when – she was asked to take on tenure in one of the American universities, it would suit all of them if they could set up Sally and the children in a flat. After all, it wasn't long, barely five years, until it was time for boarding school when Jeremy was seven. His name had been down for Malcolm's alma mater, Harrow, since the day he was born, and Rosemary, well, Cheltenham Ladies College was the obvious choice for her. America might be the home of her birth, and where her glittering career lay, but her children would have a traditional British education where every door would open to them. She might take Sally Brown into their confidence, Martha thought, there was no question of her allegiance to the family and she should be aware that should extend over the next – Martha did a quick calculation – ten years, at least. It had been a rare, spontaneous, comment when she'd said to Sally that the children should have been hers, but it was true and she would not shy away from it. Martha was not maternal, she didn't pretend to be, but she had done her duty, and now it was her time to shine.

Pleased with herself, Martha made another note. Her mind in overdrive, she sat on at her desk, thinking and planning, the world at her feet and Malcolm a willing acolyte. Then, she took her fountain pen and started to write her intentions into a final checklist. When she could see no more obstacles in her way, Martha rang for Sally to tell her how she featured in supporting the Beaumont-Harper-Smyths in their very grand goals.

23

Sally was not herself in the weeks leading up to the doctors' departure. With one week to go, she was heartily sick of the whole situation and just wanted the doctors gone, guessing shrewdly that Martha felt the same. It didn't help that it was the twelfth anniversary of the day Sally had lost – no, had taken from her; aborted. She wouldn't shy from the ugly word – her and Malcolm's baby. This year, like no other, Jeremy and Rosemary filled a very big part of her heart, so she was less distressed than angry, fuelled by the entitled and taken-for-granted view Malcolm and Martha had of their practically - orphaned children.

Sally seemed to have lived many lives this far and had known much heartache, too much perhaps. Sometimes she determined to gather up the children, steal them up to Inniscuillin and never come back; the fantasy saw her through. Sleep didn't come easily, though, and the days became dream-like. Malcolm remained his usual, frequently-absent self, but Martha was in the house much more, and while she rarely entered the nursery uninvited, she had taken to calling Sally down to the study to receive her latest list of instructions. Those, she took in her stride, practical arrangements and nothing to do with the children, but her very presence unsettled Sally. The doctor didn't make friendly overtures, it was more that her ambition was creating hairline cracks in her cool and calculated demeanour and she needed a safe and amenable audience; Mrs Somerville didn't cut the mustard, but Sally, somehow, did.

Yet, in none – not one – of their one-sided conversations did Martha ever refer to her children as living, breathing people but things that needed to be accounted for, by Sally – apparently, for the next ten years. It was after that particular encounter, listening to Martha talk, that Sally 'flipped' as she put it to herself later and decided enough was enough. She was taking control of her life and the children's – in the same way that Martha was doing for herself. The woman was an unlikely mentor but Sally decided she was learning from her, and would, in the long-run make Martha's life easy for her. Malcolm? Well, he didn't deserve any input or consideration.

Once again, Sally's life was to be packed away and a new one unfolded. This was just another chapter, she told herself, one that required a lot of careful planning. Unlike Martha, though, Sally was not running the risk of writing anything down. Instead, she ran mentally through her plans, day after day, hour after hour, as she might rehearse for first night in a London stage play.

'And have you made some plans for your own little holiday at the seaside?' Malcolm asked one evening, when Sally took the children to their parents' sitting room for a short visit. Unusually both doctors were present, Malcolm lounging on the sofa with a drink in his hand – his red face suggesting it wasn't the first of the day – and Martha, across the room, neat in her armchair, a book open on her knees.

'Yes, sir.' Sally's heart thumped. 'I thought we'd leave the day after you and Dr Beaumont. That way the children won't have time to miss you –'

'Yes, yes. Right enough. Good thinking.' Malcolm clearly saw no irony in her remark. 'And er, Eastbourne is it? Or Bournemouth? I – Oh, sorry, my dear?' This last was to Martha, whose interruption inadvertently saved Sally from the lie she had – as a last resort – prepared. Sally wasn't yet ready to admit to herself why she was keeping their actual holiday spot a secret; she was sure Malcolm and Martha would rather she took the children to Timbuktu than accompany the couple to America, and Scotland would simply get a 'rather you than me' eye raise. It didn't matter anyway.

'Really, Malcolm,' Martha said, looking up from a complicated diagram. 'Don't bother Mrs Brown for details. I have every confidence in her to do what's best for the children. Including getting them to bed on time.' In what was clearly a dismissal, she frowned slightly at her prized Waterbury grandfather clock, and Sally wondered if it was her or Malcolm being told off.

He didn't seem to notice. 'Of course, my dear,' he said heartily, getting up to refresh his single malt. 'Sorry, Nanny Brown. Off you go then. Goodnight, children.' He waved the decanter in their direction.

Sally was unsure whether to laugh or cry. She might have put herself in a surreal situation by taking on this position, but surely the doctors were already living in a very strange world of their own. After that, she offered to do some of the seemingly endless posting, collecting of documents, and fetching and carrying of the doctors' possessions, all prior to their departure. Of course Sally would deliver a box to the University, to Addenbrooke's Hospital, even to a Post Office in London – if Mrs Somerville could be prevailed upon to care for the children?

An extra box here or there, of Sally's belongings and the children's, would not be noticed if she was in charge of the mailing. After all, it made sense to send a few things ahead for their stay on Inniscuillin. Sally was well aware that transporting two young children to the other end of the country was to be an onerous enough task and the encumbrance of luggage would make it impossible for a lone lady traveller.

And then Malcolm and Martha were gone.

It was mid-morning, and there was a brief goodbye in the hallway; neither Jeremy nor Rosemary seemed concerned about the departure of their parents – or they were too small to understand. Dutifully, Sally lined up with them on the front door step and nudged them to wave.

'Big smiles,' she whispered. 'Mummy and Daddy are going off on their big adventure. We'll have ours soon, too.'

With her Chanel handbag and matching travelling rug, and without a backward glance, Martha tucked herself neatly into the car hired for their journey to London airport. Malcolm hesitated, as if wondering, Sally thought, what a good father should do before saying goodbye to his children for an extended time but in the end, he just raised his hand, and hopped in beside Martha. The chauffeur closed the door, turned the engine, and they were gone.

And with them went Mrs Sally Brown and her wards, Jeremy and Rosemary. It was Mrs Nancy Douglas, and her twins Jay and Mary who disappeared back into the house.

There was only one full day before the Somervilles also left. Sally made the most of the time, reminding them that she had a few remaining errands to do for Dr Beaumont, and that Mrs Somerville had agreed to mind the children in the meantime.

'We'll do some baking, shall we?' Mrs Somerville put her hands on her hips and looked down at the two children flanking Sally. 'How about we make some lovely Empire biscuits for your teas?'

'Yes, please, Mrs Somerville,' Jeremy said politely.

Sally wondered if he even understood the concept of baking; the kitchen was far from where the doctors thought he should be, Rosemary too. And she herself was surprised – to say the least – with the offer. This was a different side to Mrs Somerville, a holiday-side. Clearly, Sally wasn't the only one who relaxed when their employers were gone. She and Mrs Somerville shared a glance that was the closest they would ever get to complicity, before Sally kissed the children goodbye and ran lightly up the stairs to the nursery.

There, she set about collecting a few items from the children's wardrobes and drawers, packing a suitcase suitable for two weeks on the south coast. With that carefully labelled and set on the landing for Patrick to carry down, Sally set to her real work. She had already hidden cardboard boxes at the back of the huge old cupboard in her own bedroom and filled them with carefully chosen clothes – ones that Sally had bought with quite a bit of growing room – the doctors were generous with a clothes allowance – and ones that Mrs Somerville would be less likely to miss later on. Now, she added to this some of the children's favoured toys; their favourites would have to stay behind. When she was finished she had three boxes ready, taking them one at a time down the stairs, before ringing the Harper-Smyths' usual account for a taxi.

Nervously, Sally left the house. Patrick was gardening but he was so intent on the weeding that he paid her little heed and the taxi driver helped her with the parcels. 'Them doctors need an awful amount of stuff over in that America,' he said cheerfully. 'Special delivery too. Why can't they go from the local PO?'

'International Customs Regulations, I think,' Sally improvised, trying to act naturally. 'These are the last. I'm being lazy taking them all in one go.' She didn't want him to remember her as anything out of the ordinary.

At the station, a porter took the boxes and deposited them in the luggage van, and Sally eased herself into a window seat, intending to run through her mental plans once more. Instead, the train lulled her into a restless sleep. She woke five miles or so from Kings Cross Station, glad of the little rest. Once the train had come to a juddering halt she got off, the hustle and bustle jarring with her, and tipped another porter to help her get the packages to the Left Luggage office. She left two of them there and took the third with her. Sally took a deep breath, got her bearings and slipped into the Ladies. There, she ripped off the typed label addressed to the Cardinal Institute and replaced it with a handwritten one care of Inniscuillin Post Office. Next she pulled a curly wig from her shopping bag and fitted it carefully over her hair and securing a French beret on top, before making her way first out to daylight and towards the nearest Post Office. She repeated the laborious journey twice more, each time to a different Post Office, and then made a quick visit to Boots and Timothy White's, both big and busy shops.

Done.

She was exhausted as she sank back on to the train, relieved of the parcels and her wig discarded in an anonymous litter bin. Anxiety nibbled at her edges, but back at the house, by tea-time (listening to the excited children tell her all about their baking, and sampling their proud plate of biscuits and saying a farewell to the Somervilles who would be gone early the next morning) she was just glad that a major part of the plan was complete. Getting Jeremy and Rosemary ready for bed, she even felt a tiny ripple of excitement. She just had one more thing to do today.

Sally began by searching the library and the study for the family photograph albums she expected would be there in abundance; if anyone asked, she would say, 'A little project to keep the children occupied in this dreadful wet weather.' But nobody asked, and Sally was ultimately unsurprised to find slim pickings. It seemed that the Harper-Smyths' preferred studio portraits to candid holiday snapshots (although Sally, wondered, had they ever even had a family holiday?) Sally's instinct was a pang of sadness, that the children would have so few silly inconsequential and out-of-focus memories to look back on, but she equally acknowledged how much it was going to work in her favour now. The folder she found was as formal and select as the doctors' wedding album, the pick of the crop, almost Victorian in their serious poses, already adorning the walls of the hall and sitting room.

Tucking this under her arm, Sally finally made her own weary way to bed, pleased with a day of jobs well done.

The next morning, still giddy from their baking adventures, the children woke ripe for more fun. Sally, having checked the Somervilles had gone as planned and that the house was empty, didn't disappoint.

'Who's for a treasure hunt?' she asked, as they tidied up after breakfast.

'It's raining, Nan.' Jeremy objected, as he stared sadly

through the window. 'We'll get wet and the treasure will get wet. And Patrick won't let us take the spade out.'

Sally ruffled his hair. 'This is a special indoor treasure hunt, my darling. No pacing out steps or digging under trees today. It's an indoor treasure hunt and we're going to be looking for... photographs.'

Jeremy's bottom lip wobbled. 'That doesn't sound fun. I want to hunt for gold coins.'

'Who says there won't be gold coins – for boys and girls who aren't grumpy?' Sally raised her eyebrows, recognising in the child, the mutinous look his father had – had always had – when people weren't quick enough to do his bidding. 'But if you're not interested, then Rosemary and I will have our adventure while you play in the nursery, won't we, sweetie?' She plucked the little one from her highchair and left her to explore the floor; crawling was a skill Rosemary still couldn't get enough of.

'She's too small.' Jeremy, despite his grievance, was not going to be left out. 'Alright, I will come. What do we do?'

'Easy-peasy. You, Jeremy, as you're the oldest, you look in every room and if you see a photo with you in it, we put a tick on this chart – see? And I'll carry Rosemary and see if we can find any of her. Then at the end we count them up.'

'For a prize?' he asked hopefully.

'For a prize. And there's another prize for being fastest. How's that?'

Jeremy thought about it for a minute, then a wide smile spread across his face. 'I am the oldest so there will be most photos of me and I will be fastest, Nan.'

'Will you?' Sally offered her piece de resistance. 'To make sure, you will... have to ... run!'

'Run?' Jeremy looked confused. 'Run in the house?'

'Just today. Today the 'No Running Rule' is a 'Must Run Rule.' Now, no more dilly-dallying. Are you ready?'

'Ready, Nan!'

'Ready.'

Laughing, Sally and Rosemary chased Jeremy a merry jaunt through the house, as fast as his little legs would carry him. While he spied himself in half a dozen photographs in the hall and on the landing, ('Nan, nan – there's baby Jeremy; there's church Jeremy; there's Christmas Jeremy… Write it down, Nan, write it') Sally took stock of the images and, most importantly, the sizes of the frames. The large canvas above the drawing room fireplace could be safely ignored; pride of place had been given to Malcolm meeting Princess Margaret on a tour of Addenbrooke's Hospital. Sally was amused to see that Martha was not to be outdone – the opposite wall was all but filled with a montage of Martha shaking hands with His Royal Highness The Duke of Edinburgh.

'What are we doing now?' Jeremy asked an hour later, when they were back in the nursery, flushed and triumphant.

'Now, I am going to rearrange the photographs for a surprise for Mummy and Daddy when they come home. And you…' Sally's eyes twinkled. 'You are going to claim your prize.' She handed him a packet of chocolate buttons. 'Just one for Rosemary, because her teeth are too little. And you must promise to brush extra well tonight.'

'Yay hurray.' Jeremy clapped his hands and laughed. 'Nan, this is so fun.'

Drunk on the heady delights of being allowed the run of the house and chocolate when it wasn't Sunday afternoon, both children quickly lost interest in Sally's measurements and calculations.

Later, Sally went downstairs alone and removed the large canvas painting of the children. Malcolm had only hung it there before going to the States with Martha last week. She knew with the staff being laid off while they were away, she could remove the painting and change the photo albums without being discovered. As she did the deed, Sally felt that seed of excitement grow, just a little. She finished the day by cutting her own hair and somewhat messily dying it a lighter shade, nothing dramatic, and donning a pair of very weak reading glasses she'd picked up in Timothy White's. Then, before their last night in the house, Sally wrote a note and left it in the middle of the kitchen table where Mrs Somerville would be sure to find it.

This was going to happen.

It was no longer a game, and it was no longer just for a while.

24

Their journey was going to be a long one. Sally had a tortuous route worked out, one that cemented the fact that this was no holiday. It brought home to her what she was doing: she was deliberately taking Malcolm Harper-Smyth's children away from him – for good. She had no intention of returning, ever, and instead she, in the persona of Nan Douglas, was adopting (she wouldn't countenance the word 'abducting') little Jeremy and Rosemary – no, she reminded herself – Jay and Mary and giving them the life and love they deserved. The life and love her aborted baby would have received; the life and love they would have received if they'd been hers. They should have been yours; Martha's words rang in her head like a permission-giving mantra.

First they took a slow train to London, then another to Brighton. There, they had a quick bite in the buffet, before taking a bus back to London and mingling in the chaos of Victoria Coach Station. So far, so good, the children had never been on a coach before and were rallying well. It made for a long trip, a pointless one, but it was the best Sally could think of, so as not to be tracked. And it was only the start. She couldn't risk a direct train north, but that was just as well; the children would need a proper bed to sleep in.

'You look funny,' Jeremy said for the second time that day, as they settled on to the Peterborough train and Sally took off her hat and shook out her hair. He glanced at her lightened locks.

'Do you like it?' she asked and he nodded uncertainly.

'It's just for a little while.' Sally tousled his own hair. 'I cut my own hair when I did yours and Ro…Mary's, and then

I thought it would be nice if my colour matched yours so I changed it.'

'Silly Nan.' The little boy smiled, not interested in hairdressing and already nodding off lulled by the motion of the train. She looked down at Rosemary already asleep on her lap and bent to kiss her head. This is how it should be, she thought.

The mustiness of the cheap Peterborough guest house filled Sally's nostrils and her stomach threatened to retch for reasons she refused to acknowledge. 'Mrs Patricia Clark.' Quaking, Sally used the first of the temporary names she'd decided on. 'I wrote ahead to book a room for the night.' She called on the Yorkshire accent of her childhood, to change her voice only slightly, wondering how she'd become so devious.

The age-ravaged owner trembled as she handed Sally the key. 'I don't want them disturbing the other guests.' She pointed a bony index finger at the two little ones.

'My twins are well-behaved.' Sally swallowed her need to say more, for she must not be remembered. She and the children made their way dutifully quietly up the pattern-worn staircase behind the disapproving hotelier, Sally making a funny face at Jeremy, who had looked in fear at the witchy-seeming landlady. With the door closed safely behind them Sally and the children settled into the green eiderdown and melted into fits of giggles. Despite her anxiety, Sally was bone-tired, and sleep overtook them as they snuggled together.

Breakfast was a quiet affair. The other guests comprised of an elderly couple whose conversation did not go beyond 'Pass me the butter, dear' and 'Looks like it's going to be another nice day.' The lady smiled at the children as they passed, and Sally, wishing with all her being to hurry them by, paused with a polite and friendly hello – her Yorkshire accent coming to the fore once again.

As they left the guest house Sally embraced the sunshine. It was going to be alright. Looking at the children, with a big smile, she asked, 'Now who's ready for today's adventure?'

Two policemen stood at the platform as the travellers alighted from the 16.37 arrival in York. Sally had to steady herself against a barrier. You're not yet missing, she reminded herself. This is a holiday. The doctors told us to take a holiday. It might not be Brighton or Eastbourne, the southern seaside places Martha might have expected, but wasn't it natural Sally would take the opportunity to visit the county of her birth? She mentally rehearsed her story with her head down, rearranging their belongings, until the policemen had moved on. Hastily she hoisted the heavy bag over her shoulder, almost overbalancing. 'It's not far to our next hotel, Jay,' Sally said, taking Jeremy's hand and lifting Rosemary into her arms.

'You promise?' Jeremy's weary face looked up at her.

'I promise, come on, let's go.'

The Station Hotel was across the road, and once again, they took refuge – Mrs Susan Harman and her children – behind the locked door of their simple room. Sally felt a sadness join the array of emotions constantly encircling her. York was familiar to her, the big city of her childhood, more exciting than Ripon and the place for an occasional school outing or even more rare family day out from Offley Farm. If things had been different, this might have been the place that she and Robert – or, she had to face it, she and Malcolm – would have visited with their own children…

'Nan, nan?' Rosemary stroked Sally's shaking hands, and Jeremy looked worriedly at her. 'You are crying tears, Nan,' he said. 'Are you hurt?'

'No! No, darlings, I'm fine. I have grit in my eye.' She smiled brightly, brushing away her tears, and with them the feeling of disloyalty that arose from thinking of those other, mythical, children. These, Jeremy and Rosemary, should have been her children – even Martha had said so. That couldn't be, but Jay and Mary could be the children of Nan Douglas.

'Jay, Jay, come what may,' Sally sang, throwing both children on the bed and tickling them, much to their shrieking delight. 'Mary, Mary, not contrary.' Then, 'Shh, naughty Nan is making too much noise at bedtime. Cuddles?'

'Cuddles!' The children chorused happily.

In comparison, the next night's accommodation at The North British Hotel in Edinburgh, promised luxury. Standing in the generous entrance hall Sally was suddenly struck by the feeling of total unreality; she was now Catriona Sinclair, her hat back on, and her hair tucked up. She also wore her unnecessary reading glasses, small enough that she could look over the top of the frames to avoid a headache. The receptionist barely looked at her, and within minutes, Sally was crossing another bedroom, this one hearty in its proportions, and closing the curtains on the red lettering of Woolworths opposite. They could make a life of this, she thought idly, moving from place to place, a night here, a night there, drifting. But no, the children needed roots, stability, love. Was she doing the right thing? Right for them, right for her? First things first.

'Hands, face and teeth,' she recited, chasing them into the bathroom, and once done, and in their nightclothes, a fresh nappy on Rosemary, Sally settled them in to bed, easing herself in beside them.

She woke a while later, with a start suddenly unsure of where she was. She rubbed her hand over the cotton sheets and checked to her left where the children lay. They were in Edinburgh, she reminded herself, I've made it this far. Sally rose from the bed and padded over to the window, peering between the curtains she watched the hubbub of the street below.

The children – Jay and Mary, she said over and over, Jay and Mary, like a mantra – nestled peacefully while she recklessly called Room Service, waking them once the feast was laid before them. This was the last leg of their journey; they all deserved the luxury. Rose – Mary, she meant Mary, never liked waking up but the trolley of food encouraged the little girl to sit up. 'Look at this big treat,' Sally said. 'What can you see, Mary?'

'Orange juice.' She pointed, rubbing her eyes and yawning.

'Would you like some?' Sally kissed the little girl's curls, as she nodded.

Jer – no, Jay feasted on bacon, fried bread and beans. 'It's very good,' he said earnestly.

Sally ruffled his hair. 'I'm glad you like it.'

After breakfast she bathed the children in the ample bath, filled with bubbles. Mary giggled as she and Sally piled them high on Jay's hair. Then Sally risked a quick shower as the two played. She was reluctant to leave the cocoon created for them, but the room had to be vacated and they had a long journey ahead.

As Sally and the children stepped from the hotel, Sally breathed in a lungful of city air and, linking hands with Jay and carrying Mary, she smiled. 'Now, who wants to go to Inverness?' she asked.

'Me, Nan, me,' Jay shouted.

'Me, me, me.' Mary copied him.

'Okay, you two! Then let's get tickets for the train.'

And the next day it was in an Inverness back street, at the Castle View guest house that the trio woke up. Sally smiled again at its name – she realised that if she stood on her tiptoes, she could just see the castle. She had a feeling of safety here. Perhaps it was the distance from Cambridge, or was she so numb that for the moment she simply couldn't worry anymore?

After breakfast they made their way to the bus station.

'Fort William, please.' Sally struggled to hold the two little ones and climb the steps.

'Leave yer bag there, hen. Ah'll get it for ye,' the driver offered, winking at the children.

Sally settled them all in a double seat and they dozed. The journey was more picturesque than Sally could ever have imagined; she wondered at times if she were dreaming. It was a long trip though with a change of bus at Fort William, and only intermittent bouts of sleep made it pass more quickly.

'Mallaig, next stop,' the driver announced eventually.

As the bus pulled off, they made their way to a café across from the stop for some welcome refreshments, before heading over to the port. There was just under half an hour to wait before the ferry was due to leave, and once aboard, Jay and Mary pressed their noses to the window and laughed joyfully as waves dampened the glass. Slowly, the mist surrounding the vessel cleared enough to give them their first view of Inniscuillin; it seemed to be floating in front of them.

'The seaside,' exclaimed Jay. 'I see the beach and the rocks and some little boats. Can we make sandcastles and sail the little boats, Nan? Nan? Is it magic island?'

Sally's heart thumped. Was it possible to feel as if you were coming home, when it was to a place you'd never been before? 'Perhaps it is, my darlings,' she said. 'We'll just have to wait and see.'

Gill Merton

PART FOUR

THE ISLAND (1971 – 1981)

25

As the small ferry docked, Sally collected their belongings and rearranged her anxious features into anticipation and pleasure; they were holiday-makers now, long-lost family, not refugees or escapees. If she couldn't adopt that mindset and believe it, then their journey was doomed, and that she would not allow.

Sally looked purposefully around the small harbour. Miss Campbell – Aunt Maud – had promised to send someone to meet them, and the figure who emerged from the tiny harbourmaster's hut couldn't be missed.

'Look, Nan.' Jay noticed him at the same time as Sally did and nudged her in awe. 'He looks like Father Christmas.'

The weather-beaten face crinkled into a surprisingly wide smile and he strode over to meet them, holding out a firm hand to Sally, then gravely shaking Jay's hand too. Mary hid her face in Sally's shoulder but kept peeking out to look at the twinkling eyes.

'Sandy MacKinnon, gardener, handyman and general dogsbody,' he introduced himself.

Sally laughed, then took a deep breath and, as rehearsed, said brightly, 'Nan Douglas. And these are Jay and Mary.'

Sandy was a welcome sight, not least in the effortless way he helped ease the heavy bag off Sally's shoulder, all the while, showing them to the faded matt-khaki Land Rover.

'It might no' look braw but it never lets us down.' He pointed to the paintwork. 'That's what happens on these islands… Twa fine bairns ye've got there. Twins, Miss Campbell says,' he went on as they settled into the vehicle.

'Yes. Thank you,' Sally answered. Thank you, thank you,

thank you, the words repeated in her head. Here at last.

'Ye're Miss Campbell's niece,' Sandy commented – as Sally knew he would. That she had lived so much of her life in a small village was going to stand her in good stead. 'The questions will start as soon as you arrive,' she'd warned herself. 'Be ready, Nan.' I can do this, Sally told herself. I have to do this. She took another deep breath.

'Her great-niece from her father's side.' She gave the pre-agreed response.

'Aye. An' ye're English.'

'Yes. Yorkshire, born and bred.' Keep it as near to the truth as possible, she reminded herself.

'What brings ye here?'

'I need a change. We need a change.' Sally lowered her voice, mindful of the children in the back. 'Since I was widowed… Well, it's very beautiful here. Restful.' She hoped Sandy would accept her 'bereavement' as a delicate subject and leave it at that.

He nodded. 'Right enough. Ye've never been here afore, have ye?'

'No, never. I'm so glad Aunt Maud invited us. I'm so tired…' Sally's voice broke as a real wave of emotion flowed through her. She bit her lip.

Sandy took his hand off the steering wheel and administered a fatherly pat to her arm. 'Now then, lass. It'll be fine. Ye've done the best thing for yersel' and these bonnie bairns.'

Have I? thought Sally. She felt a moment of panic, because nobody must ever know what she had done. From this moment on, Sally was – had to be – all alone. But she had the children; she'd always have the children and that was worth any sacrifice. She forced a note of jollity into her tone. 'Have you always lived here, Sandy?'

'No, ah'm from a village just outside Edinburgh originally. Been here forty years or more, mind. Gie it a few more years an' ah'll be thought o' as a local.'

Sally laughed. 'I'll have a long time to wait then.'

'Maybe no', what wi the Campbells having been up at the Big House as long as Inniscuillin has been an island. Are ye biding here a while, like?'

'We'll see, but hopefully.'

Silence fell as the vehicle wended its way along the coast road.

'Ah think yer bairns are sleepin'.' Sandy said, punctuating the silence.

'It's been a long journey to get here.'

'No' long tae go now.'

Once over the brow of the hill Sally gaped at the view.

'Ah never tire o' that view, and down there's yer aunt's house.'

Nestled at the bottom of the hill, smoke billowing from its chimneys, sat Miss Campbell's generous home. A nervousness crept over Sally as they made their way down the hill. What if they knew?

Sandy whisked the ample vehicle between the gate posts and along the drive. Miss Campbell appeared quickly at the front door. She'd been watching for them, Sally thought.

The vehicle drew to a halt and Sandy turned to Sally. 'The duchess awaits yer arrival, ma'am.'

Miss Campbell, thin and angular with grey hair worn in a bun – not at all what Sally had expected – surprised Sally by reaching out to hug her. It was in the embrace that she reminded Sally to call her Aunt Maud.

'Come and meet Aunt Maud,' Sally called to the reticent children.

'Oh, they are a credit to you, Nan,' Miss Campbell declared. 'They clearly take after our side of the family.' She took Sally's arm and led her over the threshold. 'Come on, children. Welcome to your new home.'

Inside, the curious housekeeper was in attendance.

'This is my housekeeper, Margaret, who will shortly be leaving us. Margaret this is my great-niece, Nan and her children, Jay and Mary. Margaret will show you to your rooms and once you're feeling refreshed we'll have tea and sandwiches. Please take the bag upstairs, Sandy. It's the two rooms on the right.'

'Oh, Margaret, what beautiful rooms. And look at that view,' Sally said.

'She's had me titivating them for two weeks solid,' Sandy interrupted. 'Isn't that right Maggie? Wallpaperin', paintin', rearrangin' furniture, ah could've been forgiven for thinkin' Her Majesty was coming tae stay.'

Sally giggled girlishly. 'Thank you, Sandy, you've clearly done a great job.'

'Yer very welcome, lass. Ah hope ye find the life here that you and yer bairns deserve.'

Sally shivered at his words, laughing it off as needing to acclimatise to the northernmost temperatures. Once they had freshened up, Sally and the children made their way down to the drawing room, where Miss Campbell rang a little bell and Margaret made her way into the room.

'Please serve the tea and sandwiches now, Margaret,' she said. 'My family have travelled a long way and are in need of sustenance.' So saying, Miss Campbell led the way to the dining room. The smell of wood, polish and the smoke from the fire reminded Sally of her parents' house. She wanted to cry. Sandy was there already finishing a cup of tea.

'You look tired, my dear,' Miss Campbell said.

'Just a little, it's taken a long time to get here.'

'The little ones look tired too, it's an early bed for all of you, I think.'

It was a strain for Miss Campbell, too, Sally realised. She had been so busy thinking about her own role, she'd forgotten that here was an elderly woman who, for reasons of her own, had taken in strangers under the subterfuge of family; she had a role too. The two women shared a glance, and Sally knew she was right, when Maud added, 'There will be plenty of time to catch up on all these missing years later. For now, we must get to know one another as if for the first time.'

'That sounds like guid advice,' Sandy advised. 'Right. Ah'm off.'

Just then the deposed and departing Margaret entered the dining room with a tray of sandwiches and cakes. Sandy held the door open for her, before winking at Jay and tossing a 'Cheerio for now,' over his shoulder.

'He's incorrigible,' Miss Campbell said. 'He'll be the death of me – but I'd be lost without him.' The fondness in her tone was unmistakable and Sally wondered at the relationship between them; it was definitely no Lady Chatterley, but neither was it the average lady of the manor and her general factotum, either.

The children's eyes were wide as Maud invited Sally to put the plates in front of them. 'Heavens, don't stand on ceremony, child,' she said. 'Start as we must go on and treat my home as yours. It'll be all the better with young blood.'

Margaret returned a few minutes later with a silver tea pot in her grasp, and Sally, taking her aunt at her word, murmured that she'd be mother. Maud looked pleased and Margaret looked surprised; no doubt, Sally thought, the village would be hearing how the new young one, that Nan Douglas, was a chip off the old block and no mistake – making herself right at home

Sally couldn't remember a more welcome cup of tea ever, as she sipped from the china cup. She and the children ate heartily while Miss Campbell nibbled on a sandwich, and Sally thought, still looked nervous. It wasn't an emotion she would ascribe as usual to the older woman, and that gave Sally herself confidence as she realised this situation was new for all of them.

26

'This is the best holiday ever, Nan. I love Aunt Maud.' Jay
snuggled up to Sally, and she put down the Peter Rabbit she
was reading to him.

'I'm very glad to hear it, darling,' Sally replied. They'd
been on Inniscuillin for four weeks already, four blissful
weeks, but she was aware the storm was about to come. She
squeezed Mary, tucked under her arm. 'What do you think,
Mary? Do you like it here?'

Mary, sucking her thumb, looked up at Sally with big eyes
and a vigorous nod. 'Like it,' she added.

'Would you like to stay a bit longer?' Sally asked lightly,
belying the knot of tension in her stomach. Her best laid
plans, what she wanted, would only work if the children were
happy; she was doing this for them.

'A big bit longer.' Jay held out his arms wide. 'This
much.'

'This much, Nan.' Mary copied him.

'Me, too,' Sally confided. 'Shall we see what Aunt Maud
says? And if she says yes, maybe we can stay a very big bit.'

'Til I'm a grown-up,' Jay announced.

Not once in the month since their departure had either
child mentioned Malcolm or Martha. Sally had thought
ahead, deciding how she would answer the inevitable
questions or homesickness, but nothing had come.
Everything was new and fun; they were spoiled all over the
small island: lollipops at the shop-cum-Post Office; barley
sugars from Sandy Mac and something sweet and sugary
called tablet from Maud Campbell, who whispered to them it
was her secret weakness. They had beaches to play on, farm

animals to visit and haystacks to hide in; rock pools to 'fish' and a house and garden where they were allowed to run. Sally was their constant, the one they ran to, and it seemed enough for them.

There would be fallout, Sally knew, there had to be, but for now she'd enjoy it. Nobody knew how hard Sally was trying behind the scenes to make sure they fitted quietly in but it seemed to be working. The islanders, led by Maud Campbell and Sandy Mac had taken the three of them to heart, there was none of the suspiciousness Sally had expected – of foreigners and blow-ins from the big city – instead they were a novelty. Maud herself seemed incurious about Sally's background, content to get to know her in the present, and Sally returned the favour; both of them, she suspected, had secrets. The older woman was thought a mine of information about the island. She could be acerbic and not one to suffer fools, but she was also funny and quietly kind. Hints such as, 'Don't trust the postmistress with anything private, she lives her life through other people's letters,' and 'The minister is a snake in the grass and he'll want to lure you into his vipers' den,' were tempered with her fondness for Helen Brady, 'She's a veritable Girl Friday with the patience of Saint Donnán of Eigg: assistant school teacher, secretary to our solicitor and she runs the Sunday school and what passes for our Boy Scout troop,' and Sandy Mac, 'Och, he's a rare one,' which Sally quickly learned was high praise, indeed.

Sally looked forward to the quiet evenings, knitting and reading, sometimes with the radio on. In private, Maud was not the eccentric grumpy old lady she cultivated in public, but a restful companion. She saved her richest observations until the children were safely in bed and Sally looked forward to the next instalment.

'Where do I start with the two eligible bachelors on the island,' she said one night, taking a sip of the well-watered whisky that was her night-cap. She must have caught the look on Sally's face and snorted. 'Oh, I'm not aiming to set you up with a second husband, I'm using 'eligible' in its broadest sense. No woman in their right mind would take either of them on.'

'Do tell me more,' Sally encouraged. 'Who are they? Why haven't I met them yet?'

'Alisdair Conti, our solicitor, and Ewan McLeish, the police sergeant,' Maud said. 'The Conti family arrived here from Italy in the 1920s and settled on the mainland. There was family money to set up the main office of Conti & Sons Solicitors.' She raised an amused eyebrow. 'We have the runt of the litter here. Alisdair is a nice boy. Mad as a hatter, of course, and no interest in the law but he gets by. He hasn't succeeded yet in adding the '& Sons' above his office door. Nan, my dear,' now Maud's eyes twinkled, 'Don't be tempted to help him out.'

Sally laughed. 'I have no intentions. But if I had, is the police sergeant a better suitor?'

'Och, Ewan is harmless. Plodding and pedantic to the point of distraction but he keeps order. He'll be knocking at the door to meet you as soon as he's back. He's recalled to some of the other, smaller islands for a week or two at a time,' she added. 'We struggle on without him. And Alisdair is away on one of his regular fishing trips. What he's fishing for, I wouldn't hazard a guess.' Maud shook her head. 'And my dear departed mother wondered why I showed so little interest in men.'

Sally giggled. 'I'm duly warned. Nobody else I should be wary of?'

'Just the minister.' Maud snorted. 'The Reverend William Crawford to give him his full title and he's a piece of work if ever there was one.'

'Too godly or not godly enough?' Sally asked.

'I'd call him the devil in cleric's clothing, but then I'm biased. I knew him when he was plain Willie Crawfie, stealing Jimmy Mackie's jam piece and pulling Peggy-from-the-Post's pigtails.' Maud took another meditative sip of whisky. 'There was a time... well, let's just say he suggested he and I walk out together.'

'And did you?' Sally was intrigued. It was the closest Maud had come to disclosing something of her past.

'I did not. I laughed at him.' She laughed now, slightly shame-faced, Sally thought, as she joined in. 'He has never forgiven me – despite my regular reminders that he preaches forgiveness – and I won't set foot in his kirk, nor give the time of day to his God but the good minister says nothing because I know where the bodies are buried.'

'Then he won't come knocking at the door to meet me? I'm not a churchgoer either,' Sally said.

'He won't. But he will accost you in the village and command you to attend services.' Maud warned. 'And he's a bully. Word is, he treats his poor wife like a slave behind closed doors, and she's too afeared to say anything.'

'I've met his type before. Charming bullies, the need to control…' Sally's mind flew to Malcolm and she bit her lip before she said anymore.

'Och, there's nothing charming about Wee Free Willie.'

Maud looked at Sally and relented slightly. 'Maybe appease him by sending the little ones to Sunday School. It'll stop him sympathising with you over their poor floundering souls and young Helen Brady, the leader, is a lovely wee thing. She's got his card marked too: wandering hands. Watch yourself,' Maud added cryptically but Sally got the message.

'There's one thing you need to know about Inniscuillin, Nan.' Maud drained the last of her drink and set the glass carefully down. 'The island is made up of two sets of people, those born and bred here and those who have run away here and are hiding – don't look so worried, my dear, I don't mean they're bad people, just, well, different. Those who don't necessarily fit in the wider world.' She leaned over and patted Sally's knee. 'We all have secrets. And we all look after our own. And with that, I'll say goodnight, my dear.'

'Goodnight,' Sally echoed as the older woman made her way to the door. She sat on stiffly and thought over Maud's words. What was their warning? That Maud knew – or guessed – there was more to Nan than Sally was letting on? Or that there was more to the islanders, Maud included? What she did know, she thought cynically, was that she needed to be on good terms with Sergeant McLeish – she didn't want him sending off his friend the solicitor fishing into her life…

And so, it was taken for granted that 'Nan' and 'the twins' would stay on with their Great-Aunt Maud Campbell at the Big House. But as their fourth week came and went, Sally was well aware that she was on borrowed time. With no way – other than contacting Mrs Somerville – of discovering when the doctors were due home, she had to assume it could be imminent and once they returned to find Sally and the children gone, there would be a huge investigation. It was the end of the road for Sally and she had two choices: Nanny Brown and her charges returning to Cambridge after a wonderful extended holiday with a distant relative, or to live on the island as Nan Douglas with her children and wait to be caught out.

Now, as she readjusted her position on the saggy double bed, and resumed reading Peter Rabbit, her arms around the two people that mattered most to her in the world, Sally's mind was not on the well-thumbed book but on what she was going to do. She knew right from wrong. Her head knew she had taken the children under false pretences and that it was a criminal act. Her heart though insisted she had done what was right, and she had made that decision when she donned a disguise to visit a London Post Office and had altered all the photographs in the doctors' house.

Whether she had another week, month, year or more with Jer...with Jay and Mary it was worth all the anxiety and risk in the world.

27
SERGEANT MCLEISH

Police Sergeant Ewan McLeish thoughtfully rubbed his large and ruddy nose, and contemplated a metaphysical dilemma he had not previously experienced. He stood, back ram-rod straight, almost motionless at the front door facing him. Blessed with his policeman's curious and enquiring mind, he also prided himself on lateral thinking that had solved crimes which perplexed his colleagues. The case of the Inniscuillin's black public phone boxes was the one he was most proud of, and one he regularly mulled over as if he was savouring a mouthful of a vintage wine… He shook his head, cognisant of the business at hand, and reached out to rap the ancient metal door knocker.

There had been an explosion of gossip on the island on his return from the neighbouring islands – even more so than usual – this time about the arrival of the attractive young woman and her two young children staying up at the Big House with the formidable Maud Campbell, spinster of the parish. It seemed she was a niece, or maybe a cousin, and widow by all accounts, with two young bairns. She'd come to replace Maggie-the-housekeeper, as companion to Miss Campbell. It was a police sergeant's duty to make her acquaintance forthwith.

Awaiting a response to his knock, Ewan got ready to analyse, mentally, the expression on her face. This was a skill he had been taught at police training college. Police instructors loved the slightly corrupted mantra, 'A face is worth a thousand words', referring to someone's initial facial response on being confronted by a police officer. It was, in

Ewan's view, worth more than a two-hour taped interview in a police station. Not as punchy, of course, but just as apposite.

When he heard feet approaching, he cleared his throat in true police fashion (as demonstrated in the official police training manual at Tulliallan). He wondered if it was the old battle-axe herself or… 'Come on, Ewan McLeish,' he said to himself, as he detected his pulse quickening, 'You're behavin' like a lovelorn teenage laddie.' He reminded himself he was just here to find out how the woman and her children were settling in, and to satisfy his curiosity on a few wee points.

Stolid, clumping footsteps told Ewan that it was Maud Campbell – to him, always the intimidating grande dame of Inniscuillin – who would be opening the door. Even the self-styled teddy-boys and mods on the island – all three of them – quaked in their blue suede shoes and wobbled on their scooters when Maud stomped by.

'Feasgar math, Eòghann,' she said now.

'Agus feasgar math, Miss Campbell.' He curbed, as usual, his irritation that she didn't give him his formal title. 'Ciamar a tha thu?'

'Tha mi gu math, tapadh leat.'

Formalities complete, Ewan cleared his throat and in a tone that was half police-ese and half informal, explained he was just paying a complimentary visit to welcome the new residents to the island.

'And what a relief you're back with us. The island's a safer place with you in your police box.'

'Yes, well, thank you.' He wasn't sure how to take Maud's tone and he certainly didn't add that he wished to discreetly satisfy his curiosity on a number of points regarding Nan Douglas. For example: was she romantically attached? 'Ewan, that is not an appropriate question... yet,' he had already negotiated with himself, 'maybe on a later occasion.' It was as though Dr Jekyll and Mr Hyde had taken up residence in his head, as he mentally listed all his queries: Where had she come from; what were her plans for the future; did she like policemen... 'Ewan, I won't tell you again!' he mentally admonished himself... How long had she lived at her previous address; was she financially independent; did she have links, other than with Maud Campbell, in the area; did she like men with moustaches ... 'Ewan, this is your last warning!' came his other voice ... Did she have a driving licence and if so, was she planning on running a car on the islands myriad network of roads – all three of them?

Maud, looking amused – not for the first time, he wondered how she had the effect of reducing him to feeling like a wee gangling boy – interrupted Ewan's internal wrangling by announcing that the household had just sat down to afternoon tea. Then she did something that Ewan knew was totally out of character for a spinster who considered herself to be the matriarch of the island – reluctantly assisted by someone she considered her social inferior, namely Police Sergeant Ewan McLeish – she hesitated. Yes, Maud Campbell hesitated.

It was plain to him, a trained observer, that she was deliberating whether to invite Ewan into the parlour or to keep him standing on the doorstep and bring her new boarder out to him to be introduced.

'Wait here, Ewan,' Maud said, eventually.

His mouth dropped open; this was against all social convention. Irrespective of who knocked on your door, if they lived on the island you always invited them in and offered a cup of tea. The police part of Ewan's brain, which had been metaphorically parked in a lay-by by the romantic side, now gunned itself into action and roared back onto the road. Ewan knew that if you wanted to avoid having to answer potentially awkward questions, you made sure you didn't invite them in for tea… Ewan sighed; it was wishful thinking that there might be a case to answer here. Truth was, as a trained observer like him was aware, Maud Campbell was just being her contrary one-up-man-ship self. He wouldn't, professionally speaking, give her the satisfaction of seeing him piqued.

Two sets of footsteps caused him to straighten up once more and click his heels together ready for inspection.

'Sergeant McLeish.' Maud indicated the young lady at her shoulder. 'May I introduce you to my great-niece, Nan Douglas.' She turned slightly. 'Nan, dear, this is our custodian of the law, Police Sergeant Ewan McLeish.'

For once, Ewan was speechless. He stood there, mouth slightly open, as the pretty young woman stepped forward, smiling.

'Sergeant McLeish,' she said. 'My aunt has told me all about you. I'm pleased to meet you.'

Ewan gathered his wits and reached out to grasp the slender hand held out to him. 'Mrs Douglas. The pleasure is mine,' he managed.

Ewan was smitten.

28
MARTHA AND MALCOLM

In the early hours of the morning, flushed with success and full of their achievements, Malcolm Harper-Smyth held open the front door for Martha Beaumont, nearly three and a half months after they'd last left their Cambridge house.

'House' was the best word, Martha thought, dispassionately as she laid her gloves on the hall table and turned to greet Mrs Somerville. During their time away, it had lost any vestiges of home; Martha had found her feet in the Cardinal Institute, and with an offer of a visiting professorship at Harvard University expected any day, this was a temporary visit – whatever Malcolm decided.

'Madam. Sir. Welcome home.' Mrs Somerville patted her curlers self-consciously.

Martha inclined her head. 'It's been a long journey, Mrs Somerville. And I see we've kept you up.' She eyed the housekeeper's nightclothes, covered incongruously by what looked like Cook's apron. 'No – please don't apologise.'

Mrs Somerville flushed. 'Yes, madam, but–'

Martha held up her hand. 'I'm sure you have plenty to say, but not now. We'll go straight to bed and I'll see you in the study at 10am. We'll take a late breakfast and discuss anything of importance then.' She turned to look over her shoulder, where Malcolm was dragging in the first of two suitcases. 'You can tell Patrick we've managed the luggage without him. He can take them up in the morning.' Martha added pointedly.

She swept across the hall and up the staircase, leaving Mrs Somerville, the mutinous look on her face barely hidden, to close the door after Malcolm – who greeted her with a cheery, 'Goodnight, Mrs S,' and skipped off after his wife.

'Yes, madam. Certainly, madam,' Mrs Somerville muttered under her breath and made her way back to a drowsy Patrick. 'Not a proper hello or a thank you from either of them,' she grumbled as she removed the hastily-grabbed apron and threw it across the easy chair. 'And you were missed. You're to take their cases up first thing.'

Patrick grunted from his side of the bed. 'Did you tell them 'owt?'

'I tried. Madam wasn't having it.' She gave a self-satisfied shrug.

'On their heads be it.' Patrick pulled back the eiderdown. 'Get in, woman, you're creating a draught. If you ask me, the lass has had the right idea.'

'You really think they're all-three alright? Not dead in a ditch or abducted by sheikhs?' The bed springs creaked under Mrs Somerville's weight. 'Aah.'

'You read too many books. 'Course they're alright.' Patrick tapped his wife's shoulder. 'Remember what we agreed? Least said soonest mended.'

'You've no arguments from me,' Mrs Somerville said with relish. 'Night, then.'

'Night.' Patrick gave another fleeting thought to the absent nanny as he drifted off to sleep. Good on the lass, he said to himself again.

Martha didn't approve of jet lag; it was mind over matter. She was up and working well before ten o'clock. There were instructions and recommendations – disguised as generous 'thank you' notes – to be sent post-haste over the Atlantic.

Martha had prepared the groundwork; she was not known for letting the grass grow. She could, she decided, with judicious planning, be back in America in a month, two at the most. That was plenty of time for niceties and appearances to be kept up; Martha would not look desperate. Malcolm had a lucrative job offer, too, permanent cardiac surgeon at the facility attached to Royston's unit, with an eager team beneath him and as much golf as he cared for. Martha's lip curled. It was not her idea of success but each to their own. Maybe Malcolm would decide to follow on later – or to stay here, but somehow, she didn't think so. What was to keep him?

'The house is very quiet.' Malcolm himself, yawning, entered the room and disturbed her thoughts.

'Um-hm.' Martha didn't look up from her desk.

'Very sensible of Nanny Brown to keep the children away. I need to acclimatise. Maybe she's taken them out for the day,' Malcolm prattled on cheerfully. 'I rather think I'll wander down to the Club for lunch today. Won't be the same without Pa –' Malcolm's father had keeled over in his chair a month into their trip. He'd decided not to return; there was no funeral, as the body had been donated to medical science. 'Pa wouldn't thank me for it and the old man had a good innings,' he'd said to Martha, trying out the idea. When she agreed, Malcolm relaxed and raised a glass: 'To Pa.' He wasn't one for tears. 'No, won't be the same without Pa, but plenty of others to boast to.' Malcolm gave a roguish grin.

'You've plenty to boast about.' Martha looked up. 'Professionally speaking.' It was a dig at his less than professional relationships with some of his pretty young female colleagues, but Martha wasn't interested or hurt by any of his flings. He knew to be discreet. Or else.

'We both have.' Malcolm squeezed her shoulder briefly and they shared a brief but triumphant moment. 'Mrs S can tell Nanny Brown to bring the children down tonight,' he added. 'Will you sort that, darling? I expect jet lag might catch us out though.'

'Yes, I can't have a late one.' Martha frowned. 'It seems I agreed to lecture tomorrow in Leeds, and I've been reserved a seat on the 6.15 train in the morning. I'll be away overnight.'

There was a knock at the study door and Martha's frown deepened as she glanced at the clock. 'I told her 10 am. What is she thinking of…?' The knock was repeated. 'Come in,' Martha snapped. 'What is it, Mrs Somerville – oh.'

When Mrs Somerville appeared swallowing nervously, with Patrick by her side, Martha and Malcolm shared a confused glance. Martha's heart began to beat faster. Something was going on and instinctively she knew it was trouble.

'Hello, Patrick. Is there a problem?' Malcolm asked affably.

The couple ignored him. 'Madam. Sir.' Mrs Somerville licked her lips. 'I tried to tell you last night. There's something you should know…'

'What, for heaven's sake. Spit it out.' Martha lost her customary cool, causing Malcolm to look at her in surprise. He went to squeeze her shoulder again but thought better of it.

'It's Nanny Brown and the children, madam. I'm sure all is well but they're not here.'

'What do you mean, not here?' Martha glared.

'Probably at the park already,' Malcolm added. Mrs Somerville shook her head. 'No. I mean they haven't been back. From their seaside trip.' 'You're talking in riddles, Mrs Somerville. What exactly are you saying?' Martha challenged her, causing the housekeeper to look imploringly at her husband to explain. Patrick sighed. 'What the wife's saying is that she's upped and gone,' he said bluntly. 'Sally Brown has gone. And she's taken Jeremy and Rosemary with her.'

29

Sally, under Sandy's instruction, was to familiarise herself with the Land Rover. She was nervous at first but soon felt she was getting the hang of it.

'He said I did it alright,' she told Maud later.

'High praise, indeed, from Sandy.' Maud sniffed.

The idea was that Sally, rather than Sandy himself, who had 'better things tae dae than wait around for the women', could drive Maud to Innis Castle when she wanted to visit her housebound friend, the ailing Mrs Armstrong-Stuart. Sally was nervous, not only driving, but at driving in such a way that she drew the attention of the local policeman. She'd been surprised and a bit dismayed to meet him only a few weeks after their arrival, and she was afraid it might have shown on her face. She needed to get over that, she told herself. She couldn't tell if Sergeant McLeish's intense gaze was suspicion, stupidity or speechless admiration but he had no reason to think of her as the enemy, and, mindful too of Maud's words, Sally had to keep it that way - especially as she had no driving licence in the name of Nan Douglas.

'Nan?'

Maud's eyes were on her; they and the children were in the car waiting to move. Sally snapped out of it. 'Sorry. Just memorising the gears,' she improvised.

Nerves did indeed kick in as she searched for first gear, and then breathed a sigh of relief as the stick moved into place. Sally drove cautiously down the drive and between the gateposts.

'There's plenty of room,' Maud encouraged her. 'No-one has hit the gate posts in years.'

Sally hoped she wouldn't change that. She indicated right at the end of the drive and juddered onto the single-track road. 'Sorry.'

'Don't apologise,' the old lady corrected her. 'It's probably more to do with Sandy's tinkering. He's always under the bonnet and I'm not certain he knows what he's doing.'

There was silence for a few minutes as Sally concentrated on her driving. Then:

'What do you think of the island now you've seen a bit of it?' Maud asked.

'It's very beautiful. I love the sea and I'm looking forward to living beside it.'

'We'll see if you think the same, my dear, on a stormy January night.'

Sally smiled. 'I'll take whatever it throws at me.' She risked looking briefly over her shoulder. 'We all will, won't we, children?'

'Children!' Maud boomed, as she too half turned. 'You can see the seals – look over there. Like black bananas trying to stay out of the incoming tide.'

'Go see,' Mary demanded. 'Nan, nan, go see.'

'We will, in a little while,' Sally promised her.

'Turn left here,' Maud instructed.

Sally did as she was told and passed a terraced row of cottages. 'The first on the right is Sandy's,' Maud said, causing Sally to glance at the white-washed stone cottage. She imagined Sandy, feet up and his 'wee dram' in hand.

'Is it left here?' Sally tried to remember.

'Yes. There's a cattle grid at the entrance to Innis Castle, so take it slowly.'

Sally did as bidden, but still excited squeals from the back seat competed with the bouncing suspension, and Maud laughed. 'We'll make country children of you yet,' she said. Then she gave a tut of annoyance. 'Oh, fiddle. Nan, speed up,' she commanded.

'But there's a car coming towards us–' Sally had seen it too, a Ford Anglia coming down the drive.

'Yes, and it's Wee... I mean, it's Minister Crawford and that's an encounter we don't need. I swear that man stalks me. He knows this is my time for Hilary. Well, aren't I glad we were late today.'

'Sorry–'

'Don't be. He'll be vexed and I am smug.' And Maud looked it, Sally thought. 'Wave to the nice man, children,' she cooed.

Obediently, they pressed their faces to the window and waved their arms enthusiastically, Jay giving a thumbs up for good measure. Sally caught sight of the minister's astonished look as he swerved to avoid them, his bulk hunched over the wheel.

'He never waved back,' Jay objected. 'Rude man.'

'Rude,' Mary echoed.

Continuing up to the house, Sally couldn't help but laugh at the broad beam on Maud's face.

Innis Castle was much more than she had expected, with turrets and crow steps. It would be bleak on a dark winter's day but now, brightened by cool sunlight, with the Atlantic no more than fifty feet from the front door, it was impressive.

'Why is your house...?' Sally hesitated, not sure how to satisfy her curiosity without sounding rude.

Maud pre-empted her. 'Why is my house called the Big

House when Innis is so much bigger?'

'Well, yes.'

'History and habit, my dear. My father was the doctor, he took in patients at one time, walking wounded for convalescence, I think – I vaguely remember it during the war – and if there was no space, he'd billet them in the village. People would ask where they were staying and if it was ours, the doctor's, they'd say up at the Big House. Part home-part sanatorium, my mother called it. It stuck.' Then her tone changed to brisk. 'Come back at 3.30pm, Nan,' Maud told Sally. 'I'll ask Hilary to invite you to tea next week, and you can meet her then.'

With Maud safely delivered, Sally turned to Jay and Mary. 'Now who wants to explore?'

First Sally drove to the village, to hand in the weekly shopping list Maggie had left behind - the message line, she'd called it. It was the first time Sally had driven into the heart of the village and she stalled the car twice before managing to park it.

'Och, it's our Miss Campbell's great-niece, Nan,' Peggy, the red-faced lady behind the counter said enthusiastically as Sally handed over the piece of paper. 'How are you settlin' in?'

'Very well, thank you.'

'It's London you're from?'

'Yes, that's right.'

The woman clucked her tongue. 'There's no' many folks that leave London for these parts. What brings you here?'

'I wanted a change for me and the twins after my husband died.' Sally had practised this until she was fluent. 'We're going to explore so I'd better go. Sandy will collect the groceries.'

The woman nodded. 'Right you are.' She handed the delighted children a lollipop. 'See you soon, wee bairns.'

They were just climbing back into the car, when a booming voice hailed them from behind. 'Not so fast, young lady. It's time we were introduced.'

Sally whirled around and came face to face with the same Ford Anglia and the hefty man who had been driving it: the minister; Wee Free Willie, Sally added mentally.

'Oh, hello,' she said politely. 'Reverend Crawford, isn't it? My aunt told me about you.'

'Did she now.' He heaved himself out of the small car and stood towering above them. Mary shrank behind Sally's knees. 'And you are Mrs Douglas, I believe. I haven't seen you at church.'

'No, well–'

'Are you a churchgoer, Mrs Douglas? God loves a sinner and we're all sinners.'

'Yes. No, I –' Sally was at a loss. The man was a caricature of what her dear dad would have called a hell, fire and damnation evangelist. Once a year, when she was a little girl, a group of maverick Baptists used to hire the Offley Farm big barn to hold services – Sally hadn't thought of that for years but now it came flooding back – and Minister Crawford would have fitted right in. It was on the tip of her tongue to say she was a Roman Catholic convert, just to see if his red face turned purple but discretion was the better part of valour; she didn't want to draw attention to herself.

'… as it says in Revelations. Are you a Bible reader, Mrs Douglas? There's no better bedtime story for these wee folk. Have I seen them at Sunday School?'

'Yes. Yes, you have.' Sally grasped on to a question she could answer.

'Then all is not yet lost,' he all but roared at them.

Jay put his hands over his ears and stepped back to join Mary. 'Nan, is he a giant?' he asked loudly.

'We must go,' Sally said hurriedly. 'I promised… I mean, I've to collect… Goodbye, Reverend. Come along, children.' She lifted them both into the back of the car and made to get in the driver's seat herself.

William Crawford inclined his head. 'Ignore the call of duty at your peril,' he bellowed as he folded himself into the sagging Ford Anglia. 'I'll be praying for your souls. Be sure to tell Miss Campbell that I'm praying for her soul particularly.'

As they drove off, Sally caught sight of the children in the back, looking thunderstruck. 'Funny man,' she said lightly. 'He didn't have an indoors voice, at all, did he? Now, the beach?'

'The beach,' they chorused, the minister forgotten. Sally relaxed. She was with Maud in her opinion of Inniscuillin's Free Church minister. She'd keep her distance.

On the beach, the resident seals soon turned their heads curiously as the car drew up, and one or two barked.

'They're saying hello,' Jay said.

'Hello, hello,' Mary shouted as the smallest seal slunk from the rock and into the water.

'We must be careful not to frighten them.' Sally lowered her voice and led the children along the beach, stopping to handle stones, turn shells over and look for crabs in the rock pools. She was struck anew by the paleness of the sand and the turquoise sea. A sense of calm embraced her and her mind-clutter quietened. Sally felt present in the moment, not like the observer she usually felt she was.

'Nan! Come see.'

Mary's joyous cries made Sally smile. 'What is it? What have you found?'

'A beastie.' The little girl pointed at the shape from a safe distance.

'Oh well done, darling. You are clever, you found a crab,' Sally said.

'I found it too.' Jay was not to be outdone.

The trio watched it journey sideways to get as far away from them as possible. Then, 'Shall we have a race?' Sally asked. 'The first one to those little boats over there is the winner – and I'm going to win!'

'No. Me!' Jay tore off ahead, as Sally helped Mary toddle behind.

'Yes, Jay's the winner,' Sally declared, clapping her hands, with Mary joining in, while Jay took a bow. 'Now who wants a picnic?'

Two cheers went up and Sally retrieved the food from the car. They settled down on the tartan travel rug and munched cheese sandwiches, washed down with apple squash. After a while, Sally checked the time, and said, 'We'd better go and pick up Aunt Maud now.'

'Oh, can't we stay? Please? Pleeeeaaase?'

'We have to go today. But we'll come back another day,' Sally promised.

'Tomorrow?' Jay asked

'Soon.' Sally confirmed, then added, 'We live here now, remember?' She held her breath.

'Hurray,' the children chorused without a beat, and Sally relaxed.

When Maud lowered herself into the car, she was greeted happily by the little ones, and Sally asked if she'd had a nice afternoon.

'Too much cake, too little sherry.'

Sally laughed and the older woman's school ma'am expression relaxed into one of amusement. 'Oh, what must you think of me? If you don't watch out I'll be leading you into bad ways.'

'Speaking of bad ways...' Sally looked sideways at Maud. 'We met Reverend Crawford in the village.'

'Lucky you,' Maud's tone was dry. 'And how did that go?'

'Hmm. He greeted us with a few words on sin, Mary hid, Jay asked if he was a giant, oh, and,' Sally added, expertly reversing the car to return down the drive. 'He said, to say he was praying for your soul, in particular.'

'Huh. That man couldn't save the sole of my shoe,' was the reply, proving to Sally that whatever the minister thought, Maud would always have the last word.

187

30
MALCOLM AND MARTHA

It seemed that half of the Cambridgeshire Constabulary and a selection of Scotland Yard's finest had taken over their once-elegant and tranquil house as a temporary headquarters – all without a by-your-leave or any sense of imposition, Martha thought irritably as she bypassed the dining room, the sitting room and the library, and unlocked the door to her study. When she dared to complain about the booted footfall in and out (not only police but news reporters, and heaven forfend, a psychologist or two), she was greeted with something like sympathy; as if she – she, Dr Martha Beaumont – was misguided. It was like they expected her to be grateful for their bullish presence. Yes, the children were gone. Yes, it was a challenging situation. But life went on; careers as glittering as hers could not be derailed by the antics of a mere nanny.

'Aren't you worried at all about them?' The police psychologist, a dowdy, mumsy-looking woman with big earnest eyes behind her bottle-top glasses, had given up being subtle when Martha had reiterated she was quite alright, thank you and did not need to talk. She and an ever-present WPC kept sitting opposite Martha being understanding.

Martha allowed herself the luxury of a sigh. 'No, to be frank, I'm not.' She was unperturbed by being labelled unemotional or disassociated; she was both things, that's what made her a brilliant scientist. 'I am irked. I am inconvenienced. I have some curiosity. But I am not worried. You have ascertained it unlikely the children were taken by a stranger. You believe it was a planned event and that they are somewhere, possibly abroad, with Mrs Brown, and unharmed. Yes?' She paused for breath.

'Yes, but –'

Martha held up a hand. 'You wanted me to talk. Kindly let me do so.' The door opened and Malcolm entered, but she ignored him. 'Sally Brown may have committed a criminal offence by wanting to take our children away, she may be misguided and I cannot pretend to understand her motivations but, but, she loves those children and she is a damn good nanny. What she has done, she has done knowingly. And that, is why I am not weeping and wailing and acting in the way you all seem to want me to.' Martha sat back to stunned silence, her speech clearly heartfelt – even if the psychologist and the open-mouthed WPC had never seen a reaction like it. 'Now, if that's all, like you, I have work to do.'

The two women looked at one another, and murmuring something incoherent, got up and slipped out of the room. Martha knew she'd be the talk of the investigation, but that was no concern of hers.

Aware that Malcolm was hovering, Martha sighed again, and turned to him. 'Is there something you'd like to say, Malcolm?'

He flung himself down into the armchair under the window. 'All that – what you just said – is that how you really feel?' he asked.

'Of course it is. Why else would I say it?'

'And you think that Nanny Brown has the children and they're safe?'

'That's what I said.' Martha felt her impatience rising. She had an international telephone call booked and wanted to be prepared for it. The broadsheet's 'Case of the Missing Nanny', and the tabloid's 'Nanny Sally, Child Stealer' had reached her American contacts, and it seemed that both Royston and the powers-that-be at Harvard assumed Martha would be withdrawing her services, possibly permanently, and certainly until further notice. She had to put them right forthwith – Malcolm, too. After all, would it make any difference if she waited for news in Cambridge, England or Cambridge, Massachusetts?

'Why would she do that, Nanny Brown?' Malcolm went on. 'She had everything here. A home, money, the children. Why would she take them?'

'I don't know.'

'I still think they might all have been abducted,' Malcolm said. 'One hears of it, doesn't one? Women and children kidnapped for money or… or more nefarious purposes. Smuggled out of the country. I said to that Detective Inspector this morning, they should be following that angle. I'll go to the Chief Constable if I have to. He's one of Pa's old cronies, you know and –'

'Malcolm, I'm sorry but I haven't time to discuss this again. Let me summarise.' Martha raised her hands, ready to tick off her points. 'One, the police have ruled out kidnap due to lack of ransom demand. Two, there is nothing sufficiently special – outside the medical world, of course – about us to suggest our children and our nanny would be targeted. Neither do we have any sordid secrets in our pasts or present that might open us up to blackmail.' Martha paused, there was no harm in hinting she knew about his womanising ways. 'Well, I certainly don't, and I presume they asked you the same questions in one of their endless interviews.' She let that sink in and then continued, 'Three, Mrs Somerville is sure that a selection of the children's clothes and toys were taken, as were Sally's, and four, four, Malcolm, somebody altered all the photographs throughout the house so that we have no clear, up to date, pictures of the children by which they might be recognised. If that wasn't Sally Brown's work, then whose was it?' The telephone began to ring and Martha reached out for the receiver, but not before she added, with finality, 'Malcolm, Sally Brown took the children. She has the children with her now. And she's not coming back.'

31
SERGEANT MCLEISH

Ewan McLeish sighed and opened the door of his panda car. The engine started first go and he pulled away from the police station – a rather grand name, doubling as it did as his house.

He liked to drive around the island at least twice a week. It was never an onerous task as he loved the island and the effects of the changing seasons on the landscape never failed to make him appreciate his job. On days when the Atlantic rollers crashed on the shore in their incredible way, he was still left breathless at the power of nature. As a policeman though, he couldn't just be enthralled by supremely bleak scenery, he was also trained to observe. Were there any boats or ships in the distance? Were bottles of milk piling up outside old Angus' croft? Was the phone box still red? Today, he smiled as he drove past the island's only telephone box, and – yes! No-one had repainted it black with yellow spots. Ewan knew immediately who had done that. Peggy's young one, back from school on the mainland for the summer holidays always equalled trouble. He had smiled when the boy had asked, 'But Sergeant, how did you know it was me?'

His train of thought was interrupted when he saw the still much talked-about newcomers to Inniscuillin. Nan Douglas coming out of the phone box with the two bairns. It was raining hard, so he pulled over, got out, and shouted, 'Can I give you a lift?'

Ewan had met Miss Maud Campbell's great-niece only the once since her arrival. If it hadn't been ridiculous, he might have thought she was in hiding. In a fraction of a second, on their introduction – the one which Maud seemed reluctant to accommodate – on Nan Douglas' face he had detected: fear, annoyance, concern, surprise, bemusement, perplexity, invitation, stubbornness, devil-may-care, relief, bloody-mindedness. Hmm. Ewan realised that the expression was more complex than any he had ever experienced before. But then, on a small island like this, the sole expression he usually interpreted on a local's face – when they opened the door to reveal his uniformed, peak-capped figure – was either puzzlement (if they were innocent) or guilt ('gotcha ma laddie', for Ewan). Sexism didn't come into it; statistics did. If a crime was committed on Inniscuillin, 39 times out of 40 it was committed by a male. This statistical fact would cloud the analytical judgements of Police Sergeant Ewan McLeish in the weeks and months to come. In computer parlance, a spurious glitch would impair his police skills.

But the poor young woman was a widow, local gossip – mainly Maggie, formerly up at the Big House – told him. Left with two young children and uprooted from England to her only surviving family. Ewan McLeish would do his duty. 'A lift, Mrs Douglas?' he called again.

Nan stopped dead, and looked as if she was going to turn the offer down but the children had already seen the police car and were jumping up and down with excitement – a ride in a police car? The decision was made for her.

'That's very kind of you, Sergeant McLeish,' Nan said.

Ewan watched for the face opening the door, keen to interpret and analyse such a sophisticated compote, a potpourri, of conflicting impressions for a second time. Who needed cryptic crosswords? People were far more challenging. 'Och. Ewan, it is, Mrs Douglas, not sergeant.'

He gave a good snort of derision. Then he noticed the wee boy playing with the police radio. 'Now, young Jay, leave that be – or it'll be a night in the cells for you!'

Little Jay dropped the handset as if it were red-hot, and Ewan gave his mother a quick wink, before adding, 'Good wee boys and girls get a ride in my boat as well as my car, you know. Would you like that?'

Jay bounced so hard he nearly hit his head on the roof. 'Yes, please, Mr Policeman. Yes, please. When?'

Ewan laughed. 'Och, soon, young man. Very soon. When your mother says so.' He stole another look at Sally. 'Children living on an island need to learn how to row a boat and to swim,' he announced. 'I will be honoured to undertake the teaching.'

'Thank you,' Nan murmured. 'You're very kind.'

As the car moved off, Ewan observed that Angus' washing was still hanging on the makeshift line at the boundary of the croft. Odd, he thought. Surely he'd have noticed the rain. Should he call it police business and stop? Admittedly, Angus was forgetful these days. In the end he decided not to; nobody liked an overly nosy policeman – not even one called Sergeant Ewan McLeish.

'Ye'll be comin' tae the ceilidh next Saturday,' Sandy stated as Sally held the shelf in place while he fixed it against the wall.

'I can't go, Sandy, I have the children to look after.'

'Bring them wi ye. Ye cannae miss it, lass. The next one's no until St Andrew's Nicht.'

The reality of her situation hit her in moments like this and she knew that Sandy could see it in her face. She'd been on the island for over three months now and had very little contact with anyone outside the house. The exception being Peggy at the post office-cum-village store.

'It's a' very weel ye hidin' away here wi yer aunt but ye need to get out and have fun, Nan. It'll be guid for the bairns tae,' Sandy looked at her fondly. 'Ah might be speakin' out o' turn but ye cannae grieve forever.'

Relief flooded Sally's body and flushed her face.

'Ah'd offer to be yer date, but ah'll be as fou' as a puggie early doors.'

'Oh Sandy, you are a one.'

'Ye're right there, hen, they broke the mould when they made me. That's whit ma mother used tae say.'

'I'll look after the children, if you want to go to the ceilidh with that wretched man,' Miss Campbell announced at breakfast the following morning, prompted no doubt by Sandy, himself. 'Most of the village goes.'

'Have you ever gone?'

'Not for many a year, more than I care to remember. But if you go with Sandy, you'll have no truck with the likes of Ewan and Alisdair annoying you. And...' Maud's eyes bore into Sally. 'You'll not want to get a reputation for hiding away too long, Nan. The gossips will make more than your bereavement out of it. Nosy old souls.'

'Of course. You're right.' Sally concentrated on her porridge. 'We're so ordinary we don't want to become interesting for the wrong reasons.'

'Exactly,' Maud agreed.

Nothing more was said, but Sally quietly arranged to pick up Sandy and drive them to the ceilidh. Though she wondered if he was soon regretting his avuncular invitation.

Sally had overheard just enough of the conversation between Miss Campbell and Sandy to know that he was expected to accompany Sally to the dance, stay with her without fail and to restrict his intake of alcohol until Sally had gone home.

'She's trying tae get me tae sign the pledge,' he said to Sally, winking, as he passed her on the way back from Miss Campbell's study.

On the evening of the dance, the door of his cottage opened immediately and Sandy stepped out. He was wearing his kilt and a tweed jacket. As he got in the car Sally turned to him.

'You look so handsome in your kilt.'

'Aye, Ah can still cut a dash, if ah say so mysel'.'

'You're no lookin' sae bad yersel', hen, if I might be sae bold.'

Sally had chosen her one good dress, a dark blue velvet, from her very limited wardrobe and Miss Campbell provided her with a tartan wrap.

'We'll be the talk o' the island,' Sandy laughed.

'That's what I'm afraid of,' Sally replied, the truth behind her comment lost on Sandy

'Ye tryin' tae tell me ye dinnae want tae be an auld man's darlin'.'

They both laughed.

The village hall rang out as they got close. The six, twelve-paned windows glowed orange, in welcome.

'Oh. It's so pretty,' Sally began.

'Look out, lass!' Sandy grabbed the wheel, just as Sally slammed on the brakes to avoid the large, dark-clad figure that appeared to loom up from the shadows and step out in front of them.

'Bloody fool,' Sandy muttered. 'Are ye alright, Nan?'

'Fine. Luckily I was going so slowly.' Sally peered out of the driver's side window. 'What is that?' It was a bit early for Halloween, or she'd have assumed it was someone in fancy dress.

'Och, it's the minister. Mr Crawford. He makes it his business to protest any gathering that has a spot o' dancin' and drinkin'. Spoutin' the Bible and likenin' us to Sodom and Gomorrah.' Sandy shook his head. 'Don't wind down ye're window, lass. Just pull up there a bit, and that's us.'

The warmth and buzz flowed out as Sandy put his hand on the interior door. 'Ready?' he asked. When he opened it, heads turned.

Sally felt like a bride being led down the aisle on her father's arm. A wave of nausea swept over her, What if they knew?

'We'll sit there.' Sandy pointed ahead. 'Next tae Jimmy Mackie and his wife, Mary. They dinnae bite. And we'll head yer police sergeant off at the turn.' Sure enough, Ewan McLeish was striding towards them as if he'd been on the look-out.

'Aw' the phone boxes must be red the nicht,' Sandy added, winking at Sally. 'He's like the minister, he disnae usually come in tae the ceilidh,' Sandy continued, as if reading her thoughts. 'He usually just hangs about at goin' hame time tae see wha he can catch ahint the wheel wi yin too many drams in them. Big Davy Faulkner's son got done last year. Ah thought big Davy was gonna swing for Sergeant McLeish. Mind me no tae get intae a conversation wi him if ah get fou, hen, 'Ah've heard a' his stories afore and yince he starts ye cannae get away.'

But Maud had been right – as ever. With Sandy by her side, and garrulous Jimmy Mackie and his kind wife, Mary, taking her under their wing, Ewan didn't have a chance to get too close, and the nature of the ceilidh meant he couldn't ask her to dance in the way Sally understood dancing. In fact, trying to figure out the complicated dances occupied Sally's mind, leaving little room for her usual fears. She began to relax, and when – while they were enjoying their stovies – Sergeant McLeish appeared at their table, she even pointed to the empty chair.

He took it, ponderously. 'I noticed you driving in but I had to proceed back to the station. An island police sergeant is never off duty, you know.'

Sally smiled and listened politely, hoping it wasn't long before his duty called. She hoped she was safe in thinking that Sergeant McLeish was the one police officer not a threat to her – other than boring her to death. Soon his conversation got round to the black 'phone box mystery. Even newcomer Sally had heard it twice before from him and on numerous occasions from Sandy. Admittedly Sandy's story was usually preceded with, 'That man's an idiot.' Any attempt of Sally's to let Ewan know he'd told her before was ignored and she had to sit through the story again.

With the food cleared away Sergeant McLeish took his chance and whisked the protesting Sally to the floor for a Strip the Willow. It was a frantic dance, and all the birling, her worries and Sergeant McLeish's hand in hers, was too much for her. 'I'll need to sit down,' she gasped.

With concern on his face, he led her through the crowds, his arm around her supporting her back to her seat.

'Sorry,' she offered, once safely sitting down. 'I've still to get used to Scottish dancing, it seems.'

'I'll take you up for a Canadian Barn dance later,' he

replied. 'It's much more sedate.'

'Oh, I'm going home, Aunt Maud's looking after the twins.'

'I'll give you a lift.'

'No, I have the car. I haven't been drinking,' she felt the need to add.

He was clearly put out and Sally imagined he'd been brewing a few stories to tell her on the journey home.

'I can't take you away from police business,' she said. 'You might be needed here – the evening's young.'

Ewan opened his mouth as if to argue, when he was interrupted by a clap on his shoulder. 'Here you are, my old pal.' A male voice – more English than Sally had come to expect on the island and it gave her a sudden jolt – spoke. 'Not romancing on duty, are you, Sergeant?'

The policeman turned without enthusiasm. 'Ah, it's yourself back from the mainland, is it? About time. We've many a puzzle to solve of a Saturday afternoon and you'll be needing the stimulation after all that fishing.'

'Fishing is good for the soul. And the stomach,' the other man declared. 'And I've stocked up on the best single malt the Highlands can offer.' He tapped his nose. 'Ask no questions but get out the best decanter.'

'Alisdair, I am an officer of the law. If you have contraband–' Ewan puffed up and looked as if he wanted to pat his pockets for his policeman's little black notebook.

'Joke, my friend. Keeping you on your toes. It's good to be back.'

Sally, realising the stranger wasn't a stranger and hadn't come to interrogate her, was watching this exchange with amusement, knowing – primed by Maud, of course – before he turned to her that this had to be Alisdair Conti, the island's peripatetic solicitor.

'You must be Nan Douglas,' he said. 'Pleased to meet you. Alisdair Conti. I've heard all about you. I'm sorry for your loss, but I'm sure it's Inniscuillin's gain.'

Sally thanked him, muttering something banal about it being a while ago and time was a great healer – Ewan nodded along sympathetically – and mentioned that she and her twins were the lucky ones. 'It's a beautiful island and very friendly,' she said.

'Yes. The natives are good eggs. Well, come to me if you need any legal advice – and I'll recommend a good man.' Alisdair roared at his own quip, and Sally wondered if it was general bonhomie or if he'd been busy testing his new single malt. 'Drink?' He looked between Sally and Ewan.

'I was just saying it's time I was getting home,' Sally said. 'I don't want to presume on Aunt Maud's good nature.' She looked around the room and caught Sandy's eye as he made his way towards them.

'Ready, Nan? Ah'll chum ye tae the car.' He came to the rescue, managing to get between her and Ewan who had already lumbered to his feet.

'Thanks for rescuing me,' Sally whispered, out of earshot. 'From both of them.'

'Anytime, hen. Now drive home safely,' he instructed as she got in. 'Don't be running ower Wee Free Willie as he runs through the town, neither.'

Sally giggled. 'Thanks, Sandy. You can get 'as fou as a puggie' now.' She stumbled over the words he had uttered earlier. 'Whatever that might be.'

'Aye, Nan, lass, that ah will, that ah will.'

32

Sally continued to be surprised at how easily they all settled into life on Inniscuillin. Every morning, as she listened to the BBC news on the radio, she felt a frisson of anxiety – she expected - she always would – but after an initial flurry, the missing Cambridge nanny and her charges was no longer a headline and soon barely made the Scottish news. There were brief updates – 'No new leads" – in the daily newspaper delivered, with the milk, to the Big House and Sally steeled herself to read those; forewarned was forearmed – another of her late grandpa's sayings.

Maud confessed more than once that she felt years younger since they'd come to share her home. Since the children had been enrolled in the nursery class, the two women spent more time than just the evenings together, plenty of time to get to know each other. And if there was reticence on both sides, it was in tacit agreement. Time would tell how many confidences they would share, but Sally didn't doubt she and the children – already known across the island as the wee Campbell twins – had found the home and family she craved for them.

Gradually, the children segued into calling her Mum more than 'Nan' – Sally had made passing reference to the fact that Mary had struggled with her speech and couldn't pronounce her Ms for a while. Not wanting her to grow up in the shadow of her precocious twin brother, Nan had been the alternative. Nobody batted an eyelid. And if Mary remained a bit smaller and quieter than Jay, well, that was girls and boys for you. Sally marvelled at the children's adaptation. As time went on, she didn't dare ask them what they remembered, of course, but she told herself she didn't need to. They had a mother, a family, a home; they were cherished. Any slips about the past were easily put down to their lively imaginations.

It was early October, six months after their arrival, that Sally had her first real fright, reminding her how fragile their happiness was. Jay and Mary had got into the habit of playing alone in Maud's big garden. Sandy Mac had been summoned to fence off an area near the house where Sally could keep an eye on them from the kitchen window, and he'd gone a step further and made them their own set of swings and a sandpit for the days the beach was too blustery. There was even talk of a treehouse for when they were a bit bigger, but Maud had told him to hold his wind, he wasn't Robinson Crusoe and the twins didn't need broken legs and bumped heads. Sandy had just winked at the excited Jay and Mary and mused about a hidey hole playhouse instead. One day, he promised, when he'd finished all Aunt Maud's work they'd go hunting for the best spot.

Sally thought nothing more of it, as she bundled the two of them up into their winter coats – ordered from the mainland by Maud who had raised her eyes at their flimsy 'London' jackets. The nights were drawing in, the clocks about to change, and Maud was still concerned how the trio would cope with an island winter. 'Remember to stay in sight of the house,' Sally warned them. 'And we'll have hot cocoa and toast when you come in.'

Humming quietly, Sally had busied herself stirring milk and cutting into the new loaf, Maud had been teaching her how to make. The jar of jam she fetched from the larder was almost empty and she scanned the higher shelves, looking for another plum one – Mary didn't like raspberry seeds in her teeth – and then had to fetch the step ladder to reach it. Back in the kitchen, tea ready, Sally glanced towards the window, smiling, and then froze. Whereas usually Jay would have climbed onto 'his' swing, legs pumping for all he was worth, while calling to Mary to watch him from the sand, today there was no sign of either child. The swings were still, the sandpit and tools untouched.

Sally stumbled to the back door, flung it open and shouted. 'Jay? Mary? Where are you? Stop hiding, please and come in. Right now, children!'

Silence. She ran to the edge of the fenced area and looked over the larger garden – nothing. Still calling, Sally then made her way to the drive and the old stables – both places forbidden to the unaccompanied children – expecting any minute to see their apologetic little faces peeping out of the barn, aware they'd gone too far. But there was nothing.

'What is it, lass?' Sandy appeared from the depths of the barn, wiping his hands on a rag, at the same time as Maud's figure filled the kitchen door, calling, 'Nan? Nan? Is everything alright?'

'It's Jay and Mary – they're gone. They were playing. They're not here. I…' Sally was near tears.

'Dinnae worry, lass.' Sandy patted her arm. 'The cheeky wee bairns have wandered off, that's all. We'll find them in twa ticks.'

But they didn't. The grounds were scoured – and Maud even checked the house, though it would have been virtually impossible for two small children to have sneaked past Sally and back inside.

'I shouldn't have left them. They're just babies.' Sally sat at the kitchen table, wringing her hands. 'The sea – they can't swim, Maud. What if they're looking for the seals? Or one of the dinghies came loose and they're in it? What if someone's sailed off Skua Beach with them?'

'Nan. Pull yourself together,' Maud said sternly. 'They're far too little to get to the water, or even the beach, alone. We're on an island where everyone knows everyone and they all love the twins. Nobody has taken them. We have some misguided fools on Inniscuillin but nobody is evil.' That checked Sally's hysteria, but she didn't see Maud semaphoring over her head to get the car out and go and fetch the police sergeant.'

'Yer aunt's right, hen,' Sandy added. 'Like ah said, they've wandered off. Have yersel' a warmin' cup o' tea wi plenty o' sugar and I'll fetch Sergeant McLeish – just to help us find them quicker, mind.'

'We look after our own,' Maud reminded her, when Sally cried again in a mix of terror and gratefulness.

Ewan, in his element, bounded into action and was organising a search party of half the island, when Alisdair Conti arrived up at the Big House in his fancy Land Rover. Sally was watching and ran out to see two frightened little faces peering out from the seat beside him. She wrenched the door open and scooped both up in her arms, scolding and crying in equal measure. That caused the dirty and tired 'twins' to cry too, and wail that they were sorry for not listening and they didn't mean to get lost and – through their sniffles – could they have their cocoa and toast now, please?

Sally's tears turned to relieved laughter, Ewan disappointedly stood down the proposed search party and Alisdair brushed off all thanks but said he wouldn't mind the cocoa too – with a wee dram, naturally. Maud obliged, while Ewan – not to have his nose put out of joint by his friend's victory – had a quiet, gentle word with the children about 'minding their ma.'

'Where did you find them, Alisdair?' Sally asked. 'Half way down the lane, that away.' He pointed vaguely towards the road. 'Cuddled up in the old bothy up the hill. I saw a flash of colour–'

'Mary's red coat,' murmured Maud, and Sally was glad she had chosen the somewhat garish colour.

'– and thought I'd better take a look. Always the hero.' He smiled modestly, causing Ewan to frown at him.

'We were looking for the hidey hole playhouse,' Jay piped up.

'Sandy Mac said,' Mary added, looking up adoringly at the aghast Sandy – who was mortified his words had led to the drama. He, too, needed a wee dram to get over it, several wee drams to accept Sally bore him no ill-will and Maud snapped at him 'to mind himself and stop maudlin.'

It turned into quite a party and it was only later when the children were safely tucked up and Sally's adrenaline sputtered into empty that she realised with a sinking horror, what it really felt like to have your children missing, lost, possibly abducted... Was Malcolm...? She felt Maud's eyes on her, and tried to smile. The children were safe again now, that's all that mattered, and what Sally had done, she'd done for them.

'Don't agonise over it, Nan,' Maud said quietly. 'I might not have been blessed myself, but I believe these challenges are all part of being a mother, aren't they?'

Sally nodded. That was it, wasn't it? She was a mother now, and with that came a lifetime of responsibilities. Suddenly, being 'caught' was no longer her chief concern; being a good mother was.

33
MALCOLM

Malcolm made up his mind: he was closing up the house and moving into his club. It was just too big for him to rattle around in, yet he still felt guilty under the gimlet eye of Mrs Somerville. It was as if she suspected him of something – Lord knew what, he thought indignantly. He was the victim here. Yes, he was aware – and, to add insult to injury, the police had made no bones about it – that most unsavoury actions relating to missing or murdered family members were the work of someone known to them, frequently the father-figure, but the investigation had ruled him out entirely. Malcolm had made sure that outcome was leaked to Fleet Street; he'd called in a favour and was the focus of a rather good, very sympathetic, piece published alongside The Times leader. If anything, his medical practice and his social standing had risen; it was a sympathy vote, but he wasn't complaining. The Somervilles were the exceptions and Malcolm could imagine them musing on the fact that it was unfortunate to lose one's children, but to lose one's wife, as well, was – to misquote one of those literary fellows – altogether careless. As if he had any control over any of it.

Martha had issued an ultimatum not long after the initial police investigation into the abduction had been scaled down. (It was not being closed, he was reassured. Whilst the children were missing, it would never be closed and the case would run quietly behind the scenes, new leads followed up diligently). No, Malcolm's thoughts reverted to Martha, it wasn't an ultimatum, one of those suggested some level of choice. Rather, his wife had announced she was returning to

America where she would split her time between Harvard University and the Cardinal Institute – hedging her bets, he thought, maliciously – and what Malcolm did was entirely his own concern. They would remain married, whatever happened. After all, they were already touching on notorious, they didn't need to bring scandal upon themselves by admitting personal failure and filing for divorce – that was something they both agreed upon. So Malcolm stayed in Cambridge, resumed his work, ate out on his temporary 'bachelor' state and accepted the ministrations of anyone who offered him sympathy for his missing children (especially if they were young and pretty) and absent wife.

So, yes, he was definitely closing the house and giving Cook and the Somervilles notice, and he would gain an unkind pleasure from the latter. It didn't take long to make the necessary arrangements, and then he sat back, in Martha's chair, at Martha's desk, using her stationery, and enjoyed the feeling of being master of his own life.

Malcolm's mind wandered to the missing children – six months gone. He still couldn't get over the fact that everyone believed the mousy and biddable Nanny Brown – what was her name, Sally – would have had the gumption to plan and carry through the kidnap of his son and daughter. She was good at her duties, of course, but looking after children didn't take brains or ability, one just did it, and it came naturally to females anyway. But he supposed Martha and the police were right, the other alternatives were even more far-fetched: Nanny Brown was not one to inflame passions and the children, much as he had a father's love for them, weren't yet old enough to be interesting or to have had money settled on them. It was a mystery and a damned impertinent one.

Malcolm slapped the desk in a sudden burst of anger. His life had been going along very well, thank you very much, and now look at it. Oh, he'd recover, but he really didn't need any of this upheaval. And he missed his children, he reminded himself hurriedly. He might not have seen them all that much, but they were his and they should be in his home with him. As should his wife.

In a fit of pique, Malcolm dialled Scotland Yard and demanded to speak to the detective following up the Harper-Smyth abductions. 'You'll need to speak to Cambridge Constabulary, sir,' he was told, which didn't improve his temper. Ready for strong words, he was therefore surprised when the affable voice at the end of the telephone, thanked him for calling.

'I'm PC Flynn,' the voice said – PC, thought Malcolm, a constable. Was this what his case was demoted to? 'You've saved me a call, sir. Would it be possible to pay you a visit at home? I'm afraid to say we don't have any definite leads,' PC Flynn added quickly, 'but we'd like to talk to you about some information that might have bearing on the case.'

'Alright.' Malcolm was grudging. 'Come today at two o'clock. I've a very busy schedule.' He hung up without waiting for an answer, determined to keep the upper-hand. Then, while he was in the mood, he had a large drink, and went to give the Somervilles notice.

'Hello, sir. I'm PC Flynn. We spoke on the phone. Briefly. And this,' the boy – he looked like a recruit straight from Hendon – pointed to the older, grey-haired and plain-clothed figure beside him, 'Is Detective Inspector Carruthers of Scotland Yard. May we come in?'

'Dr Harper-Smyth.'

The detective shook hands firmly, and Malcolm, who had answered the front door himself, showed the visitors into the library and nodded at them to sit down. He'd planned to have Mrs Somerville greet them, while he kept them waiting, but another restorative drink had seen common sense prevail; he didn't want to put their backs up or let it be known he was anything but the charming and concerned doctor. 'Drink?' he offered, and when both men demurred, he went straight in.

'Now look here, chaps,' Malcolm had already decided the 'all boys together' approach was the way forward, 'I'm sure you're doing your best but an update wouldn't come amiss. These are my children we're talking about.' He left a pause for sympathy but none was forthcoming – the policemen looked solidly plod, he said to himself later – so he cleared his throat and went on. 'Six months, nearly seven, and you're telling me there's still nothing?'

'I'm sorry, there have been no further developments, Dr Harper-Smyth.' DI Carruthers was very well spoken, enough to go up in Malcolm's estimation. 'Be assured that all avenues have been explored, and will continue to be so, but the trail is cold. It's as if Mrs Brown closed this front door sometime during the month of May and vanished into thin air.'

'It might have been later,' the PC put in. 'Remember the note the nanny left for the housekeeper. It was dated June the... the...' He ran out of steam.

'Red herring,' the detective stated. 'She was probably gone weeks before that. That's what makes this so difficult.'

'Yes, that's what I thought,' Malcolm said eagerly. 'In fact, maybe the Somervilles... Well, one wonders.' He hadn't liked the couple's attitude on being given notice and didn't see why they shouldn't be questioned again.

'We have no reason at all to believe your other staff are involved, sir. They understood, as did you, Mrs Brown and the children were on an extended holiday while you were away. And I understand your own trip was much longer than the six weeks you originally planned.' DI Carruthers raised his eyebrows. 'Yet you didn't directly contact Mrs Brown during that time?'

Malcolm bristled. 'Now look here –'

'I'm just stating a fact, Dr Harper-Smyth,' the detective said mildly. 'If it will make you feel better, Flynn here, will go and have another word with the housekeeping staff. Off you go, Flynn.'

'Yes, sir.'

Malcolm watched PC Flynn scuttle off as if he was to interrogate armed criminals and relished the thought. 'He won't get much out of them,' he said morosely. 'I gave them notice today. House is too big for me. Alone.'

Again, there was no expression of sympathy, but the senior policeman's attitude changed once his junior was out of the room. He loosened his tie, sat back and said, 'You know, sir, I think I will have that drink, after all. Whisky and soda would hit the spot.'

Malcolm obliged, pouring generous doubles for both of them. 'Cheers,' he toasted. 'You said you had something to tell me?' Then the penny dropped: PC Flynn had been deliberately sent out of the room. Malcolm felt a twinge of unease. He should have nothing to fear – he'd nothing to do with the abduction of his children and he'd swear that on a Bible in a court of law – but police privately strong-arming the public to get a conviction was something he'd read about. 'Well, out with it, man,' he blustered.

'Ah, well, it's a little delicate, sir.' DI Carruthers coughed, but it was probably for show. 'However, we're men of the world, aren't we? Unlike that keen whipper-snapper currently grilling your help.' He allowed himself a little smile. 'It's come to our attention, sir, in our character checks, that you have... er... a way with ladies, shall we say.'

A response was clearly expected and Malcolm tried to laugh it off. 'Come, now, Inspector, a young man, medical student, wild oats and all that. Surely you understand.' No need to admit to more recent dalliances, he thought.

'I do, indeed, sir. And in the general course of events, your er...romantic liaisons would be of no interest to anyone but you and the young ladies in question – and maybe your wife.'

That was uncalled for. Malcolm opened his mouth to object then thought better of it. 'But?' he snapped instead.

DI Carruthers made a show of consulting a small black notebook, pulled from his top pocket. 'Do you remember a particular young woman from your medical school days, let me find her name... A long time ago now; 1958 it was, I believe. She was a first-year student, you were in your final year... Ah, here it is.' He looked up. 'A Miss Sarah Power. Ring any bells, sir?'

Malcolm got up to refill his drink; so be it if it looked like a play for time. There had been so many pretty young girls, ripe for the taking, to pick out one was needle and haystack territory. But all of a sudden, mid pour, his hand shook. He was sure Carruthers noticed. 'Sarah Power,' he repeated slowly. 'I think I recall the name, but remiss of me as it is,

I'm afraid not the details.'

'That's a shame, sir. Are you sure?'

'No, I'm not sure.' Malcolm spoke firmly to hide the lie. Sarah Power. She was the pregnant one, wasn't she. The first one. The one he'd performed the D&C on, a bit out of his depth. Unfortunate business. And illegal as hell. Where the blazes had they dug that up? He tried a roguish smile. 'As you said it's a long time ago. And forgive me, Inspector, I'm a busy man. What has this to do with my children? You're not saying some bit of a girl from nigh on ten or eleven years ago stalked me, waited 'til I was overseas, then stole my children and their nanny because I once broke her silly little girlish heart.' Malcolm gave a genuine bark of laughter, which died at the look in the detective's eyes.

'That's not what I'm saying, sir, no,' Carruthers said. 'What I'm saying is, that silly little Miss Sarah Power grew up to be clever Mrs Sally Brown.' He left a minute for it to sink in, then added, 'Sally Brown, your missing nanny. Sir.'

34

On the first Sunday of Advent, Jay and Mary left Sunday
School full of their roles in the forthcoming Nativity play,
and Sally realised that Christmas was almost upon them. It
promised to be an event such as hadn't been seen in the Big
House since Maud was a girl. Everyone was pressed into
action.

Sandy Mac half-carried, half-dragged the carefully-
selected spruce into the drawing room, leaving a trail of
needles in his wake.

'Watch where you're walking,' Sally instructed as Jay and
Mary ran to greet him. 'There are jaggy needles on the floor.'

Sandy manhandled the cumbersome tree into the metal
stand, where Sally held on to it as he adjusted the screws
until confident the tree was steady. 'Solid as a rock, that.' He
shook the tree vigorously, to prove it.

'There'll be no needles left at this rate,' Miss Campbell
commented as more fell.

'A cannae dae right for daein' wrong. Nae tablet for poor
Sandy wi his tea today.' Sandy winked at the children, who
giggled back.

'You've done well, Sandy, it's a handsome tree, thank
you,' Miss Campbell conceded.

'Light it. Light it.' Jay jumped up and down.

'Sandy will get the lights and decorations for us in a
minute, won't you?' Miss Campbell said, smiling at the two
little ones.

'Ah will that.'

While Sandy made his way to the attic Sally cleared the
needles up as best she could.

'Is Sandy Mac Father Christmas?' Jay's earnest little face looked up at Sally. Mary's, too.

'Do you think he is?' Sally asked carefully.

'Uh-huh,' Jay replied, nodding. 'We saw him on the boat day. The day we came from that place we lived before.' The little boy looked puzzled.

'Probably best not to ask him,' Miss Campbell advised, before Sally could speak. 'It's a good secret, isn't it?' Then turning to Sally, she muttered, 'No saying how he'll respond.'

Soon Sandy was back with two well-used, dusty, cardboard boxes. 'There's still two more to come.' He laughed as the children crowded in on the boxes.

Kneeling on the rug Sally showed the children how to carefully take the little parcels from the boxes and unwrap the tissue to reveal the delicate baubles. Mary's chubby little hands worked away methodically; Jay lost interest after the first half dozen but was fully engaged again when Sandy, after much untwisting and unknotting of lights, finally snaked them along the floor by the tree, and announced he would be testing them.

'Right, fingers crossed everybody,' Sandy said as he moved to plug them in.

They lit – to a loud cheer.

Sandy fixed them in place and rechecked on the tree, 'Just in case,' and after a further bit of adjustment by Miss Campbell, the decorating began.

Mary was in her element as she placed the lower baubles, her tongue lolling in concentration. Jay pushed in for the 'biggest ones' to hang in the 'bestest place.' And Maud was in the thick of it, assisting Mary with the fiddly decorations and lifting her to reach the higher branches. Pre-empting an argument Sally declared Aunt Maud should place the angel on the top and as they all ooh-ed and aah-ed, Sally felt a lump in her throat. This was exactly how Christmas should be. But as she cleared the packaging into the boxes and removed them to the hall cupboard, an uneasiness gripped her – this was someone else's Christmas she was acting out. She shook herself and ran back to the fun, calling out, 'Now, hands up who's for cocoa around the tree?'

That evening, as the children slept, cosy in their beds, Sally tasked herself with wrapping their presents. She imagined Mary's face when she saw her new pram and dolly. Jay would be delighted with his shiny, green bike, he'd ride round and round the house until he had them all dizzy. Sally flicked through the six storybooks: 'Another story, please, Nan. Just one more,' they'd plead, except these days, it was more often, 'Another one, please, Mummy.' It still came as a shock to Sally, though she cherished it and never said a word. Thinking about it, her heart began to race and her fingers stumbled over the wrapping, so much so that she placed the gifts still waiting for their Santa-clad coating, into two carrier bags, to be finished the next evening. She'd ask Maud to help. Sally consciously let her breath deepen and slow, but thoughts of Malcolm crowded her racing mind. How would he be this Christmas? Where would he be? The newspapers would be bound to do a heartrending seasonal update about the missing children and the wife, who a stray copy of the Daily Mirror had informed Sally, was now back in America. Well, she was sorry if he was suffering, she was really, but he had had his chance at family Christmases and she was sure he hadn't appreciated them. Neither had he allowed his oldest child to experience even one happy, joyous day.

The children were awake just after 6am on Christmas morning. Maud was already up and had put a match to the fire which Sally had set the night before. Soon it was roaring in the grate. The children delighted over their presents and it was all that Sally could do to stop them breakfasting on the selection boxes Sandy had given them.

'I'm exhausted already,' Maud declared. 'And it's only 7.15. I'll be asleep before Her Majesty's Speech.'

Sally laughed as she cleared the discarded paper from the sitting room floor. She felt lightheaded and dreamlike. She hadn't expected to make it this far. Every day since they'd arrived, she'd expected to catch sight of Ewan's panda car appearing over the brow of the hill, coming to take her and the children away. But here they still were. And, her lips tightened, here they would stay.

Sandy had offered to lend her a hand with lunch, which Sally was very pleased to accept – telling Maud her Christmas present was to be waited on hand and foot – and slowly and surely the Christmas meal came together. Sitting at the table, surrounded by those who meant the most to her, Sally felt happy; happier than she had in such a long time. They were just finishing tidying up in the kitchen when the telephone bell rang, making them all jump. It had only been installed a few weeks ago – on Maud's orders, after the scare with the twins running off – and there was great excitement (and trepidation from Sally) on the rare occasions it rang. Miss Campbell went to the hall to answer it and soon appeared back in the kitchen, her lips twitching.

'Her Majesty's Constabulary, on the telephone for you,

Nan,' she announced.

'For me?' Sally turned from the old lady, pretending to busy herself, for her face had gone clammy and she knew the colour had drained from it.

'For you. Run along and don't waste the minutes.'

Sally's legs would hardly take her to the hall; her hands didn't want to reach out to the green slim-line receiver on the telephone table. She lifted it with trembling hands. 'This is Nan Douglas speaking. How can I help you?'

'Merry Christmas, Nan. Are you having a good day? Ho. Ho. Ho,' came the ponderous voice.

'Ewan! Ewan, it's you. I thought… never mind.'

'Were you expecting the Chief Constable?' he chortled. With half her mind, Sally guessed he and Alisdair Conti had made inroads into a new consignment of single malt over their turkey, but the rest of his words were lost to her. She had to reach for the hall chair and ease herself into it for support. When the call ended she stood unsteadily and made her way to the toilet under the stairs where she sank to her knees. She might have been there a minute or an hour when she roused to a gentle tapping on the door.

'Nan? Nan, dear, are you alright?' Maud's voice was low.

Sally found hers and replied as naturally as possible. 'I'm fine. I'm coming.' She struggled to her feet, washed her hands and face, and discovered Maud by the roaring fire.

'Sandy's taken the children to play in the garden. Come and sit down, my dear.' Maud patted the sofa cushion beside her. 'You've been working too hard. All this is too much for you.'

'No. Not at all,' Sally protested. She sank down beside the woman who had become her honorary aunt – and, if she were honest, though Maud wouldn't thank her for it – Sally's saviour. 'It's just all so lovely. Christmas, being here. After everything that's happened, I got a bit overwhelmed. I don't deserve to be so happy.'

'Of course you do,' Maud said briskly. 'I thought it was Ewan's telephone call that caused you some consternation,' she added bluntly. 'Is everything alright? Is he becoming troublesome?'

'Ewan, no. Ever the gentleman.'

'Then what is it, Nan. Can you tell me? Perhaps I can help.'

Sally wasn't sure how to reply. This lie of a life was a complicated one. For days she almost forgot, others it came rushing to the fore. How could it be any other way? She couldn't – wouldn't – drag Maud into it. Even if the older woman understood, a gamble that Sally couldn't afford, she didn't deserve the pressure it would cause. 'I just hadn't expected Ewan to call, that's all.' Sally forced a smile; that was true. 'For a moment I was afraid he was going to spring a Christmas proposal on me.' That wasn't the case, and she was sure Maud didn't believe her for a moment and her next words bore that out.

'You know you can tell me anything, don't you?' The old lady placed her hand on Sally's arm. 'I might look and act the part of spinster of the parish but I have had a life, you know, and at my age, there's not much I haven't already heard.'

Sally wanted to cry. I bet you haven't heard this one, Miss Campbell, she thought. 'There are things in my past,' she said carefully, 'things I have moved on from but I can't always forget. I'd rather not... not taint you and this house and Inniscuillin with them. That's all.'

Maud gave a dry laugh. 'That I certainly understand, better than you think, my dear. Remember when you first arrived I said that half the island was hiding from something? Usually themselves.' She sighed. 'Nan, dear, I feel that, in a very short space of time, we have become a family. I sincerely hope you feel that way too. And I like to think that families are always there for each other. It's important to me that you remember that. I know that life doesn't always follow the path we expect, or that we make the decisions people expect of us. I speak from personal experience. Like yours, maybe they are best left unsaid, but suffice to say I lived a life, albeit for just a little while, that would have shocked my parents to the core. I have not followed the well-trodden path and for that reason I do not stand in judgement of others.' A smile began to play on her lips. 'Well, perhaps I do a little,' she added, returning a lightness to the conversation.

Sally hoped her surprise didn't show on her face – Maud Campbell with a chequered past, who would have believed it. Sally did, actually. Sally was in no position to pry. But she was touched by Maud's sincere words. Spontaneously, she leaned over and gave the older woman a tight hug, which was reciprocated at first tentatively, and then with conviction.

'Thank you, dearest Aunt Maud,' Sally said earnestly. 'I do so appreciate all that you have done for us, I'm not sure where we would be without you. Bloodlines or not, we're family, aren't we?'

'Indeed, we are. And as for me saving you, Nan, I can promise you that my life is all the richer with you and your dear children in it.'

35
MAUD

Long after her honorary family had retired, exhausted, and Sandy had gone back to his cottage, Maud sat on. Late nights were a rarity for her, but there was something about this Christmas night, the lights on the tree and the warmth of a family Christmas denied to Maud since she was a girl that made her want to extend it as long as possible. Her conversation with Nan, too, had put her in reflective mood, ghosts of the past playing in the firelight. Maud sighed contentedly as she dozed by the warmth of the open fire. She'd no time for those new-fangled electric ones, a fire wasn't a fire to her, without the crackle and scent of peat and pine cones.

An involuntary smile caressed her face as she mused over the past six months of her life and the blessings that Nan and the children were to her. Granted, initially she'd had doubts and reservations about taking these strangers into her home, and even more about passing them off as family – her widowed niece and offspring. She'd always tried to be honest – ever since she'd deceived her parents with such disastrous consequences so long ago. But things done from love, could they ever be totally wrong?

It was true what she'd told Nan, it wasn't a platitude to make the girl feel better about her own demons, whatever they were: Maud's had been a life less ordinary than the good folk of Inniscuillin gave her credit for. And it had all started with Colin. Oh, how she had loved Colin.

A single tear squeezed between Maud's eyelids as her memory re-opened old wounds. They were less painful now, and there was something healing in shedding a tear of remembrance. Colin and she had been sweethearts – barely out of the schoolroom, she realised now – and both sets of parents had declared them too young to marry. They had no experience of the world, of real life, nothing to fall back on in troubled times; 'each other' was not decreed sufficient. No, they must wait until Maud was nineteen and had seen the world beyond Inniscuillin.

Neither Maud nor Colin had wanted the world though, they just wanted each other, to be together there and then, not later on.

So, they had eloped to Edinburgh – two seventeen-year-olds, full of the joys of love and rising sap of spring. It was early April 1916, and nobody could have foreseen the night that the German Zeppelins were to bomb Scotland's capital city. The targets were Rosyth and the Forth Rail Bridge, but they missed these and hit the Grassmarket and then the Whisky Bond in Leith, which caused such a blaze that it illuminated – and so facilitated – the further bombing of Leith Docks. Germany had been the first country in history to mount a sustained aerial bombardment and one that had killed Colin outright. Maud herself had lain unidentified in the Royal Infirmary, suffering head injuries and concussion. When her condition had improved and her parents came to claim her, they had taken her home, back to the island to mourn Colin's loss, and face his poor bereft parents. They, and her own parents had forgiven Maud the impetuous elopement that ended so tragically – she was a child, Colin no older – and if anyone was to blame it was the Germans at war. But Maud never could forgive herself, never would. It led to a period in her life of which Maud wasn't proud. She didn't regret it exactly, but it had no lasting impression, she'd done no good – and that, she did wish she could change. Towards the end of the Great War, she'd insisted on going to Glasgow, to nurse the wounded and shell-shocked soldiers. But Maud was no nurse. Instead of a Nightingale-esque mopping of brows and lifting spirits, her stomach heaved at limbless, disfigured young men who were surely left worse off than her Colin.

Instead, she took to waitressing in a Lyons Corner House, then to dress-making in a factory where she became a fierce advocate of Trade Unions and equality for the workers – women workers. It took her into a seedy underworld that shocked her Highland innocence, meeting prostitutes and opium addicts, women who found love in the arms of other women – though they who had nothing but abuse from men could hardly be judged for that. It was there she'd stumbled across Willie Crawford, now minister of the kirk. His work, like hers, was saving these women who were no better than they should be, he'd insisted. She said that him paying to take them to bed and to carry out violent acts – yes, the women spoke frankly to Maud and told her these things – was a funny way of going about it. William had turned tack after that, begged her forgiveness and suggested they walk out together. That's when she'd laughed at him. What Maud hadn't told Sally was how he'd slapped her face in anger and would have done much worse if one of the working girls hadn't hit him over the head with an empty bottle. That was the night she stopped believing in God and vowed never to set foot in a church again. Sicker than ever, Maud returned to Inniscuillin and looked after her parents and the Big House. She'd hardly left the island after that, even after her mother and father died, enclosing herself in a defensive cocoon against further horrors of the world beyond. She had found contentment in a simple life, finding the brother she'd never had in her sparring partner, Sandy Mac, and a best friend in Hilary Armstrong-Stuart, who, after a stroke, was all but locked up in Innis Castle.

In the past few months, though, Maud Campbell had come to realise how narrow and mean her later life had become: existence; unloving and unloved. In front of the dying embers of the fire, she wriggled in her chair as her thoughts shifted and she thought of little Mary. Tonight, the little girl had asked if Maud could be her grandma – her friends had a grandma and she'd like one. Maud had said she couldn't really, not as such, but that she was definitely Great-Aunt Maud – and that was special because not everyone had a great-aunt. The precious child had been so happy, and Jay had jealously checked that Maud would always be great-aunt to him, too.

She determined to make an appointment with young Alisdair. He might not be of the same calibre as his father and brothers, but even he could write a will and form a Trust Fund. Maud would sign over the house to dear Nan as soon as possible; Nan would appreciate the lack of legalities and necessary paperwork if it was done now. There would be a legacy for the twins and Maud decided, also, to set up a separate fund for their education. Maybe they wouldn't have to leave the island for high school… Maud's thoughts were limitless. A private tutor could be employed, someone to help all the children stay on Inniscuillin until they were ready to go to the mainland. Life was safe and happy here, and Maud herself knew the temptations of the city on youngsters. As for

Jay and Mary, if later on, the world did cause them grief, they would always have her island and her house to return to – to call home. Exactly as her parents had done for her. And exactly as Nan was trying to do in coming here.

Maud's tears flowed freely now, but they were happy tears. Yes, indeed, her life was rich now in love and blessings – her cup full and running over, and if the Minister Crawford dared say a doubter like herself had no right to such words, well, she would happily tell him exactly what she thought all over again.

36
ALISDAIR

Alisdair Conti was in his office, typing with gusto. It was
something he'd taught himself to do from a book, a skill he
kept to himself, which would surprise even Ewan McLeish if
he caught his friend in the act. But needs must; there were
some things he could definitely not ask his secretary to type
up.

Bzzzz. The intercom startled him, as it always did.
Alisdair checked the time and deftly slid its black cloth cover
over the typewriter before answering.

'Ewan McLeish will be here in fifteen minutes, Mr Conti,'
Helen Brady said. 'And I'm off for the day now.'

'Thank you, Helen. See you on Monday.'

When there was no better gossip, the working relationship
between the solicitor and his secretary was often speculated
about, and one wag on the island had suggested that the word
'working' was a wee bit of a smokescreen. Alisdair wasn't
averse to being thought a bit of lad, but he had enormous
respect for Helen Brady, who worked as many hours she
could to fulfil her dream of travelling to Australia – she'd
sworn him to secrecy about that, fearful she'd be seen as
having 'notions' – and between them they had soon nipped
that idea in the bud. Alisdair liked women but he didn't want
to live with one and rather gallingly, Helen thought he was an
ancient specimen anyway. Speaking of amoré, he mused, he
must put Ewan out of his misery today and confess he had no
interest in Nan Douglas. The fun of pretending he was a
romantic rival somewhat waned in the shadow of the
genuinely lovelorn face of his friend. Maybe it would give

Ewan a kick up the proverbial so that he'd actually approach Nan about walking out with him. Alisdair couldn't see it happening – everyone except Ewan knew she had eyes only for her dead husband and those little twins of hers, but stranger things had happened.

Alisdair moved from the side table that housed his typewriter to the oak desk in the centre of the room and settled himself there. Without being consciously aware of it, he glanced at the crystal glass decanter on top of his filing cabinet – the level of the Talisker would drop by a quarter by the time the afternoon was out. No matter. They wouldn't ever go short.

There was a rap on the inner door and Police Sergeant Ewan McLeish entered the office with purpose.

'Ah, Ewan,' Alisdair said. 'Business or pleasure?'

'One or the other, Alisdair. One or the other,' Ewan replied, with what passed in him, for wit.' He, not very subtly, stared at the malt, and Alisdair did the honours. It was a charade they went through every week. 'A wee dram, Ewan?'

'Well, Alisdair, that's very generous of you. Just a wee nip to keep the chill out of my bones.'

'To be sure, my friend. I'll join you.'

Ewan made himself comfortable, removing his uniform jacket; he wouldn't be accused of drinking on duty, and received the glass with the gravitas it deserved. 'Sláinte.' He raised it before taking a hefty gulp.

'Sláinte,' Alisdair repeated. 'And what mystery have you for us today?' he asked – another ritual.

On an island where little happened, a mental exercise enjoyed by them both, was to solve usually non-existent crimes, just using logic and intellect: Jack the Ripper; Black Dahlia; Bible John; and the disappearance of the wee lass from Inverness– they had a solution for them all. The spirit of Sherlock Holmes lived on in the two sleuths, who craved a real criminal to intellectually spar with.

'Well, now. There is something. A somewhat different kind of puzzle.' Ewan shifted his bulk uncomfortably. 'It involves the Campbell twins up at the Big House…'

'You're referring to the children of a certain, delightful Nan Douglas? Interesting.' Alisdair's eyes twinkled as he watched his friend decide whether to take Nan's name in vain. Clearly he was smitten if he was not only dredging up mysteries about her but potentially incurring the wrath of her battle-axe aunt – all nothing but a smokescreen to talk about her, of course. 'Spit it out then, man.'

'It's nothing but a wee bit of curiosity,' Ewan back-tracked. 'And I must insist that it's not to go anywhere near one of your secret lurid books.'

'My secret lurid books, as you call them, are the things that keep you in this.' Alisdair held up his glass of Talisker The police sergeant was the only other person on the island party to Alisdair's alter ego as Jack Lambert, author of slightly risqué mass-produced paperback books mostly published in the United States of America. His hard-drinking, womanising detective, the grandly-named Humbert Madison solved crimes in New York City – a place Alisdair had never visited – and generated Alisdair an income that supplemented his modest trust fund. Aware his family would disown him at the sniff of another scandal (and this would be scandalous to the Conti clan) if his writing career was ever to become known, his so-called 'fishing trips' were sessions with the

Edinburgh publishers who handled his international rights.

'That's as maybe,' Ewan acknowledged. 'But I still need your word.'

'It's unlikely that a puzzle involving two – what are they? Three-year-olds? Four? – would feature in that old rogue Humbert's shenanigans but you have my promise. Or shall I swear on the word of God?'

Ewan ignored him, the desire to tell his story obviously paramount. He coughed his regulation policeman's cough, clearing his throat as if about to give evidence in court. 'As you are aware, I have recently been a guest of the Inniscuillin nursery and infant class, as I am every year as… er… representative of the Tufty Club.' He glared at Alisdair, daring him to smirk; Alisdair just turned away to refill their glasses. 'I proceeded to speak to the children about road safety, water safety, stranger safety and seeking help from a policeman. They were very well-behaved. Your Miss Brady is a fine teacher,' he added. 'She's wasted here with you.'

'I know,' Alisdair said, cheerfully. 'But she hasn't yet worked that out for herself. So, what did these Douglas-Campbell infants do to raise your police antenna. I'm intrigued.'

'I am proceeding to that point. The boy, Jay, asked me why I didn't wear a 'proper' policeman's helmet, the one that looks like,' Ewan harrumphed, 'and I quote 'an upside-down cow's udder'.'

Alisdair burst out laughing. 'Do I hear Sandy Mac's humour somewhere in there! Sorry. Shocking. What did you do, arrest him for insubordination?'

'That wasn't the key issue,' Ewan admonished. 'I went on to talk about the vagaries of a Police Sergeant's attire, although I fear I lost my audience somewhat. They started to ask for milk and a biscuit… To which end Miss Brady closed proceedings by suggesting Jay had seen a Metropolitan police officer in London. She showed the class a picture in a book. And that's when he said it.' Ewan sat back and looked expectantly at Alisdair.

'Said what, Ewan?'

The substantial sergeant cleared his throat again and from the depths of his leather chair acted out a small boy speaking in a falsetto voice – complete with his size ten boot kicking the chair leg as Jay must have done. 'I saw him when I was the other boy. The time when I had a different name and wasn't a twin and I lived with the other people.' He reverted to his own tones. 'What do you think of that, then?'

Alisdair's initially startled and bemused expression, caused by his friend regressing so effectively, was replaced by a raised eyebrow. 'What I think is that if you had failed in your application to the police force, you would certainly have been snapped up by RADA.'

'Most hilarious, Alisdair. Do you not find it – the boy's words – strange?'

Alisdair considered. 'Not really, Ewan. He's a small boy. Small boys make up stories. They lie. Didn't you? Probably not, you were born upstanding, my friend. But I know I did.' He took a glug of his drink. 'Did you interrogate young Jay further?'

'He ran off. I mentioned my suspicions to Miss Brady but she took your attitude,' Ewan admitted. 'So, I drove the child and his young sister home; the car remains a treat, you know, and I asked to speak to Nan –'

Ah ha, thought Alisdair.

'–but she was away collecting the messages. I thought not to mention it to Miss Campbell.'

'A better man would have second thoughts there,' agreed Alisdair. 'And what did Nan say? I assume you happened to go straight to the village and she happened to be in the shop?'

'Nan looked at me somewhat oddly and said that Jay was an imaginative little tyke and that his bedtime story was currently about a small boy who lived in London and was evacuated to foster parents on a country farm in the war. Everything Jay had said came from the story.' Ewan looked disappointed.

'Well, there you go.' Alisdair wagged a finger at Ewan. 'My dear fool, court the woman if you will, but don't come between a mother hen and her flock.'

'There's no mystery?' he checked. 'Not even when we note that Nan, Miss Campbell's unknown niece appeared from nowhere?'

'Ewan, let's recap. The child listened to you reading a Tufty Club story, looked at your hat, and made up a silly story that his mother had a perfectly valid explanation for. As for Miss Campbell, isn't she a closed book at the best of times. Just the old spinster-type to have long-lost family. Is that all correct?'

'Aye, Alisdair,' replied Ewan. 'You're saying we let it go?'

'I am indeed. Unless you're thinking Nan Douglas is a secret kidnapper of small children, whose names she changes and crosses the country to bring them here to Maud Campbell who's in on the crime?' Alisdair laughed at his own joke.

'I'm saying no such thing.' Ewan drew himself up stiffly. 'As well you know. That sort of slander might fuel that detective in your books, but he's not an officer of the law as I know it.'

'Yes! I knew you'd read the old Jack Lambert books.' Alisdair punched the air. 'You sly old dog.'

Ewan maintained his policeman's poker face. He raised his eyes to the wall clock. 'Talking is thirsty work,' he said pointedly.

'One for the road.' Alisdair took the hint. 'And a special one at that – a Glayva?'

'Glayva, indeed?'

That caused a raised eyebrow, as the solicitor had known it would. He poured two measures of the whisky liqueur, saying, 'Now, I really wanted to ask you about motiveless crimes–'

'No such thing.' Ewan downed his drink. 'I really must go.' He stared somewhat blearily at his old friend 'This was fun, as always. That Glayva really is glayva!' As he stood to go, he tore off the top three sheets from his notebook – those which he'd filled with thoughts about the Douglas-Campbell clan, Alisdair assumed – and crumpled them into a ball, which he threw expertly into the raffia waste-basket. Alisdair automatically bent down and lobbed it instead into the fireplace before following his pal to the door, with an irreverent,

'Haste ye back, PC Plod, haste ye back.'

Old Ewan was clutching at straws with that one, Alisdair thought. They'd have to do better for next week. Still… maybe something could come of it. A plot for Madison? NYPD's finest had never dealt with a child abduction before. 'I must do some research,' he said to himself.

37
MALCOLM

Malcolm was still getting over the shock of that impertinent policeman, Carruthers', parting shot. Sally Brown and Sarah Power – one and the same? Ridiculous. Impossible. There was no similarity – none – between that fresh-faced, adoring medical student and his family's dull and deferential nanny. Malcolm was self-righteous in reflection; he should have sent the detective away with a flea in his ear and a complaint to the Chief Constable. Instead, he had stumbled and blustered before lapsing into a stunned silence and the visitors had left him to it. Though not before Carruthers had lain a manila envelope on the desk, saying quietly, 'The evidence is definitive, sir. I assume Sally Brown's motive to be one of revenge directed at you. We'll be in touch. Good day.'

In the ensuing silence, Malcolm resisted his first instinct, which was to rip the offending papers into shreds, but he did shove the envelope off the desk with an outburst of the kind of language Martha would never have tolerated. Martha! He almost froze in horror, what if she'd been here, heard this nonsense? Thank Christ for small mercies. But his whole day was ruined.

He drank too much, then spent a sleepless night – unheard of; Malcolm usually snored snug and smug for a healthy eight hours – refusing to face the truth. Not long after dawn, he got up, retrieved the folder from his bedside cabinet (where he'd hidden it for fear Mrs Somerville would rifle the downstairs desk), opened it and began to read.

Sally was Sarah. Sarah was Sally. There was, as the police had reported, no margin of error. Clearly Cambridgeshire

Constabulary had been diligent behind the scenes and dug deep into Malcolm's past. Questions here, interviews there, names, places: two and two together making hundreds – Malcolm wondered if the eager PC Flynn had done the donkey work and would get a promotion on foot of it. Was there a similar dossier on Martha, at this moment winding its way in Telex form across the Atlantic Ocean? He doubted it. Malcolm felt trapped, out of control and couldn't see a safe path out. It was an unfamiliar feeling and he didn't like it. Should he telephone his solicitor? What was he going to do? More importantly, what were the police going to do? He had a sudden, crazy urge to ask Martha's advice – she would know exactly what to do, she always did; hard decisions were her forte and she carried them out with relish and moved on. The compulsion left him as quickly as it arrived. This time, she'd leave him wallowing. Maybe she was doing that already, maybe she knew... knew what?

Malcolm frowned and read the neatly typed sheet through again, and then once more. Slowly, his analytical and precise surgeon's brain worked its way through the maze. The report listed his relationships – alright, his affairs – and the evidence turned Sarah Power into Sally Brown but that was all. As it stood, he was still the wronged party, the victim of a scorned and delusional woman who had never got over her thwarted relationship with the young doctor. Sally Brown was the criminal here, stealing his children because she had had none of her own. There was no mention of, well, of that other unfortunate, really rather sordid medical business that could have wrecked his career – and, he knew, still could.

Malcolm watched the clock, seconds passing, until he deemed it respectable to phone the police station and ask for

DI Carruthers, whose, 'We'll be in touch,' was ringing
ominously in his ears. Why? Were they baiting him? Was
there more to come?

He needed to hear exactly what else, if anything, the
police knew about his relationship with Sarah Power.

And the answer was a big fat, heady and reassuring
nothing; Malcolm put down the phone in giddy relief. Once
he – charming and apologetic personified – had stressed his
shock and embarrassment and agreed that yes, Sally Power
had been one of his 'short-sighted student conquests' as 'a
young man sowing his wild oats'. She had misunderstood his
intentions and become clingy and frankly irrational before –
rightly – throwing in the towel. He'd had no idea, none
whatsoever, that she was Nanny Brown. In fact, he still found
that hard to believe, although he was no longer questioning
the evidence. Would they like to ask his wife? She would
never have employed an 'old flame', and he certainly
wouldn't…

Malcolm, breathing heavily, ran out of steam at that point
and Carruthers had already seemed to lose interest.

'Thank you for your candour,' the man said mildly. 'That
clears up the matter. We have our motive. And you can think
of no specific reason, nothing untoward that occurred
between you, other than the ending of the relationship?'

'Nothing,' Malcolm said firmly. 'Nothing at all.'

'In that case, sir–'

'Wait. Does this information have to be made public? I
have a reputation, you know, and my wife, too. It doesn't
bring my children back…' He let the sympathy plea hang.

'I don't see that it's relevant to the public, sir. Your
'secret',' the Inspector said the word distastefully, 'is safe

with us.'

That's what you think, Malcolm thought as he put down the telephone. As if he'd trust anyone with his real secret.

38

Sally cut the newspaper article from The Times and reread it before storing it along with other similar articles in her locked, wooden chest kept below her bed. The headlines which alerted her attention had all been there. She wasn't sure why she kept them, it was a ridiculous, dangerous, thing to do, like a murderer keeping a trophy from his victims. Periodically she retrieved the sheets and burned them, one by one, standing over one of Sandy's bonfires until her face was red and her eyes gritty with ash. It was strangely cleansing.

From a world away, Sally never entirely switched off from the news. In the early months of their disappearance, the newspapers that arrived on Inniscuillin were a constant reminder: a paragraph here, a headline there, an expert opinion or – the worst – what the press called a 'potential sighting' of them. Sally nearly had a panic attack the first time she read in black block print that she and the children had been seen boarding a ferry. The print swam in front of her eyes – until she focused enough to realise it had been a ferry from Liverpool to Dun Laoghaire in Ireland. There were other suggestions, too: they were hiding out in a Women's Liberation commune on the Isle of Wight; gone overland to Greece on a Magic Bus; on another boat, this one to Orkney, which shook Sally all over again. It was too close to home. How long did she have 'til plodding Ewan came knocking…When it transpired that an indignant young Orcadian woman had identified herself and her two boys travelling home, Sally had breathed again. Thank goodness, in all of the gossip, false leads and speculation, nobody ever considered 'foul play' as it was called in the papers. Sally didn't think she could bear it if people believed she had harmed the children.

Locked in her bedroom, she studied the grainy photographs of Jeremy and Rosemary, long out of date, and was sure not even their own parents would recognise them now: taller, older, with different haircuts and warm island clothes. Sally, nor Maud for that matter, did nothing to discourage them being labelled the 'wee Campbell bairns', nor the rumour – wherever it came from – that young Mary was the spit of Maud as a girl. Sally's other saving grace was that they had not been reported missing until several weeks into their settlement on Inniscuillin. And before their arrival Maud had let it be known they were expected (mostly to get up the smug Maggie's nose, she admitted wryly to Sally) so who would ever guess that Nan Douglas, Miss Campbell's great-niece, was Sally Brown?

As time went on, the reports became less frequent and a year on, then two, three, ran to barely a trickle. Other kidnappings, disappearances, world news took over, and 'The Missing Nanny Case' joined the annals of the unsolved, downgraded from abducted children to a common or garden missing person's enquiry and mentioned only as an addendum.

But still, Sally had to steel herself to read any news stories that mentioned kidnapping or abduction or missing children; all of them were a possible catalyst to re-open the Nanny case. It was only natural that they would come up in conversation and Aunt Maud, who knitted a drawer full of matching Arran jerseys for the whole family – Sandy, too – liked Sally to read the news aloud as she concentrated on her cable stitch. Together, they shook their heads in horror that the deaths of Susan Blatchford and Gary Hanlon went unsolved; smiled when three missing fifteen-year-old girls were found living their version of the high life in Wales; wondered aloud at how the parents of Jeremy and Rosemary Harper-Smyth could be so careless of their children and their nanny… They sipped tea in between their conversation and Sally attempted to remain nonchalant.

'Any good news today?' Maud asked as a matter of routine.

This was Sally's cue to pick up the two-days old Times and flick through. 'More about the attempt to kidnap Princess Anne and Captain Mark Phillips...' she reported. 'Hmm… 'armed man confronted them on their way back to Buckingham Palace by driving his car in front of their car forcing them to stop... carrying two guns... in the skirmish which followed he shot and wounded two policemen and two civilians. He carried a long ransom note to the Queen'. Can you imagine, Aunt Maud? That happening to royalty.'

'Shocking.' Maud clicked her tongue. 'I haven't much time for the English monarchy but they're due some respect. That poor girl.' She sighed as she held up the half-finished jumper into the light and squinted through her glasses. 'I say thank you every day that we're all safe on our strange little island.'

'Mmm…' Sally was only half listening, scanning the print for any passing reference to her, quickly relieved that missing nannies obviously didn't warrant mention in a royal story.

It was a different matter the next January when both the newspapers and the radio were full of the kidnap of the heiress, Lesley Whittle. Sally was in the Big House kitchen, making bread and half-watching the children out of the window. It was a dull but dry winter's day and the twins were revelling in it; Sandy's swings and play-house had been adapted as they got bigger and today, the children were in harmony rather than squabbling. It was lovely watching them but Sally felt a pang – they were growing up quickly. She was half-listening to the radio and half-listening out for the telephone; Maud was over at Innis Castle visiting Hilary Armstrong-Stuart who was growing frailer by the day, now bed-ridden apparently, and she would summon Sally with the car when she'd had enough 'sick visiting' her old friend. Despite herself, as soon as she heard the word 'kidnapping' her heart rate quickened and she turned the volume dial up: '...Police were called in after Lesley's brother received a ransom demand for £50,000 ....' She was seventeen. Her mother was said to be 'devastated'.

'What a stupid thing to say,' Sally said to herself, looking out at Mary in her red boots and woolly scarf, knowing how she'd feel if Mary – or Jay – were taken. A fleeting, uncomfortable image of Martha Beaumont ran through her mind, quickly banished, but not before Sally wondered what she was feeling – then and now.

She was prepared then, when Maud came home, and spoke of it, following on the conversation she and Hilary had been having.

'What is the world coming to?' Maud said, over her tea. 'You'd think as you get older you'd become used to the horrors, but believe me, Nan, dear, it's just more sickening. And all for money.'

'It makes me want to bring Jay and Mary in and wrap them up.' Sally shivered.

'Och, we're safe enough here.' Maud patted her hand.

'There's not fifty thousand pounds on the island, nor a bad apple amongst the islanders – some strange bodies, mind, but that's island life. That's life.'

'You're very wise, Aunt Maud.'

'I'm old. I can pretend wisdom comes with it.' Maud's eyes twinkled. She wasn't looking at Sally though, as she added, after a minute, 'I see they're talking about what they so horribly call, the Babes in the Wood murders and the missing Nanny case, as well. Suggesting that there may be reconstructions…'

'Really?' Sally reached over to the teapot, oh so casually, and refilled their cups. 'After so long? They both must be, what, five years ago? Six. What could they gain from reconstructions now?' She felt the bile rise in her throat at being linked with such a horrific unexplained murder of two innocent children.

'Heaven knows. It's all speculation.' Maud shook her head. 'Forget it, Nan, dear,' she repeated. 'Like I said, we're fine here. I don't know why I brought it up. Hilary has got to me; she's developed a morbid fascination for crime stories in her old age.'

'Mrs Armstrong-Stuart? Really?' With difficulty, Sally pulled her mind to local gossip. 'I imagine her as more a Regency Romance type.'

'That might be worse.' Maud snorted. 'I'm going to take her a pile of Alisdair's pulp, they'll open – oh.'

'Aunt Maud? What do you mean?' The old lady put her hand to her mouth, but to Sally it looked theatrical; she wanted to be asked. 'Alisdair has a hidden stash? Are you telling me he's a secret lurid crime reader?'

'No, dear. I'm telling you – though I shouldn't be – he's a

secret lurid crime writer.' Maud broke a large piece of tablet in half, smattering flakes over the scrubbed table.

'No!' That lifted Sally out of the doldrums. A smile crossed her face. 'Aunt Maud, tell me everything.'

'Have you heard of the author, Jack Lambert? I found out by accident.' Maud lowered her voice, conspiratorially. 'He doesn't know I know...'

So well did Maud distract her, Sally only thought about the Panorama programme later in her bed. Surely not. Surely, surely not... Sally didn't usually pray, but she prayed then. And they were answered, she supposed, but in the most horrific way. There was no television reconstruction, just a brief mention on an episode of Panorama, because two months later, the country was distracted by the news of Lesley Whittle's body being found. Be careful what you wish for, went round in Sally's mind for weeks, be careful what you wish for.

Despite herself, her ear was honed to pick up snippets of information from the medical world – a magazine in the doctor's surgery on the mainland, a perusal of the bookshop in Mallaig; more radio news – all filed away at the back of her mind. Sally learned how Malcolm had advanced steadily upward, a promotion here, an accolade there. Chief Medical Director of the Executive Council for Greater London, she'd read somewhere, a candidate for the local Conservative Party, preaching old-fashioned family values and apparently indispensable to Edward Heath.

In 1977 he was filmed on a platform – grown portly, slightly balding – accepting his election to the Wimbledon constituency. Three years later The Right Honourable

Malcolm Harper-Smyth MP was appointed Her Majesty's Principal Secretary of State for Health & Social Care, holding responsibility for the National Health Service.

Martha, meanwhile, rarely made the newspapers, her work specialised, but a Radio 4 programme mentioned her – cold, no, glacial – Dr Beaumont as the darling of Harvard, excelling herself with a breakthrough into cloning the 'oncogene' and developing a scan enabling observation of functional changes within the vital organs.

There was an element of reassurance in their progress: as time passed and the more the doctors had to lose, the stronger position she felt herself in. And that was something Sally desperately needed, because she was suddenly, acutely aware that things – on Inniscuillin, which never changed – were going to do exactly that: Maud was ageing, as was Sandy; the children were heading towards double figures.

'Mum? Why are you staring at Aunt Maud as if she's growing a dinosaur head?' Jay asked her one day, as he and Mary were enjoying an after-school snack of hot drop-scones and treacle and telling Maud about their day. Jay wolfed down his food, apparently always on a growth spurt; Mary was daintier, licking her sticky fingers carefully.

'Was I?' Sally was brought up short. He'd caught her checking Maud for signs of old age, of strain or illness. But she looked the same as ever.

'Because maybe I am.' Maud raised her eyebrows. 'Haven't you heard the Tales of Skua Bay? Not dinosaurs but reptiles…'

'Tell us, Aunt Maud,' the children chorused.

'Och, I'm no storyteller. Ask Sandy Mac. Now, you two, tell me about school. Are you still learning?'

'Of course we are.' Jay looked affronted.

'Mr Crawford came in today for religion,' Mary said. 'I don't like him. He waves his Bible in the air and says we mustn't let the devil in. But what if he sneaks in?'

'Yeah, and he's got horrible hairs sprouting out of his nose,' Jay added.

'Who? The devil?'

That brought giggles from both children. 'No, silly Aunt Maud,' Jay said. 'Minister Crawford. And when he shouts, he spits. Miss Brady got some spit in her hair but she didn't tell him off. Not fair.'

'Aunt Maud, can the devil sneak in when I'm not looking?' Mary was looking nervously towards the back door.

'Nonsense.' Maud was brisk. 'Poor Mr Crawford just doesn't quite understand…'

Sally's lips twitched as Maud managed to reassure Mary and put William Crawford down in the way that would irritate him most: politely and with sympathy towards his shortcomings (as Maud saw them) all in one short speech.

She loved their stories of school. It brought back her own happy days, in a very similar two-room village school, each heated with a coal fire. Inniscuillin School was much smaller, though, only twenty children aged four to eleven. The twins had been welcomed with open-arms. In name, a Miss Thomson was the headmistress, but she lived on the mainland and had responsibility for several tiny island schools. Helen Brady was the day-to-day teacher – assistant in name only – and they all loved her. Unlike Miss Thomson, who had the Schools Board at her back, Miss Brady wasn't averse to turning a blind eye when her class halved during the lambing and harvesting seasons.

'Aunt Maud?' Mary asked now. 'Have you and Mum finished your talk about us getting bikes? And if you have who was the winner?'

'Silly. If they've finished their talk, of course Aunt Maud was the winner,' Jay said – and they all laughed.

Maud tapped her nose. 'Work hard, my dears. Wait and see.'

Aunt Maud planned to buy the twins a couple of bicycles for their birthday enabling them to cycle to school and to visit their friends but Sally said it was too great an expense. She would buy them; Sandy Mac could do wonders with second hand machinery. Jay was right though; Maud had won out, but Sally shook her head, it was a secret for now.

'Come on, Sandy will be here in a minute. It's time for Brain of Britain on the Home Service,' was all she said. 'Mary, you clean the table – and your hands while you're at it and put out Sandy's tea. Jay, you tune the radio.' It was the time of day Sally liked the most. Her makeshift little family, the most important thing in the world to her – to all of them, she thought – all cosy and safe. She'd potter around tidying, but really listening to the children piping up outlandish answers, Sandy and Maud arguing over the more obscure questions, and Maud always – always – having the last word about the questions put to the two panels in that week's radio programme.

PART FIVE

THE REUNION (1986)

39

'Friends, we are gathered here today…'

The voice of John Hunter, the humanist celebrant from the mainland, rang out through the village hall, packed to the gills with islanders past and present, all come to say their fond farewells. The single dissonant face was that of William Crawford, who stood at the back, his arms folded across a Bible held tight to his chest, his glare thunderous. He was, Alisdair whispered to Sally, like a big black cloud that promised storms ahead. Sally herself was glad she'd warned John what to expect. He'd run a self-deprecating hand through his thinning hair. 'Don't worry,' he'd said. 'I always prepare to lose another fistful when I come face to face with this particular Wee Free at the forefront of his fiefdom.'

Truth was, John had known Maud and liked her (surely she'd been a humanist before the term was even coined), and he would not fail her last wishes now.

'We are here to celebrate the life of Maud Campbell,' he went on, ignoring the rumblings from the door. 'And we are doing so in the simple way she wished. Think not of this as a funeral service, but as a memorial of the past and a glance to the future. A celebration carried out in the sense of brotherhood – and, indeed, sisterhood,' he added pointedly. 'Maud left me clear instructions to add, in her words, that anyone not here in that spirit, should… er… 'Leave now and forever hold your peace. But you're still welcome to the refreshments afterwards'.' John paused for the ripple of suppressed laughter that went around the room.

Sally felt another poke in her back from Alisdair, seated in the row behind her. 'That's one in the eye for our Minister of the Free Church. Maud would be loving this.'

'Ssh.' Ewan McLeish, beside his friend, gave a hiss that was stentorian. He was resplendent in full dress uniform, mothballed since the passing of President John F Kennedy in 1963, when he'd been part of a guard of honour in Glasgow.

But John would not have Maud's send-off turned into a farce either. 'Maud was a native of this island, a spinster of the parish, who lived most of her life here, but whose presence spread quietly far and wide. In true form, Maud has requested no eulogy and no fuss. She was a good woman with little religious conviction, choosing to believe in the overall goodness of mankind – and the power of a good party.' John smiled. 'And we'll get to that very shortly. As you're all aware, Maud was privately cremated–' Everyone ignored the snort that came from William Crawford '–and her ashes will be interred alongside her parents, in their family plot in the graveyard.'

Despite herself, Sally – in the centre of the front row, flanked by Jay and Mary, with Sandy further along – couldn't help but turn slightly to see the minister's reaction to that; it stuck in his large craw that, 'Miss Maud Campbell, heathen to the last', would be buried in the churchyard, and there was nothing he could do to stop it. She, along with the rest of the congregation, was just in time to see Mr Crawford raise his Bible and turn to the door with a muttered, 'Heed ye sinners well!'

If he'd hoped for it to close behind him with a thunderous bang, he was disappointed as it merely rattled closed with a 'click' but it meant the latch was on and he was locked out.

'Well Maud aye did like tae hae the last word,' Sandy said loudly and this time nobody held their laughter in.

Neither did they catch the eye of the long-suffering Mrs Crawford who made no effort to get up and follow her husband. She didn't move, just sat there, relatively unnoticed with a resigned and apologetic smile fixed on her face. Everyone felt sorry for poor, meek Mhairi, and nobody held her accountable for her husband's brimstone ire. She bore the brunt of it.

John Hunter smiled broadly and gave everyone a moment. 'Maud did ask me to say a few words about her family,' he went on, looking along the front row.

Sally squeezed Mary's hand and was rewarded with a teary smile. Mary had adored Maud and since she was a little girl had insisted a Great-Aunt was far better than a Granny. Jay, at almost eighteen (and so like his father, that Sally sometimes still gave a gasp) sat stoic, his hands in his jacket pocket, but his tense shoulders and thrust out bottom lip showed how much he really felt. Sally herself was just sad. Maud had died quietly in her bed on a sunny morning; she was old, she was tired and it was what she would have wanted. Sally took comfort in that, but the hole her adopted aunt left was going to be impossible to fill.

'… Maud frequently said how much finding her family meant to her in these, her later years,' John Hunter was saying. 'She counted the fifteen years since Nan, with Jay and Mary, arrived on Inniscuillin, as amongst the happiest of her life. And she was delighted that the Big House would stay in the family for many years to come.'

There was a murmur of approval from around the room; Miss Campbell was an old stick but she had her priorities right. Sally let the tears fall unchecked, even when Ewan leaned forward, his chair creaking ominously, with a perfectly laundered white handkerchief.

'And finally, to Sandy Mac.'

'Well, ah'll be...' Sally heard him mutter.

John smiled again. 'Maud loved a sparring partner. She loved having the constant companionship of the man she would have liked as her brother. Quite simply Maud loved Sandy, though of course, she'd never have dreamed of saying so.'

The hall was delighted now; long-lost family and a love story – albeit of the purest kind. Sally sneaked a look at Sandy's face, which was red; a mix of proud and mortified.

'Which is why she's saying so now – and, yes, Sandy, having the last word!'

The mourners roared.

And so, when John Hunter asked if anyone would like to stand and say a few words, it was Sandy who rose – Sally felt a pang at how much he had aged since Maud's death – and shuffled up to the lectern. He surveyed the small company of mourners and she realised nearly all of them he had known since they were children – with one noticeable exception: Nan and the children.

'The last word?' he said. 'Ah'll no be lettin' Miss Maud Campbell, the best friend a man ever had, outwit me wi that.' His voice cracked. 'She's right, though. Ah'm no' a man o' words. An' ah'll no' be startin' now.' He nodded at Jay, who, Sally realised was sitting up straight, eyes fixed on Sandy, and fiddling with something he'd drawn from his over-sized pockets. 'Maud detested pop music wi a passion,' Sandy went on, 'but there was one song she loved. This is for her.'

Everyone in the hall shared glances of mystification, Sally and John Hunter amongst them. Only Jay knew what was going on, and followed his cue precisely. He stood up, little portable cassette player at the ready, and at a signal from Sandy, everyone else got to their feet. When Jay pressed the 'Play' button, and John Lennon's song 'Imagine', emanated tinnily from its wee speaker, there was no other sound to be heard. And as the last echoes faded away, there was barely a dry eye either.

'Mak' yer way tae the kitchen folks for a wee dram an' a bite tae eat,' Sandy called, as the congregation prepared to file out, finding their voices once more.

A week later, as the sun was rising, and the island was quiet, Sally, Jay, Mary and Sandy, made their way to the graveyard. In a well-tended corner, the Campbell plot lay ready, and Sally bent to lower the plain box containing Maud's remains into the small space beside her loving parents. Then Mary read a few words she herself had written, folding over the paper at the end and slipping it in beside the urn. It was easy for Sally to comfort her daughter, but her son was harder to read. Jay stood, head down, attempting to be the adult he already thought he was, and Sally's heart ached for him.

She stood back, linking arms with the two of them – Jay didn't resist – and they watched in silence as Sandy fetched a spade and a small bucket and began to cover Maud up. He was obviously struggling, and Sally wasn't sure what to do – to offer help and offend him, or watch him stumble – when Jay stepped forward. He laid a hand on Sandy's shoulder, took the spade and finished the job. Sally's eyes filled all over again. Mary had gathered a bunch of flowers from the Big House garden, mostly wild roses and thistles – Maud's favourites – and laid them gently down. 'Goodbye, Aunt

Maud,' she whispered.

She knelt in front of the simple, temporary cross, and Sally joined her. Jay and Sandy standing to one side. The four of them read the inscription that Maud had chosen:

Maud Elizabeth Campbell of Inniscuillin, born 1899 died 1986, beloved Aunt of Nancy, Jay and Mary Douglas, honorary sister of Sandy MacKinnon.

As they made their way back to the house – their house – Sally's grief was tempered with true gratitude. Dear Aunt Maud had died supporting her adopted family to the last and taking Nan's secrets – the ones Maud didn't actually know – to the grave. She'd handed over the house to Sally years before, saying it meant less paperwork if it was a gift during her lifetime; it was as if she knew Sally had no legitimate claim to the name Nan Douglas and no way of proving who she was in legal matters. She'd also left generous legacies to the children and the rest to Nan. Alisdair was party to the decisions and if he'd seen anything odd in the arrangements he hadn't said. Sally had felt safe, then, cocooned in the arms of Maud and the island. Maud had saved Sally Brown and she'd made Nan Douglas. Now, with her gone and the children, almost of age, and soon wanting to forge their own lives, the outside world crept nearer – and Sally was afraid.

40
ALISDAIR AND SERGEANT MCLEISH

'Hello, Ewan. Come through. Miss Brady's off on other business today. Now, I want to hear more about our dastardly money-laundering Peggy the Postmistress.'

'What?' Ewan puffed up. What had he missed? Instinctively he reached for his little black book; a policeman's eye should never be off the ball.

'Calm down, old friend. I'm teasing you.' Alisdair waved the decanter at him in a gesture of peace. 'Peggy's an old gossip and I wouldn't put her above steaming open envelopes and listening in to the switchboard but the only laundering she does is her rather large smalls!'

'Now, really, Alisdair… Wait, are you telling me that the postmistress interferes with the island's private mail? That's a criminal offence–'

'Lighten up, Sergeant. You're getting too serious in your old age,' although, Alisdair thought, had Ewan ever been anything but? 'Investigating poor old Peggy reminds me of the daft time you were all fired up over Nan Douglas having abducted her children and hidden them up at the Big House. Here. Try this.' He thrust an amber-coloured single malt towards Ewan, who looked slightly mollified by its size.

'Aye, well. If it's true that Maud Campbell left her money as well as the house to Nan and the bairns…' Ewan paused for Alisdair to confirm or deny but Alisdair just grinned and zipped his lips '…then they're her kin alright. Blood being thicker than water and all that.' He took an appreciative sip of his drink. 'Now back to Peggy…'

Two hours and their customary half-bottle of Talisker

later, the two diligent, and unpaid, volunteer sleuths, had proven, without a shadow of a doubt, that Peggy-the-Post's money-laundering enterprises had been set up to finance a trans-national narcotics syndicate, based partially in Colombia, Florida and Inniscuillin. And Peggy had provided incontrovertible proof of her guilt, herself: Ewan devised a cunning trap. Invoking the long arm of the law, he telephoned the post office, daringly disturbing Peggy on her afternoon off, and asking how much it would cost to send a letter to Colombia and another to Florida. On neither occasion had Peggy hesitated – she knew the prices off by heart. And she knew the Colombia national currency was the peso. QED.

'Pass over the handcuffs, could you, old friend?' Alisdair toasted him. 'Too easy. Shall we do Lord Lucan now. Or a brand new one?' But the fire had gone out of Ewan and he was staring down into his glass, unusually half-full, his shoulders slumped. 'Something tells me your heart's not in it,' Alisdair added. 'What's up? Has a Merry Widow turned you down again?'

It was no secret between them that over the fifteen years Nan Douglas had lived on the island, Ewan had scraped up the courage instilled in him at police training college – mind, that was supposed to be more about facing up to bank robbers and hostage situations, alien to Inniscuillin – and harnessed the techniques, more than once, to ask Nan to marry him. She always said no, but he lived in stubborn hope.

'Not yet,' he said now. 'Though now Maud's gone and the young ones are teenagers, maybe...' He shook his head. 'Ah, Alisdair, everything's changing, do you not feel it? I never thought I'd say it but the island's not the same with the lady of the Big House gone. I'd even go as far as to say I miss her. Hilary Armstrong-Stuart was the first to go and old Sandy Mac's on his way out. Soon none of the old ones will be left.'

'Anno Domini. Catches us all. I agree about the dowager Campbell, but the new mistress of the Big House will make her mark.' Alisdair winked. 'You didn't hear that from me but yes, as rumour suggests, Nan's the new owner. Has been on paper for years, come to that. And, come on, Ewan, there's life in us yet.'

'Aye. I just wish I could do something to cheer Nan up. She's taken Maud's passing hard. Sandy Mac too, he's lost his spirit since Maud died.'

'Young Mary's good for everyone. She's a cheerful wee soul. The spit of her Ma.'

'How will Nan manage Jay though?' Ewan clucked his tongue. 'He's what I hear them call a charmer – but he'll need an eye kept on him. Must take after his father.'

'Hmm.' Alisdair thought for a moment and then slapped his leg. 'Got it. Let's have a picnic.'

'A picnic?' Ewan looked dubious.

'Yes. On the beach – Skua Bay end. There's no currents there and it's shady. Tea and lemonade on the table and a bottle of something stronger underneath it. Cake and jam pieces gritty with sand. Rounders teams. Paddling. And a bonfire when it gets dark. Come on, Ewan, it's a great idea. Like the old days that you're hankering for. You can even wear a hanky knotted on your head if it pleases you.'

'Well...'

'We'll invite everyone. We'll call it a memorial to Maud. The old girl deserves it after that debacle of a funeral –

granted she would have got a kick out our dear minister making a fool of himself, but still. Yes, a final farewell. I'll pay for it and Helen Brady will arrange it. She's a whizz at that kind of thing and it will be like a farewell for her too – she's finally bought that ticket to Australia, you know. You can take Nan for a walk along the sand and whisper sweet advice about how to manage her teenage boy. How could she resist you then?'

'You might just have something there.' Ewan spoke slowly but there was a light in his ponderous eyes. 'We could have it before the midsummer ceilidh. Oh. The minister won't like it though.'

'Then the minister can go into his kirk, shut his ears and lump it,' Alisdair said cheerfully. 'Let's make a plan.'

41

Alisdair telephoned the Big House the following day, on the pretext of a few legal matters still to be cleared up in relation to confirmation of Miss Campbell's will and testament.

Sally was surprised. 'I didn't think there was anything more 'til confirmation comes through,' she said.

'Just one or two small matters,' Alisdair said easily. 'They don't concern the estate. Just you, Nan.'

'Me? What?' Sally's radar went up.

'Don't worry, Nan, you're not about to be evicted or lose your inheritance.' Alisdair picked up on her tone and sounded amused. 'Maud had some papers here for safe-keeping and I want to pass them on privately. That's all.'

'Oh. Oh, right, of course. I'll come to the office, shall I?'

'That might be best.'

Once they'd made the arrangement, Alisdair said, 'And one more – nice, I hope – thing…' He then casually mentioned that when Ewan was in touch, inviting her and the children to a picnic at Skua Bay, that it was his lumbering way of trying to do something nice, there was no ulterior motive, the whole island would probably be there, and would she please agree?

'Of course, I will. Alisdair.' Sally smiled down the phone. 'We need a lift, and with the long days here, it will be good to get out.' She paused. 'But on one condition: that Ewan does not insist on giving me a free swimming lesson!' He'd been meticulous in teaching Jay and Mary to swim, in the couple of years after they'd arrived on Inniscuillin. No island child had any business not being confident in the water, he'd said, and for once even Maud was impressed with his plan for swimming tuition. Sally herself couldn't swim and didn't feel the need; looking at the water was enough for her, but she pushed the twins to learn until they were veritable fishes. It meant that when Sergeant McLeish did his annual Water Safety lecture up at the school, he still tried to persuade Sally to join his classes.

Now, Alisdair laughed, and assured her Ewan would bring his trunks and the swimming rings and water wings – he couldn't be stopped – but he would be chief lifeguard – no lessons.

'What about food?' Sally was ever practical. 'Shall I organise that?'

'No need. My treat,' Alisdair said. 'We're going fancy. Oh, not that your food wouldn't be good but I don't want to impose–'

'It's fine, Alisdair,' she broke in. 'I shall enjoy being waited on. Thank you.'

'Good. I'm ordering in a spread from Strathern's in Mallaig. My spendthrift ways shall be the talk of Inniscuillin and take the Reverend Crawford's shocking behaviour at Maud's memorial service off the gossip list.' With that he rang off.

He wasn't wrong, Sally thought, as she went through to the sitting room to finish polishing; she loved the smell of beeswax. Everyone would speculate over how Alisdair got the money to splash out; there was already talk that he'd helped Helen Brady with her long-saved for ticket to Australia. Maybe he had – but if so, he certainly wasn't also planning on eloping with her, which was the extension of the rumour. Sally was sure of that. His latest Jack Lambert book must have made a mint, she thought as she picked up her cloth, and grinning at her insider knowledge, she resumed her housework. Maud had continued to order Alisdair's books from the mainland, inconspicuously tucked amongst a handful of her favourite writers and kept on the bookshelf in her bedroom. Sally had never seen her read one openly, but their spines were certainly creased, and out of curiosity, Sally had begun reading them herself. They were... well, they were totally unlike the Alisdair she knew: violent, sexy and fast-paced. Pure escapism. Sally wasn't sure if she enjoyed them, but the novelty of Alisdair Conti, island solicitor and keen angler, writing them, kept her hooked.

'What are you laughing at, Mum?' Jay poked his head around the door.

'I'm smiling,' Sally objected. 'Alisdair and Ewan are planning a picnic at Skua Bay. With food delivered from Strathern's – you know, the posh hotel?'

'Cool.' Jay was already showing a taste for life's luxuries; Mary was more of a homebird, happy with her nose in a book. 'D'you think he'll let me drive the Hillma'?' Ever since they were little and Alisdair's original Hillma' Super Minx had been missing an 'N' that the solicitor gravely told the twins was due to too little glue on the assembly line (not his reversing widely as he drove off the ferry), his succession of cars had been known as Hillma'.

'If you ask him nicely, perhaps,' Sally said. 'Now, were you looking for me, love?'

'Yeah. I'm hungry. Can I have something?'

'You're always hungry. I'll see about lunch. Where's Mary?'

'Reading in her room. I'll help you.'

'You will?' Unlike his sister, Jay wasn't known for

helping out; Sally was suspicious. 'Alright, Jay, what do you really want?'

'Nothing.' Jay gave her his – his father's – charming smile. 'But now you've brought up the subject and I have some money coming. 'A car of my own would be a very good idea, wouldn't it, Mum? And a proper wee boat, a skiff. Those old rowing boats have been on the beach since the day we arrived. They're antiques. Mary would like that, too.'

'We'll see.' Sally was increasingly falling back on the trite motherly phrases she'd vowed never to use, but Jay had an ever-growing list of wants, or what he would call 'needs'. There were things he was entitled to, he told her, and Sally wondered where had she heard that before? Jay didn't sound like Malcolm, his accent was pure Inniscuillin, but the tone was identical. Sally worried how much Jay the teenager brought Malcolm to mind these days. Thank heavens there was no Martha in Mary, she thought. As for a car, that was one thing, and maybe the one thing she could give in and accede to. It would buy her time, wouldn't it? Because Sally was sure Jay was soon going to start looking for things she really couldn't provide.

'When will you see?' Jay asked.

'Soon.' Sally ushered him into the hall and along to the kitchen. 'Cheese and pickle sandwiches?' she asked. 'And you can get the cake tin out. Sandy will be in shortly. Then call Mary –'

But a thunder of feet on the stairs and along the hall announced that Mary had pre-empted her. 'There's someone coming,' she announced breathlessly, almost falling through the kitchen door. 'The car's half way up the drive.'

'Oh, it'll be Ewan, come to invite us to the picnic.' Sally

was concentrating on grating cheese; the old mandolin-style implement Maud had favoured was a devil for slicing the skin off fingers.

'No, it's not Uncle Ewan, it's – I think it's – the Reverend Crawford... Wait, what picnic?' Mary looked from Sally to Jay.

'What? Are you sure? What's he doing coming here?' Sally bristled immediately. William Crawford hadn't been welcome in Maud's home during her lifetime, had he the neck to try to get a foot in the door when she was barely buried.

'I think so. It looks like his car. Mum – what picnic?'

'One Ewan and Alisdair are arranging on Skua Bay. Jay?' Sally turned to him. 'Go and peek out the window, see if it's really him. You'll recognise a Ford Anglia better than me.'

Jay was back in two ticks. 'It is him. He's just getting out. He's got a bloody nerve coming here. I'm going to warn Sandy. He won't like Wee Free Willie catching him napping.'

'Jay. Language.' Sally spoke automatically but she hadn't the heart to reprimand him; they were her sentiments exactly.

'Shall we hide?' Mary suggested. 'We can pretend we're not in.'

'He'll see the car. And he'll go and annoy Sandy in the workshop,' Sally pointed out. 'And if he wants to see us for something he won't be put off, he'll keep coming back. No, love, let's brazen it out.' But she was damned if she was letting him into Maud's house.

Mary nodded. 'Maybe he's come to say sorry for being rude at Aunt Maud's memorial.'

Mary always saw the good in people. 'Maybe he has.' But

Sally didn't think so.

The shrill ring on the front door coincided with Jay and Sandy crossing the yard to the back door.

'Let him come tae the back, like the rest,' Sandy grunted. Nobody – except Ewan when he was in his official role as Inniscuillin's police sergeant – ever used the front door. 'Are you gettin' on wi that cup o' tea, Nan, lass?' He winked at Sally.

'I certainly am,' she said. 'Lunch for four, then.'

42
THE REVEREND CRAWFORD

It was the last straw. After the farce of Maud Campbell's funeral and her cremation – cremation! Who did she think she was? – he, William Crawford, the Free Church minister of Inniscuillin for nigh on a half century, had been summarily escorted from the so-called Big House by that plodding fool of a policeman. And – and! Adding insult to injury, McLeish had had the nerve to 'warn him' they were having a picnic in her honour and 'any protests, stand-offs or otherwise anti-social behaviour' would be dealt with by a night in the cells. Cells! William snorted. If McLeish had notions about the glorified shed off his kitchen being a police cell, and that he, a man of God, would ever cross its threshold, well… Words failed him. Anyway, that was the least of his pre-occupations.

He stomped back to his car, crushing the impulse to run over the officious sergeant who was now signalling to him that the road was clear – in the name of heaven when was it not clear? – reverse over him and grind him to pulp. William Crawford drove his Ford Anglia in the direction of the manse, his already filthy temper mounting. Would that infernal woman never let him be? Was she always going to be the spectre at his feast? William thumped the steering wheel. What would be next – a monument to Maud Campbell on the quay? A renaming of the island? Over his dead body. He'd not be attending any hedonistic picnic and neither would his wife. He'd forbid the congregation too… but there William's shoulders slumped; time was they'd have listened. Not anymore.

By God, Mhairi would suffer for this tonight. It was all

her fault anyway, everything to do with… with that Maud Mary-Magdelene Campbell was Mhairi's fault and he made sure she didn't ever forget it. William prided himself on his ascetic lifestyle, and Fridays – today – meant stale bread and hard cheese for their supper. His incompetent wife was bound to cut the cheese thickly, or use fresh bread, and he would lambast her for doing so. The woman never learned, and in all their farce of a married life he'd never known if she was contrary or plain stupid. He got great satisfaction in beating the Beelzebub out of her. Not for his own satisfaction, of course, but because it was the Lord's work, the only way to save a woman from such poor stock, who bore her own abhorrent youth and spoiled reputation barely as a cross; she accepted what she was! If self-flagellation hadn't been a Papist sport, William would have instigated it from the first. Instead, it fell to him to save her soul.

William could feel pounding against his temples. High blood pressure, the doctor called it and gave him pills – that were flushed immediately down the old outside privy. How dare they? Maud Campbell's so-called family: a decrepit old man who had all but shacked up with her; and a far-flung great-niece who might once have been a nice enough girl. Contaminated she was now, no better than she should be, cavorting with the two eligible bachelors of the island and wed to neither of them: uncles, those unfortunate twins called them. Aye, right, it was no secret what that meant. All of them, in a row like a silent picket, had stood there and barred him from entering that house. He could see the food on the table beyond them, the steam from the kettle boiling on the range, but was he invited to break bread? No, he wasn't.

'Heathens and sinners, the lot of them,' he snarled. He'd

swallowed his pride and gone up there like a good Christian: let bygones be bygones; the seats he'd kept warm for them in the kirk; how prayer and penance now would save their departed relative and themselves from the eternal fires of hell and damnation... They'd said nothing, heard none of his wisdom. Had they called the police sergeant on him? Or was it a regular uncle's afternoon visit? Either way, let them rot, McLeish as well. Purgatory was the best place for the likes of them.

But by the wrath of God, he would have his say first. He'd been impotent while Maud Campbell was alive; if he were party to her secrets then so was she to his. It was an impasse, a devil's bargain. But now she was gone to cower before her Maker and there was nothing stopping the Reverend Crawford from speaking out. He owed it to his flock.

There had been bad blood between him and Maud Campbell ever since she had returned to the island and taken up permanent residence in her parents' house. He'd gone up there with the best of intentions. They were much of an age, and he'd even wondered at that time whether he might bestow on Miss Campbell the honour of her becoming Mrs Crawford... He was willing to forget her unfortunate elopement with that wet fish, Colin Murray, and would revel in teaching her the ways of a good God-fearing wife... He had shuddered many times since, and still did to this day, each time thanking God for his intervention. Maud's incredulous smirk as William broached the subject had stopped him in his tracks. She'd upped and gone to Glasgow and look what that had brought her.

He hadn't followed her to the city; God's calling, in its mysterious way, had simply taken him along Maud's path.

And that was how he knew – William's erratically thumping chest swelled and his blood surged – the starchy old woman's dirty secrets, carefully hidden as she lorded it up there in the Big House, with that pandering acolyte, Sandy MacKinnon, her bodyguard. How much of that heathen lifestyle had she shared with Nan Douglas? How much had she saved for the end, confessing to John Hunter? And what had he told her nearest and dearest and all the nosy onlookers?

Indignant as he was, it still didn't quite remove the nagging doubt about what Maud might have passed on about him.

Roaring down the road – God help the Anglia's throttle and any innocent vehicle coming his way – William Crawford's thoughts went to dark places. Maud Campbell had been this far from an institution after her so-called fiancé was killed. William all but cackled; divine retribution if ever it was – young people running off together in sin, what did they expect? He found he wasn't able to forgive it, after all. She was lucky her god-fearing folks had taken her back in, and cosseted her. And what had she done? Run off again, to do Good Works with the Salvation Army. The woman didn't even believe in God! William ground his teeth. Gone to the Gorbals, she had, taking a job in a sewing machine factory and living in a rooming house – with women no better than they should be. As if that wasn't bad enough, he'd heard rumours that… that… William gulped, hardly able to stomach the word, a thrill of horror coursing through his veins, that Maud Campbell had scorned all men and preferred the company of women.

William wiped his sweating forehead and wriggled uncomfortably in his seat. By the 1920s she was mixing with a very Bohemian crowd. Scandalous! Tongues wagged. And official police records that McLeish couldn't cover up, showed she'd fallen into the Suffragette movement. 'Fallen in' – William's throat was sore; such was the snorting he was doing – she'd no doubt run the coven! Single-handedly responsible for getting women the vote! No doubt those heathens up there in the village hall had dabbed their eyes and applauded her, imagining her chained with handcuffs to some railings, skirts riding above her ankles, her lip-sticked mouth shouting obscenities at the innocent...

William had to pull over, so passionate was his ire. 'Opium,' he muttered as he collected himself and drove on. She would have been taking opium in a den of vice. Depraved. 'Whore,' he whispered daringly. It was all spilling out now, every feeling he'd harboured ever since he was a young man.

How much of that, had John Hunter told that crowd of sheep at her so-called funeral? Eh? 'How much?' This he roared out of the window at a couple of real startled sheep.

He held his hands up to the heavens, trying not to think how much Maud would have enjoyed this loss of control. Gulping fresh air, he gained a modicum of equilibrium, enough to continue his drive home. Home to his wife. William had courted and married Mhairi within a year of meeting her. She had been one of Maud's Good Works: beauty gone bad, weak-willed but willing. And, by God, she was no Maud – and none of them had ever forgotten it. Mhairi was William's biggest mistake... No, he revised that. His biggest mistake was that Maud knew exactly what Mhairi was. And, even worse, why she was.

Back then, it had been William's intention to save the

woman from what she was, a common Glasgow prostitute. He'd thought it would make him holy, more than a mere mortal, nearer to God than Miss Maud Campbell, but what it did was make him feel dirty and diseased.

He flushed when he remembered how Maud had spoken plainly to him about his relationship with the brand-new Mrs William Crawford. He'd come home early, from the mainland, one afternoon and found Maud and his new bride, Mhairi, taking tea in the manse garden. Tea! In the garden! With his wife! William had minded his manners for a few minutes, until Mhairi had crept away and Maud had looked him in the eye as she gathered up her wrap. 'Be kind to that timorous wife of yours, William,' she'd said. 'Or else.'

'Or else, what?' he asked, despite himself. 'What will you do about it?'

'I'll do what I'll do,' she'd said. 'Surely you should be worrying what your God will do.' She'd not mentioned the name that was on both of their lips, a name William had never spoken aloud since. She'd just smiled, an evil smile, and William had had a primeval urge to throw her down to the ground and wipe that look off her face with a strong and purposeful pounding. But he was a man of God, he'd not laid a finger on her; Mhairi, though…

'Mhairi? Mhairi, where are you?'

Back at the manse, William barged through the front door and threw his car keys at the bowl on the hall table. He shrugged off his overcoat, dumped it over the banister and yelled again; the woman should be watching out for him. He put his head into the dining room and frowned when he saw the table laid but no bread or cheese evident. Marching back down the hallway, he glanced at the clock. He was twenty minutes early. That was no excuse; the woman knew to keep on her toes, and what could delay her with their scant Friday collation anyway?

'Mhairi? Where the devil are you?'

'In the kitchen, William. I didn't quite expect you.' She sounded flustered, as well she might, and when he flung open the door, there she was pink-faced, with her hair falling down, scuttling around the ageing kitchen like an even more ageing mouse.

What the –? He couldn't believe his eyes. 'What are you doing, woman?' William thundered.

'I'm sorry, William, but the bread... well, it was very stale... Your teeth...' Mhairi looked up from the grill, where she was toasting the bread. 'I thought...'

'You thought? You thought? What you mean is that in a moment of weakness, you summoned Satan and told him to take the cheese and roast it in the flames of hell.' William lost the run of himself altogether and he screamed at her.

Mhairi flinched, but nearly sixty years of marriage had inured her to his worst fits – something William was not happy about. 'No, William,' she said. 'Welsh rarebit is not a devilish dish. I'm sure God wouldn't mind just this once.'

'What does someone like you know about what God wants?' he sneered, pushing past her to switch off the grill. 'Well?' He didn't like the strange look on her face.

'More than you think, William,' Mhairi said quietly. She felt in the pocket of her apron, and with a shaking hand, held out a letter to him. 'I didn't open your post. You'll see it's addressed to me.'

'To you?' He snatched the piece of paper.

'Maybe you'd like to sit down to read it?'

'Don't tell me–' But William had seen the signature. He groped blindly for the nearest chair and collapsed into it. He didn't even notice that Mhairi turned away, switched the grill back on and calmly went on toasting the bread. All he saw were the words on the paper, the black ink boring a hole in his brain:

My Dear Mhairi,

Please tell William that I have no secrets. My life, the good and the bad, is an open book to my friends and family. Ask Sandy, if William must have proof. He may slander me from the pulpit but it will have no effect on me or on those close to me. If it makes him feel better, let him.

Your secrets, my dear, are safe with me. They are also safe with William, who is a bully and a coward, and has been, I'm sure, for the eighty-six years of his life. I can't begin to understand why you have stayed with him, but I know you deserve better. To this end, William's secrets are not safe with me, I have not taken them to my grave. There is a letter in the care of Alisdair Conti that details – precisely – the love affair between William Crawford and Chrissy Fraser during the summer of 1922 in Glasgow. The letter explains that following Chrissy's unexplained death, that William targeted you, paying for your services, until you agreed to marry him.

I take no pleasure in this, Mhairi, though William will scarcely believe that. However, if you are in any way ill-treated from this day on, you have only to contact Alisdair Conti, and that letter will be made public. Will anyone care, sixty-plus years on about the sordid details of a homosexual relationship? William will. He can't take the risk, my dear.

You, finally, are safe. And Chrissy's untimely death is avenged. He, like you, was an innocent, dear Mhairi, a victim of the Reverend Crawford.

I regret that the years have passed and I have not been more of a friend to you. You chose your life, as I did mine. However, there is also a sum of money lodged with my letter. Should you wish to live out the rest of your years without William, it will see you through. It's only what you're entitled to. William's entitlements will be decided by his God. Will he find solace or fear in that? I don't know.

Your friend,

Maud (Campbell)

William sat there for so long after Mhairi carried the cheese on toast into the dining room, that she dared to say her own blessing and eat hers. She sipped from her water glass and thought for a while. Then she collected William's meal and took it back through to the kitchen, where she plucked Maud's letter from his limp hand and tucked it back into her apron. In silence, she placed his plate in front of him. The food was cold, the cheese like greasy rubber, but William would like that. It was extra penance, after all.

43

The day of the picnic was overcast, but that was no dampener – as Sally said (like a true native) if they waited for sunshine and high temperatures on the island, they'd probably get snow in June. Outdoors events might be a gamble further south, but they lived on an island; they just dressed in the right clothes.

Sandy had perked up no end with a project to work towards: digging out and mending old windbreaks; fashioning a sun-cum-rain umbrella; even painting deckchairs that were found tucked away in a boxroom up at the school. Sally was so relieved to see him humming as he worked, she was able to ignore how heavily he lent on Jay for help. And it was good for Jay, too. Sandy brought out his gentler, kinder side, and if Mary thought of Maud as her granny, then Sandy was Jay's grandad.

Sally didn't want to admit it but her boy was showing himself just a wee bit too inclined to play the man of the Big House without any skills or ambition to support it. As Jeremy, he had been such a precocious little boy, razor-sharp and way ahead of his years, even at ages two and three; little Rosemary had lagged behind, partly, of course because she was actually a good year younger than her 'twin'. But as they'd grown into teenagers, Mary had come into her own, and was now set on going to university – maybe even as far as Edinburgh – and studying to become a primary school teacher. Her ambition was to return to Inniscuillin and teach. Sally hadn't the heart to say that the little school's days might well be numbered, and anyway, there would always be rural schools that did need dedicated and sensitive staff, the kind of teacher Mary, she thought proudly, was bound to be.

Jay, though, was a whole other being. Yes, he had his father's charisma, but he also had his self-centredness. He was bright but lazy and he showed no interest in a particular career or training for a job, he wanted to live off his inheritance and had a vague notion to travel. Sally loved him dearly, but there was no getting away from the fact he was a constant source of her headaches these days – but then again, never forget how lucky she was to have been given motherhood and all of its challenges.

Sally shook herself out of her daydreams and set her mind to the day. The picnic was just the distraction they all needed, and Ewan and Alisdair were like two small boys putting it all together. Most of the island seemed to be going - even Peggy was going to close the shop for the afternoon – and rumour was that Alisdair was even going to drive out to the manse in his Hillma' and take Mrs Crawford for an hour or two. The Reverend, presumably an answer to his flock's prayer, was allegedly attending a conference on the mainland. The man was in his eighties, Sally thought. How much longer would he be permitted to continue his increasingly erratic ministry. She presumed that out of sight out of mind, amongst the dwindling congregation on Inniscuillin was precisely where the Church wanted him. When he died, so would his position.

'Mum?' Jay's voice floated up the stairs. 'Me and Mary are driving Sandy to the beach with all the stuff, alright?'

'Bye, Mum,' added Mary. 'I'm going to help Uncle Ewan with the food delivery. He's a bit put out that Uncle Alisdair has left him to it. I'll cheer him up a bit.'

'You do that.' Sally smiled. 'See you both later. Be good!'

'Oh, Mum, honestly…' That was the two of them in

unison. Sally smiled again.

She glanced at her watch, not having told them that Alisdair was busy meeting her to go over whatever it was Maud had left outstanding in her affairs. They'd rearranged it so he came to the Big House and then would drive her to Skua Bay, collecting Mhairi Crawford en route – 'Alone with a man that's not the minister might just be a step too far for her,' Alisdair had said cheerfully. She'd make a pot of coffee and they'd have it in the sitting room, Sally thought. Unlike Ewan, who always dropped in for a cup of tea, the solicitor liked his coffee strong and bitter. Neither did he have a sweet tooth so she couldn't feed him the boxes – large and small – of tablet Maud had stashed in her bedside cupboard and Sally had found and taken down to the pantry; they'd be eating it until Sally was in her dotage. That was a thought – she'd take some of the tablet down to the picnic.

'No time like the present,' Sally said aloud and made her way to the kitchen, dragging the tiny stepladder into the pantry. She reached up for a couple of boxes of Maud's sweet treat and seeing the familiar lid, she realised all over again how much she missed the older woman. She gave an inadvertent sob, and in doing so, dropped two of the bigger boxes. 'Oh, bother. Sorry, Aunt Maud… Hmm. What's that?'

Well aware she was talking to herself, Sally frowned and climbed down. One of the lids of the sweet boxes had come open and packed inside, instead of the crumbly fudge, was a brown envelope. Curious, Sally removed it, at the same time hoping she wasn't going to find something very personal – love letters, perhaps. But no, it was a paperback book, one of Alisdair's alter ego, Jack Lambert's. What was Maud playing at? She'd been far from a dotty old woman but everyone did weird things sometimes. Sally shook her head, smiling. The book was one she hadn't seen before but it had all the lurid, sensational detail she'd expect: Stolen, the title screamed, featuring a crazed-looking woman running across railroad tracks, a cameo of the FBI agent, Humbert Madison, looking steely-eyed and moody, in the bottom corner.

Idly, Sally turned it over to read the blurb – and froze. Surely not. It couldn't be. There was no way… She sank to the floor, leaning against the open cupboard door, and forced herself to read the dramatic teaser again, slowly and carefully. Her eyes wouldn't obey, they darted over the words apparently at random, her brain refusing to process them: '…babysitter… kidnaps two children…hide-out in an island commune…race against time…Madison versus the crazed baby-stealer…'

Sally felt sick. More than sick. This was her – this was her, Sally Brown's, story, wasn't it? Over the top and dramatic, maybe, and, God forbid, not all of it, but there was no mistaking the gist. It couldn't be coincidence, could it? Alisdair knew what she'd done and he'd written about it. Maud had then seen the book and hidden it, which meant, Sally's mind worked it through, which meant Maud knew what Sally had done. She'd never said a thing though, never implied…and Sally, was certain, it wasn't Maud who had told Alisdair, she would stake her life on that, so – who had told him? And why had he done nothing about it, 'Except write a stupid, bloody, bestselling book!' As Sally shouted the words, she threw the offending book across the room, where it skidded to a halt against the range.

Just as quickly, she got up and retrieved it, fumbling through the first few pages to find the publication date. 1979.

Seven years ago, and a good eight after Nan and the twins
had arrived on Inniscuillin. What did that tell her? Absolutely
nothing, that's what. Quickly, Sally wrapped the offending
book back up in the brown paper and tucked it under the
sink, behind the Vim and bleach; nobody would look there.
She'd move it when she decided what to do. She couldn't ask
Maud, probably a blessing in disguise, but could she, would
she, should she ask Alisdair? Or did she leave it? Leave it
and see what happened?

Sally washed her face at the kitchen sink, hoping the cold
water would shock her into calm. It didn't. She put on the
kettle, for something to do more than wanting a drink, which
reminded her that Alisdair himself was due to call in less
than an hour. She put her hand to her mouth; she couldn't see
him, she really couldn't. She rushed to the telephone, trying,
as her shaking finger dialled, to think of a reasonable last-
minute excuse to cancel. There wasn't one, and it didn't
matter anyway because there was no answer at his office or
at his home. Alisdair was on his way. 'Think, Sally, think,'
she said to herself, then shook her head crossly. No, it was
Nan who needed to think. She was Nan, had been for well
over a decade, and it would be Nan who got her out of this
mess.

When the Hillman crunched over the gravel, and Alisdair
called a cheery, 'Hello? Anyone home. Nan?' from the
kitchen door, Sally was settled in the sitting room.

'In here,' she shouted back. 'Just in time. I'm pouring the
coffee.' Her hand was steady as she did so, and when
Alisdair appeared, she gave him a bright, and she hoped,
natural, smile. 'This really is an official visit, then.' He raised

his eyebrows and Sally pointed at his briefcase. 'I presume
you have Aunt Maud's papers in there, rather than your
swimming trunks and a towel.'

'I'm an underestimated man of many talents; maybe I
have both,' he replied. 'But you're right. Let's get the
business out of the way.'

Was it her imagination, Sally wondered, as she handed
him his coffee, or was he as nervous as she was? Aware she
was probably projecting her feelings on to him, she took an
inward breath and prepared to act as she hadn't acted since
the first few months she'd sat, a newcomer with a lot to hide,
in this very room. All she had to remember was that Nan's
life was an open book.

44
ALISDAIR

He seriously hoped he was doing the right thing here, Alisdair thought, as he faced a curiously bright-eyed Nan. He wondered if she'd been crying and had overdone the eye drops. She must really miss the old lady; her last surviving relative, well, the twins aside, of course. He sipped his coffee, gathering himself to the task in hand. Right thing or not, he had no choice. This was one of Maud Campbell's last 'unofficial' wishes – not the wackiest by any means, that accolade went to either the letter and money she'd left for Mhairi Crawford or the letter and ticket to Australia she'd left for Helen Brady – but it was up there as, well, out of the ordinary. Rather like Maud herself.

'Alisdair?'

Nan was behaving oddly, he thought. He hoped Ewan hadn't proposed again – and Lord forbid, she'd said yes, this time. She was hiding the unease well but she hadn't touched her coffee and sat up straight as if she were in a job interview – she looked as uncomfortable as he felt. Or maybe he was imagining that? Come to think of it, why was he, himself, a bit out of sorts when all he was doing was passing on some of Maud Campbell's papers.

'Right,' he said briskly. 'Let's get on with it, shall we – if you're up to it?'

'What do you mean? Why wouldn't I be?' she said quickly.

He was right, there was something up. 'No reason. I mean, it's hard talking about a loved one who's passed. You can be fine then – blip! Takes you unawares,' he improvised. It worked; she relaxed.

'That's true.' Nan nodded. 'I keep expecting to see her around the house…'

'She loved you like a daughter, Nan,' Alisdair said. 'She has done everything she can to protect you–'

'Protect me? From what? Why do I need protecting?' Her eye twitched, and she rubbed at it,

'Well, life, I suppose.' Alisdair was surprised. 'Money worries, housing repairs, the twins' education. What did you think I meant?'

'Nothing, sorry. I'm just on edge this morning.' She smiled but it didn't reach her eyes. 'I was clearing out the pantry of tablet, you know, for the picnic. And I found a couple of things Aunt Maud had hidden. Oh, nothing of any value, it just… brought her back.'

'Then let me make this as painless as possible.' Alisdair opened his briefcase and pulled out a slim sheaf of pages, held together with a rubber band. 'You know, of course, Maud turned over the house and all its contents to you, some years ago, along with a life income, a separate sum for upkeep. At the same time, she bequeathed the bulk of her money to Jay and Mary in trust, which, now they are of age, they can access. There is also a generous settlement for Sandy, and various other bequests.'

Nan frowned. 'I know all this, Alisdair. I've known it for years. And I'm very, very grateful. I thought there was something new? You're acting very solicitor-ish,' she added, clearly trying to lift the mood.

'There is something more. Maud came to me several times before she died. There were papers her father must have saved since Adam was a boy, mostly incidental, but I promised to go through them all, just in case. She wanted to save you the bother.'

'That sounds like Aunt Maud.' Nan flashed him a genuine smile.

He rifled through the papers and brought out a sheet, smaller and thicker than the rest. 'This is your birth certificate, Nan. Or rather it's a replacement of the original, which was water-damaged – burst pipe in the attic, I daresay.' He held it out towards her.

When Nan just gaped at him, making no attempt to take it, he pointed to the typescript. 'Nancy Campbell, born 14th April 1932, registered in the district of Perth on the 25th... Oh, Nan, don't cry.'

She had burst into big noisy tears, and he rooted for a packet of tissues he knew he didn't have. There was a box over on the sideboard, plonked on top of an untidy pile of books, and he rose and fetched it for her, passing one over and patting her awkwardly on her shoulder; in all Alisdair's fifty-odd years, he'd never had much experience of crying women.

'She never said anything much when she gave the box to me, just warned me to be very thorough. She said you'd had to come north with nothing, no proper ID except that you were a Campbell... There were other certificates there, too, marriage and deaths as well. Nancy's – yours, I should say – was the only one without a corresponding death certificate. It seems that several children didn't reach adulthood...illness, the war, you know. I put two and two together and came up with you. Mind, you look a good bit younger than your actual age, not that one should ask a lady her age – you've never even confirmed when your birthday is, have you? In all the years you've been here – it's good genes, isn't it, as Maud would say…'

'Aunt Maud really has looked after us to the last, hasn't she? Far beyond the call of duty.' Her eyes bore into him. 'Don't you think, Alisdair? And you, too.'

'Me? I'm only the messenger.' It was on the tip of his tongue to ask what she meant, but Alisdair bit it back and said nothing. There was something between Maud and Nan that he didn't quite understand, and he really didn't want to know; he wasn't above sailing close to the wind but least said and all that. 'Shall I make more coffee?' he asked instead. 'That pot's rather gone cold, in all the excitement.'

'Yes. Yes, please,' Sally said. 'I need a minute. I'll just go and wash my face.'

She disappeared into the cloakroom and Alisdair, glad that it had gone well – had it? He didn't really know but Nan seemed pleased – brewed up another couple of drinks. He carried the tray back through to the sitting room, set it down, and glanced out of the window. The weather was picking up a bit; and they'd need to watch the time to make the picnic. Alisdair felt a twinge of guilt for leaving Ewan to fetch the goodies but the old boy was going to have to get used to finding things to do in retirement; the police force wasn't going to let him plod on much longer, even in a backwater like Inniscuillin. Rumour was he'd already got his papers but Alisdair hadn't broached the subject yet.

He sipped his drink and looked around for something to do until Nan returned. There was no television in the sitting room, no newspaper either. He placed the tissue box back on the sideboard at the same time as running his eye down the spines of the books piled there – and did a double-take. Jack

Lambert. Who in the Big House was reading Jack Lambert's books? Alisdair felt a prickle of unease down his back. Coincidence, surely? As far as he knew, only Ewan was aware that he was Jack Lambert and Ewan was a dry old stick but he kept a confidence. Had Maud known? Did the woman know everything? And had she told Nan? It really wasn't a side of his life he wanted coming out.

'Take it if you like.'

Nan, groomed and looking her usual self, made him jump; he hadn't heard her soft shoes.

She nodded towards the garish cover of Stolen that he still held loosely in his hands. Stolen – of all the stories. 'Maud has a whole set. They seemed to be her secret vice – that and the tablet, of course, though that wasn't secret.' Nan held his gaze.

'Er, really?' Alisdair laid the book down carefully. 'Not really my sort of thing. Nor Maud's, I would have thought.'

'She once said she knew the author.' Nan's back was to him as she spoke. There was a pause before she turned. When she did, she was smiling. 'Do you think Maud was secretly a witch? She always said that everyone had secrets. And she certainly seemed to know all of ours, didn't she?'

'Looks like it.' Alisdair nodded; all he could manage. Did Nan know or didn't she? And did she know it was a chance remark of Jay's that had given him the idea all those years ago, led him to all that research – that he'd promised Ewan he wouldn't do. How did he play this?

'Yes. Lucky she's taken them with her, really,' Nan went on. 'The secrets, I mean. Some things are better left unsaid. Oh, thanks for the coffee. We'd better drink up and leave. Move on in Maud's honour.' She raised her cup.

'Indeed.' And that seemed to be that, Alisdair thought. If Nan knew she wasn't saying. 'Don't forget to put your birth certificate somewhere safe,' he said, putting himself on firmer ground.

'Don't suppose you happened to come across Jay and Mary's birth certificates, too, did you?'

'Sadly, not. Don't you have–'

'I'm joking, Alisdair. But no, I don't have them. It's true I came here with very little,' she said carefully. 'It had been a difficult time in my life. The children's father...'

'Nan, you don't owe me any explanations,' Alisdair said as her words trailed off. 'It was a long time ago. Maud implied things had been... painful... and that you were to be accepted here on merit.'

'Oh, I wasn't a battered wife,' Sally assured him. 'I'm a common or garden widow, but, well, my husband drank. He drank himself to death, actually.' She smiled up at him. 'But as you say, that was a long time ago. A different life.'

Alisdair nodded. 'If there's ever anything – anything at all in this life, Nan, come to me, won't you? I promised Maud I'd take care of you. And I mean to keep that promise.'

Nan moved towards him and kissed him on the cheek. 'You've already done so much, Alisdair. Thank you. Now, we've had enough drama. Shall we head off to the picnic? You don't think Ewan will propose again today, do you?' she added.

'He'll keep proposing 'til you say 'yes' and then –'

'And then he'd run a mile.' Nan grinned. 'Don't look at me like that, Alisdair, I know it's all about the chase for Ewan. He wouldn't know what to do with a wife. He's more of a confirmed bachelor than you are.'

'We're in it together,' Alisdair agreed. 'Though,' he added gallantly, 'I would like the opportunity to play my Sandy MacKinnon to your Maud, Nancy Campbell Douglas.'

'Och, away with you and your sweet-talking silver tongue.' Sally's mimicry of Maud was spot-on. They both laughed, and Alisdair was glad that the two of them headed towards Skua Bay, leaving all cross-purposes behind.

45

The picnic at Skua Bay heralded the beginning of a new
phase of their lives, it seemed to Sally later on. Outwardly, it
seemed to be a great success: the rain had held off; Sandy's
rejuvenated furniture was praised and the windbreak came
into its own; the food was pronounced 'fancy' and overpriced
as everyone happily tucked in; nobody had to be rescued
from over-zealous paddling, or cautioned about careless
swinging of the rounders bat by Sergeant McLeish; and it
was even rumoured that Mrs Crawford had gone home with
Peggy-from-the Post's for her tea.

Later, as they unpacked the car and Sally swept up all the
stray sand that inevitably trailed its way up from the beach,
Jay and Mary were full of it. Thankfully, all Sally had to do
was cock an ear in their direction and laugh when cued
because for her it was all something of a blur. Leaving the
twins to make sure Sandy was safely settled in his wee
cottage, Sally proclaimed herself exhausted from all the
excitement and went off for an early night. She was wideawake, her mind in overdrive, but she needed the space to
process what had happened with Alisdair that morning.

She sat on her bed, looking at Nancy Campbell's newly
replaced birth certificate as if it might hold the answers to the
dual life of Sally Brown and Nan Douglas. It didn't, of
course. There was no magical way that she was this Nancy
Campbell, Sally was under no illusions as to that, and neither
would Maud have thought so either. Theirs was no fairy story
in which real long-lost relatives had defied coincidence to
come together; Maud and Sally – Nan, rather, had certainly
never crossed paths until that first phone call more than

fifteen years ago. Had Maud done this, Sally wondered; come upon the documents and had a brainwave, a way to cement Sally's security on Inniscuillin. And if so, was it simply a loving, family gesture, or had Maud had her suspicions about Nan's identity? They'd celebrated birthdays in a low-key way, and Maud knew Nan's birthday was in February, not April and that she'd be born in 1940 not 1932. The old lady could have forgotten; it could have been wishful thinking. Sally could wrack her brains for all eternity, she thought, run her mind over all their conversations over the years, and yet she'd never know for sure.

Restlessly, Sally paced the bedroom. Maybe Maud was totally innocent, maybe it was Alisdair. He said he'd promised Maud he'd look after Sally – and he clearly meant it. What if he'd discovered the birth certificate and come up with this plan to make Nan Douglas into Nancy Campbell… Sally shook her head impatiently. The whole situation was crazy, but there was no reason for Alisdair to do that. Was there? 'Aargh,' Sally groaned into her hands; if she hadn't really had a headache before, it was pounding now. She would run a hot bath, emerge herself in bubble-bath and pretend her life was ordinary. All she did know, she said to herself as she put on her dressing gown and headed for the draughty bathroom, was that she and Alisdair had talked all-round the houses, each with their own agenda – his, the birth certificate, hers, the careful placement of the Jack Lambert books, to get a reaction from him (which she had, hadn't she? Non-committal and overshadowed as it was) – and each had gone to the picnic aware the other was holding back.

They were at stalemate, Sally realised. Or was it a sort of mutual resolution? 'Speak now or forever hold your peace,' she said aloud. They hadn't spoken, so…The best thing Sally could do for everyone, surely, was to take Nancy Campbell's identity and run with it. She was in too deep to do anything else.

Jay was not one to miss an opportunity. As Sally had known he would, he latched on to the fact of the document itself and the onslaught began. She sighed, for here they were, a day, a week, a month, later, having the same conversation again, and it wasn't going to go away.

'It's not up to you anymore, Mum,' Jay told his mother, his tone full of the confident arrogance of a newly-turned eighteen-year-old. 'You stopped me going to France with school. But please don't stop me going to Spain. Anyway, you can't. I need to get a passport. Alisdair got you a copy of your birth certificate, let's ask him to get ours, mine and Mary's. What's the problem?'

What had happened to her gorgeous little boy, Sally wondered. What a shame they had to grow up. But no, that wasn't fair. Logically, he was right; there shouldn't be a problem. She remembered that school trip to France, two years ago now. Mary hadn't wanted to go, but Jay? He had been so upset, so angry, when she hadn't let him join his friends and she couldn't blame him. She'd weathered the storm then, but Sally knew then it was only a matter of time before Jay brought up the subject of a passport – something he and Mary hadn't got because, of course, they needed their birth certificates to apply. She was lucky they'd got through the education system without needing proof of the children's identity – that was Maud's doing, she'd always vouched for them – but a trip abroad wasn't possible. Sally had already had many sleepless nights wondering how she was to deal with this and she was still playing for time. The solution was something she wasn't going to face until she absolutely had to.

'I told you then, darling. Our birth certificates got lost when we moved here.'

'I know that. You're not making sense, Mum. Just let's get a replacement.'

'It's not that easy–'

'Yes, it is.' To Jay it was obvious. 'You're just saying that to keep me here - just because you and Mary scarcely want to leave the island. I'm not like either of you. I'm leaving, Mum, whether you like it or not. And I will get my birth certificate somehow. I'll… I'll go to Glasgow or London or wherever I need to and then I'm going to Spain.'

Jay slammed out of the room, and Sally sank into the nearest armchair. She was cold, an icy spike struck her heart. She hadn't felt this level of despair since, well, since Malcolm, really. Not even leaving Cambridge with the children and making their way to the island, had been so worrying. She felt so – trapped. But just thinking of what she'd done back then, how much she'd come through with her children, helped Sally square her shoulders. She wasn't giving up now. She couldn't give up now. That was part of the deal.

Jay would have his passport somehow, she would see to that, but it couldn't be with the help of a birth certificate that listed him as Jeremy Harper-Smyth, son of Malcolm, and of Martha Beaumont. Sally had toyed with the wild idea of finding a forger, someone who could produce the necessary document on the black market – surely there were people in the underworld of Glasgow who could help? But how did a respectable, middle-aged islander go about finding out? Her mind crept to Alisdair but she firmly shut it down. It was a non-starter. Her one saving grace was that Jay had no inkling as to why she was so reluctant to oblige him, he genuinely thought it was all a matter of her being over-protective.

That night, as many previously, sleep didn't come easily; the hours ticked slowly by. As the dawn chorused Sally finally came to terms with the decision she had to make, much as it made her sick at heart. She got up and sat before the window, pen in hand, a growing pile of crumpled Basildon Bond revealing her turmoil. Sally read again the letter she had toiled over and gave a slight nod. She fed a new sheet of paper into Maud's old typewriter and began to slowly hit the keys. Once she was finished, she carefully pulled the letter from the roller, the tension in her shoulders jarring, and before she could change her mind, Sally eased the folded paper into the typed envelope, checking the address, inserted it into another envelope already labelled with a box number from which it could be forwarded, licked the stamp and lined it up carefully with the edges. She would post it from Fort William on Monday.

Sally wondered how long it would take to reach the recipient. She had a lot of planning to do.

As it happened it was a long fortnight later that Sally, feeling more alone than she had since the time of her ignominious departure from university, climbed aboard the waiting train. She'd barely registered the rolling ferry to Mallaig, so deep in thought was she. She was resigned to what she was about to do, knew it was inevitable, and had planned as best she could, but her mind was blank when she attempted to imagine how it would all work out. As the train ate up the miles, Sally twisted her silk handkerchief and bit her lip. Poor Jay, she thought, why couldn't he be satisfied with the island, even the mainland. Why did he need Europe, the world?

'Because he's a perfectly normal young man.' She could hear Maud's voice saying it, and she stifled a sob, for it was so much more than that. Jay would never be satisfied until he got what he wanted; he was so like his father. Or his mother.

It was a huge risk Sally was taking. Not heading south like this, she had done that a few times over the years, no, it was what she was intending to do when the train reached its destination. It made her nervous, as if time was flawed and the years collapsed – every time she spied a uniform, she was certain she was about to be arrested on sight for the abduction of two small children getting on for two decades ago, with a secondary charge of impersonating the late Nancy Campbell for a little over two months; she had the birth certificate with her but it didn't make her identity any clearer to herself.

This woman she had invented for today, in her elegant red dress, heels and carefully coiffured hair, made-up face, was unrecognisable as Nan Douglas, let alone Sally Brown, which in one way was a good thing but... for the first time another thought crossed her mind; might it actually work against her? Well, it was too late now. As Sally and as Nan, she had fought for her children before, and she would fight again. Jay and Mary were free to live their lives in all their fullness, and it was a mother's role to ensure that happened.

Blackmail was an ugly word and a strong weapon. It was also, she was convinced, the only way for everyone concerned. Sally had been acting ever since the day she learned her unborn baby would be taken away by its father and today she would play the part of her life. Other lives depended on it.

46
MALCOLM

Being Tuesday, it was a quiet day in Claridges and the man tipped to be the new Minister of Health in the Prime Minister's forthcoming Cabinet reshuffle, was in situ, incognito, at a corner table, poised to watch everyone entering and leaving the restaurant. The meeting was unorthodox in the extreme but his curiosity still always got the better of him, so he had ditched his security for an hour and rescheduled meetings at short notice. He wouldn't have admitted it to anyone, but the thought of the New Year's Honours had crossed his mind. He had an inkling that the powers-that-be sounded out people in this sort of low-key way. Well, he wouldn't disappoint. He had dressed in his usual work attire, Savile Row suit and tie, complete with gold tiepin, a pale blue shirt with gold cufflinks – rather nifty in the shape of a stethoscope – his Rolex on his wrist and impeccably polished shoes. It was a long time since Dr Harper-Smyth had worn his surgeon's scrubs; these days he cut a fine figure as a politician, one who was noted for his ability not to antagonise the Iron Lady. An unexpected bonus of his marriage to the original Iron and Ice Lady, Malcolm was wont to think when he'd ingested rather too much Talisker.

Malcolm looked over the short letter once again, turning it over and over, seeking more information or clues to who had sent it.

'I apologise for the inconvenience but I need to meet with you confidentially to discuss two mutual acquaintances and a

request that has bearing on your position. I suggest
Claridges' Tea Room at 11.30 on the last Tuesday of this
month.

Malcolm had read and re-re-read the peculiar note. He could
not make out the signature: a simple medic's scribble and no
printed name below it. On second thought, common sense
told him it wasn't from Buckingham Palace, discretion would
not have precluded monogrammed paper and a proper
signatory. He had given fleeting thought to blackmail, then
discounted it. His life was an open book, well, the story he
paid his publicist and personal assistants an adequate fortune
to share: a brilliant doctor and grief-stricken father who had
rebuilt his life, brick by brick, on a framework of family
values.

No, Malcolm had come to the conclusion that it involved a
rather more common-or-garden scandal. Probably two of his
medical colleagues, possibly with their sights on political
ladders, who may have overstepped the BMA's code of
ethics and were in danger of being ousted. It might be an ill-
advised affair, not discreet enough, but it was usually the
pilfering of drugs for recreational pleasure or private papers
for financial gain. It wasn't the first time he'd been
approached for help and it never hurt to have favours to call
in – or to be in a position of knowledge.

He nodded to himself; sure, he was correct with that
inherent arrogance which led to the belief that he was more
intelligent than he actually was. Yes: formal note; illegible
signature; 'sincerely' not 'faithfully'… 'Quod Erat
Demonstrandum,' he murmured. 'QED.'

Malcolm signalled to the waitress, rather a pretty little

thing of the type he would have pursued at one time, to refill his coffee and sat back to watch her neat bottom in its little black skirt. Whatever today was about, he would be the one doing the favour – and ultimately calling the shots. Nobody would expect less of the Minister of Health-elect.

47
SALLY AND MALCOLM

Sally knew immediately that her tight-fitting red dress was just right for her meeting. A black silk jacket slung over her left arm gave her a glamour that fell on the right side of sophistication; she'd no wish to look like a high-class call girl. The way she paused in the doorway bore no resemblance to the last few minutes she'd spent shaking in the ornate Ladies Restroom. Rather, she deliberately ran her eyes over the upper crust clientele, making sure he noticed her doing it. Oh, not as anyone he'd know, of course, but just another fanciable brunette in the figure-hugging dress – and more in his league than the teenage waitress he had been ogling from under his bushy eyebrows.

He hadn't changed.

Without a second's hesitation, Sally walked towards him, her stride confident, her soft smile becoming more brilliant as she reached his table.

Dr Malcolm Harper-Smyth was so busy congratulating himself that he hadn't lost his touch, even if – regretfully – his position meant he had to be a trifle more circumspect these days (though money always talked, of course) when she reached him, leant over and pecked him on the cheek. She was pulling out the chair opposite him before he could gather himself. She did it all with a familiarity that would make a casual observer dismiss the encounter as wife, fiancée, or, if they were in France, mistress. Before he could speak, she picked up the menu.

'Some tea, doctor?' the woman asked sweetly. She held

up an elegant hand to summon the waitress, adding brightly, 'And I suggest you keep your eyes on me, rather than the body of the child who is going to bring it to us.'

'What the...' Malcolm blustered. But the look on her face, a flash of pure loathing quickly replaced with a beaming, insincere smile – plus the arrival of said waitress – stopped him in his tracks.

Was this the sender of the letter? Or was she some unhinged socialite who prowled the better establishments looking for a husband – one heard of that kind of type. Hysterical, his colleagues would once have called them, though Malcolm was careful not to express such outdated views. He bit back a retort. Whatever this was, whoever she was, he needed to go carefully. Was he being set up?

'Who are you? What is it you want?' he asked, as soon as the waitress had taken her order for Earl Grey tea with lemon.

She just sat there, a little smile playing at the edge of her red lips, as if she were waiting for him to recognise her. He hesitated – was she vaguely familiar? He couldn't place her; maybe from a long time ago... but there had been so many women over the years. None of them had ever been a threat though, and, by God, they weren't going to start now.

Malcolm regained some of his arrogance. 'What's going on?' His voice rang out. 'I'll call the police –'

'You won't,' the woman said quietly. 'You'll do nothing, Dr Harper-Smyth. Yes, you see, I know who you are, doctor. I know all about you, but do you know who I am? No? Look. Look at me carefully. It's been a long time.'

She suddenly flashed a brilliant smile at him, it took years off her, and in that second Malcolm recognised her as... as

who? He frowned. 'You... Sarah?' She watched him
struggle, as full recognition – and the implications of it –
struck. If it was Sarah, then... His face paled and he put his
hand on the table to steady himself. 'Nanny... Sally Brown?'

'Two thirds right,' she said pleasantly. 'But we'll come to
that. Tea first, I think. It's good for shock. But you're a
doctor, you know that. Have a sip.' She nodded to the pot in
front of him. 'Don't wait for me.'

With supreme self-control, Malcolm stayed quiet until her
tea was served; his brain was in over-drive but it was telling
him not to make a fuss, not here, not in public. Was this
Sarah or Sally or whatever she called herself these days, or
some imposter who was out to fleece him? He heard his late
father's voice in his ear: 'Play your cards close to your chest,
boy,' Pa always said. 'Give nobody the upper-hand.'

'I seem to be at a disadvantage,' he managed to say.

'Shall we start again?' the woman suggested. 'We've a lot
of ground to cover. It would be a shame to get off on the
wrong foot, wouldn't it?'

'Sally? Sarah? Can you prove it?' He couldn't help
himself; he didn't really believe it was her.

'Hello, Malcolm,' she said. 'Yes, indeed. Sally Brown neé
Sarah Power. Your former nanny. The girl whose baby you
aborted. Mother of your children for the last fifteen years.'
She shrugged, still smiling, but there was steel in her eyes.
'Take your pick. Actually, don't. I'm someone different now
– but you can call me Sally. It's easier that way, isn't it?'

Malcolm's brain took a while to compute this. He couldn't
compute it. He wanted to believe this was a mad woman, a
constituent with an axe to grind, but deep down he knew it
wasn't.

'How are you?' Sally enquired of him, switching tone and character as if they were two friends meeting for an amiable afternoon of chat. 'Your career seems to be going well, doctor. I've read about your rise through the political ranks – tipped for Minister for Health, no less.'

Blood pulsed to his temples and they beat in anger. 'How am I? How dare you waltz in here and ask me how I am.' His tone was low and menacing. 'Where are my children?'

Sally smiled sweetly. 'My children? All in good time.'

'You evil bitch,' he whispered, leaning threateningly close to her. 'Have you any idea what you have put me through? I'm going to call the police and have you arrested.'

'Are you?' she enquired. 'To answer your question, yes I do have an idea of what I put you through or have you conveniently forgotten what you did to me?'

'You're deranged –'

'Minister for Health, of all things.' Sally stirred her tea; the clink of the spoon against the cup was driving him crazy. 'You were born to it, Malcolm, even innocent little Sarah knew that. What is it that all that all first-year medical students learned?' She gazed at him as if she was really expecting an answer. He clenched his fist under the table as she went on, 'Ah, I remember. Firstly: Do. No. Harm.' She spelt it out slowly. 'Isn't that what you were taught? Maybe you've forgotten – it was a long time ago.'

'Listen... er, Sally–'

'No. You listen.' Her voice changed again; she was hissing at him now and despite himself, he shrunk back. 'I should have had you struck off back then for what you did to me. I still could. Perhaps it should be me calling the police... or the press. I think the press would have a field day with what I could tell them about Mr – sorry Doctor, Family Values, don't you?'

'You bitch, you fucking bitch.' He found his voice. 'Where are my children?'

'*Your* children? I know where mine are, and that's safe and loved and wanted. The children I would have given birth to myself, but for you. You butchered me. Minister of Health? That's a laugh.' She did laugh, but there was no humour in it.

'Why are you here?' Malcolm asked abruptly. 'Has something happened?'

She seemed to ignore him. 'I came to ask you if I should go to the police, hand myself in as the missing Cambridge nanny? What do you think?' she mused.

'Keep your voice down,' he hissed. 'And yes, you bloody well should.'

'You're sure?' She raised an eyebrow. 'Imagine the headlines. The great Dr Malcolm Harper-Smyth, MP, back-street abortionist who didn't recognise his own children's nanny. Think about it for a minute. The tabloids. The trial. Our lives, your career. Which of us would go to prison for the longest, do you think?'

'You…' Malcolm went quiet. He watched this stranger drink her tea with something akin to fascination, trying to marry the adoring and naïve Sarah with the competent and deferent Sally. She was right; she was neither of them and nor was she crazy. She was stone-cold serious.

'Yes. Me. I know all your secrets, Malcolm,' she said. 'I have your children, which is bad enough, but worse, much worse, I have your glittering life – everything you've worked for, built-up, dreamed of, and yes, everything you've done to eclipse Martha – in my hands, don't I, Malcolm?'

Malcolm struggled to stop his jaw from hitting the tablecloth. She was right and she knew it; knew too, that if push came to shove, he'd put himself above his children in the way he always had. That didn't make him a monster, he assured himself, it made him human. He'd come to terms with his children being gone; he'd had to – what else could a man do?

'I took your children, Malcolm,' she said quietly. 'I could quote the mitigating circumstances but I made a promise, back then, that I never would.' She looked straight at him, her words mirroring his thoughts. 'Are you going to let me take the rest of your life, as well?'

Bitch. Clever, conniving, bitch. But he didn't say it aloud this time. Even if he called the police now, she probably wouldn't reveal the whereabouts of the children without a fight and once the fuss had died down, what would he do with two teenagers he didn't even know? And where did Martha fit in to all this? Malcolm wanted to howl with fury – and fear. She'd go to prison; he probably wouldn't but his reputation and good name would be destroyed. He was in a bind, for sure, but he was looking at damage limitation and she wasn't getting off lightly.

'Do you need money?' he asked abruptly. 'Is that what this is about? Blackmail, like abduction, is ugly.'

'No, I don't.'

'Then, what? Why now, after all this time?'

'My children are eighteen,' she said. 'They want to travel. They need their birth certificates in order to get passports. Much as it grieves me, Malcolm, I am asking for your help. I need you to fix this. For the children I cared for when you and your wife abandoned them. For the child you ripped from my body that started all this.'

'Fix it? Now, wait–'He wasn't sure if he was shocked or gratified to see tears glitter in the corner of her eyes, but she collected herself quickly.

'No. You don't get to tell me what to do,' she said. 'As I see it, you and I are bound to one another, whether we like it or not. Each of us can ruin the other or we can live in a state of truce. I know which I would choose. Give two of the children the lives they deserve, Malcolm.'

She had some nerve, guilt-tripping him like that. He bristled. He would... he would... his shoulders sagged. He would give in.

'Tell me what you need,' he said and their eyes locked. Theirs wasn't a healthy trust but it was a form of trust all the same.

'Birth certificates in the names of Mary Maud Campbell and Jay Alexander Campbell. Their mother's name is Nancy Douglas.'

'And their father's?' He watched her composure slip again.

'I can't answer that, Malcolm. I've thought about it and I don't know. If you insist on your name, you must be ready for the consequences. Martha, too... when they come looking. If you don't, if you choose a clean break, I'll confess to them they were illegitimate.'

'A clean break,' he repeated, almost to himself. He shook his head and narrowed his eyes. 'Out of interest,' he said, 'Where exactly do you think I can conjure these birth certificates from?'

'Don't tell me you haven't friends in very high places.

And very low ones,' she said. 'I don't want to know. I just want the documents. Sent to this PO Box number.' She opened her bag and removed a small white card, which she slid across the table.

He took it and slipped it in his top pocket. 'Is that it?'

'That's it.'

There was a second's silence, then Malcolm added awkwardly. 'How, er, are the children?'

'Very well. Very happy.'

'I suppose you won't tell me where –'

'No.'

'I could always find out, you know,' he tried, one last attempt to unsettle her.

'You could,' she agreed. 'But then our agreement falls down, doesn't it? Once I have the certificates and they have their passports, then,' she shrugged, 'things may be different.'

'You mean when I've broken the law for you,' he hissed.

'I mean, when you've done the right thing by two innocent children,' she corrected him. 'Now, I think we're finished here, aren't we?' She gathered up her bag and put it on the table in front of her, then slowly she rose. 'Malcolm?'

'Yes?' He tensed.

'Do you have any contact with Martha?'

'Martha?' Malcolm gave a bark of laughter. 'No. Why?'

Sally shook her head. 'Idle curiosity. I'd say it's better that way, wouldn't you? Well, goodbye.' With that, she crossed the room, and was gone.

'Bye,' he echoed automatically, wondering what the hell had just happened, and what the fuck that final comment had to do with anything.

Malcolm sat on for a few minutes, thinking. All in all, he'd handled an impossible situation quite well, he decided. It was unfortunate but it was all contained still, wasn't it? He thought it was. Nothing had changed. Nothing would change – and if it did, he'd be the catalyst next time. Maybe he should have had her tailed, he thought. Maybe it was one huge bluff and he'd been hoodwinked. But in his heart of hearts, Malcolm Harper-Smyth knew that Sally was exactly who she said she was.

Sally kept her composure as she made her way sedately through reception, via an empty function room and ornate French doors into a courtyard. From there she opened the gate, hurried down the alley into the next street and hailed a black cab.

'St Pancras,' she instructed, removing a pack-a-mac from her handbag and shaking it out. She zipped it around her, hiding the red dress. 'I'm late for the Penzance train, can you hurry?'

'Long way to go, love,' the driver remarked. 'Rather you than me, but I'll get you there.'

He was as good as his word, and Sally made her way from there to Kings Cross and awaited the train north. Safely on that, then on the next, then waiting for the ferry, her trembling lessened with every mile covered. What had she just done? Exhilarated and horrified in equal measure, Sally was also interested to reflect that, when push came to shove, she did still possess the nerves of steel that had seen her through this leg of the same journey more than fifteen years ago. She hadn't exactly traced the circuitous route their little threesome had taken way back then. It wasn't any kind of nostalgia – at least she didn't think it was – rather that she wasn't sure whether Malcolm would have had her followed. Then, of course, she'd had two small children in tow, determined never to let them go. Now, whether he came after her or not, she was going to have to do exactly that.

Realistically, it was inevitable he would find her – them – if he wanted to, and his pride wouldn't let him do otherwise, but she needed a head start, time to get herself in order.

Time, Sally thought bitterly. Wasn't fifteen years enough? It would never be enough. Her gamble had paid off though, hadn't it? She and Malcolm were at an unholy stalemate: if he outed her as the abductor of his children, she'd out him as an illegal abortionist; Sally was fairly sure that Jay would have his passport soon enough.

The biggest relief of all, of course, was that Sally still held the trump card, something of which Malcolm remained blissfully unaware. Something of which everyone but Sally was unaware… Her final remark had been calculated and it had paid off. Not once prior to that had he mentioned Martha. And if Malcolm hadn't mentioned Martha, then he didn't know – and the most sordid secret of this whole affair could remain safely buried.

Couldn't it?

But if he insisted on playing games and hurting the children in the process, she'd tell him. She'd tell him everything.

And that would be a worldwide scandal.

48

Home.

As the boat lumbered into its berth, jostling the sea wall, Sally inhaled deep, deep breaths of the crisp air, as if oxygen had been rationed on the mainland. She was the first of the few travellers to disembark, anxious now to get back to the house and the children. If she was quick enough – and she was, just – she would be able to avoid Ewan slurping back the dregs of his tea in the harbourmaster's office. She gave him a cheery wave and hurried to the car. Good old Ewan, Sally thought, boring as hell but consistently sweet on her still, after all these years. She couldn't face him today. She hoped she wouldn't have to throw herself on his mercy any day soon.

Sally felt a pang of regret as she unlocked the rusting Fiat. It wasn't the same without Sandy there, waiting in the old Land Rover, ready to fill her in on the local gossip and Maud's present gripe with him. She'd go up to the cottage later on. A chat with Sandy would ground her, let her regroup and gather her wits. The past was another country and she couldn't go there... who had said that? Maud would have known.

She still missed Maud, more than she could put into words. If Dr Malcolm Harper-Smyth had been her nemesis, then Miss Maud Campbell, spinster of the parish and maiden aunt extraordinaire, had been Sally's saviour – even if Maud would have scolded her for using that term. Sally grinned, in spite of herself. Theirs might have started out as a business arrangement but they'd grown fully into the family they had pretended to be.

Driving along the coast road, waving absently at the odd car coming towards her – Alisdair's friendly salute (Sally mimed she was in a hurry); the minister's glare (his most recent words to her were: 'Your great-aunt's mantle cannot but have fallen upon your own shoulders,' an intended insult that pleased her no end) – Sally thought back over the few times she'd almost confided in Maud. Not blurted it out, Sally was no blurter, but on those rare occasions when it all became too much for one person to bear, she was glad now she'd kept it to herself. It wouldn't have been a problem solved, just a burden crippling both of them. The two women had been so close, yet each had kept their own counsel on their pasts. It was a tacit agreement; Sally was sure that Maud had her own secrets – and the strange appearance of Nancy Campbell's papers bore that out.

'No,' she said to herself as the car bounced over the cattle-grid at the top of the lane leading to the house, 'it's better this way. Definitely better.'

The only ones who knew the full story were Sally and her partner in crime. Malcolm would probably put himself in that role, of course, but he was wrong. It was nothing to do with him. That honour belonged firmly to his wife. To Martha.

'Dr Martha Beaumont.' Sally declaimed the name suddenly, as if presenting one of the many awards the icy, calculating, self-absorbed professor had earned over the years. Scientist. Trailblazer. Even 'genius' had been bestowed upon the woman. 'All that, and what else?' Sally said aloud to herself.

Oh yes. Dr Martha Beaumont – the cunning and manipulative instigator of her own children's kidnapping.

There was nobody at home. Sally recognised that hollow feeling the empty house always had. Just as well. She wrenched open the door of the back porch and dropped her bag there. Mary had left a note – complete with smiley faces and hearts above the i's – on the scrubbed pine table, saying she was out with her friend Eileen for the day. Nothing from Jay, who was clearly still playing it cool. There was a hefty chunk of his father in that young man, Sally thought, London uppermost in her mind. She sighed, and hoped for Jay's sake, the charm and genuine kindness in him would outweigh the arrogance. As for Mary she took after none of them, not Malcolm, Martha or even Sally. Mary was sweet and gentle – and dogged to the core.

Once the kettle was boiling, she foraged in the pantry for food she didn't want but knew she needed. They'd left her the heel of a loaf and the scrapings of the last plum jam. Sally would have to go back into the village and do a shop. Some things never changed. Sally dipped a camomile teabag into her mug of water. It was a vain effort to calm herself down; a triple Laphroaig might have hit the spot but a few leaves of damp-smelling plant was the grown-up option.

Sally took her tea and swirling thoughts out to the garden, begging the benign safety of the house, the land, the island to wash over her. When she allowed her thoughts to stray in that direction, it was a constant conundrum. Had she really abducted the children even if it was done by arrangement with their own mother? It was a legal question she'd never ask (the solicitor) and a moral one that she ignored. Whatever spin she put on it, Sally wasn't innocent. She'd taken the prizes and run.

And she didn't regret a single second of it.

Nor, she guessed, did Martha.

There was peace in the silence, but today, not enough to soothe Sally's rattled brain. For the first time in many years, she forced herself to confront that long ago night. The night that Martha had laid out her plan and turned Sally's life upside down…

'I know about Malcolm,' she'd said. No preamble, no bedside manner.

Martha was sitting behind the Chippendale desk in her study, her eyes fixed on Sally who lurked, like a naughty schoolgirl in the head-mistress's office, just inside the door.

'I know all about Malcolm,' she'd repeated. 'About his behaviour in medical school. About his inappropriate relationships with female undergraduates, including with you. And about the two illegal abortions he performed.' She looked dispassionately at Sally. 'I'm right, aren't I?'

It wasn't a question and Sally didn't treat it as such – it was much later on that that 'two' registered with her. Instead, she slowly crossed the room and sat down in the leather chair angled towards the desk. 'How did you find out?' she asked, as if it mattered.

Martha gave her a brief nod, as if to acknowledge it was cards on the table time. 'I'm not sure it will help any of us for you to know the details,' she'd said. 'Suffice it to say, a girl who wasn't as lucky as you are. Her diary. A pathologist who has always looked out for me. And ultimately a very expensive and very discreet private detective.'

It sounded like something that should have been on at the picture house, not that the censor would have passed it. Sally was shell-shocked. Numb. 'What are you going to do?' she managed to get out.

Martha had steepled her fingers together. 'I shall do nothing but exercise patience. I will wait until Malcolm has another of his – these days more sophisticated – transgressions. Then I shall accept a fellowship in the States and quietly leave.' Then she leant forward, and her voice was smoother – almost seductive, Sally was to remember later on. 'It's not about what I'm going to do, Sally. If I'm right, and I usually am, it's all about what you are going to do.'

Sally had left the study that night, a mother. Had there ever been a question that the deed would be done? Honestly? She didn't think so.

Over the years, she'd battled her indistinct feelings about Martha, but there was no resolution. How could there be? There was no rulebook listing how to feel about the woman who had handed over her children out of punishment? Revenge? – An eye for an eye, and all that – towards her husband. Who had handed them over as a consolation prize to her nanny, whose entitlement to be a mother had been stolen from her? And whose objectivity was shocking, whether it was styled plain indifference, or for the greater good. It made Sally and Malcolm both victims, didn't it? In a way that Martha wasn't.

It was a philosophical minefield as much as it was an emotional one, but that was something Sally could appreciate only in hindsight. It was a debate that Ewan and the solicitor would love – she gave a bark of laughter – but only hypothetically. The trade-off had been a life of deceit and fear of being found out, but Sally had learned that you couldn't live in a heightened state forever, and it was easier than she'd ever thought possible to isolate herself – literally – and raise two beautiful children.

Her children.

Martha had worked out the blueprint and Sally the details. 'Keep them to yourself,' Martha had said harshly. 'I do not want to know where you are or what you are doing. The children will never know about me. Nobody will know about this discussion. If they find out –' the implication being that if Sally now or later lost her nerve, or had such a poor escape plan that the police found them '– I will deny we ever had this conversation and you know what that means.' It wasn't a threat. It was a fact: Sally would be treated as a psychiatric criminal and she would take the rap and lose the children.

Her children.

She'd had no contact with Martha or Malcolm since their extended trip to America. No contact for fifteen years. Until now. Now she would live, once again, waiting for the phone to ring, for a rap on the door, for an official visit from Ewan. She would live waiting for Malcolm to turn up and reclaim his children.

Her children.

Somewhere a door banged and voices called out. A shudder ran through Sally. She poured her tea onto the grass, and squared her shoulders – literally. She needed to get back to the house, plaster a smile on her face, and sort out whatever today's trials were.

After all, that's what mothers did.

And Sally wouldn't have it any other way.

THE END

ABOUT THE AUTHOR

Gill Merton is the nom de plume of five writers based around
Edinburgh and the Lothians:
Simon Bramwell
Coreen Connell
Sheila Corrigan
Anne Hamilton
Elizabeth Nallon

Entitled is their first collaborative novel, adapted from an
original short story by Sheila Corrigan, and was made
possible by funding from The National Lottery Awards For
All.

Earlier publications include:
The Writing Group: an original stage/radio play (First
recorded 2017)
A Way With Words: an anthology of prose and poetry (Pilrig
Press, 2015)

Gill Merton

ACKNOWLEDGEMENTS

With thanks to all the staff at Gilmerton Community Centre, in particular Lilian Taylor, for their many years of support, and to the NL Awards for All fund, without which the book might never have been finished.

Sincere thanks are also due to Paul Fitzpatrick for his many early contributions to the story, to Claire Morley of My ePublish Book for making it into a 'real' book, and to Marta Lis for designing the cover.

Printed in Great Britain
by Amazon

79471311R00185